CARDINAL VIRTUE

An Eastfall Novel

J.R. LESPERANCE

Copyright © 2020 by J.R. Lesperance

ISBN-13: 978-1-7349012-0-7

Cover design by Caroline Teagle Johnson

Cover images © AdobeStock

Map of Eastfall by S.E. Davidson

For my dad, who always wanted to read my writing, but I never allowed him to. I know he read over my shoulder as I wrote this novel.

This one's for you, dad. I hope you like it.

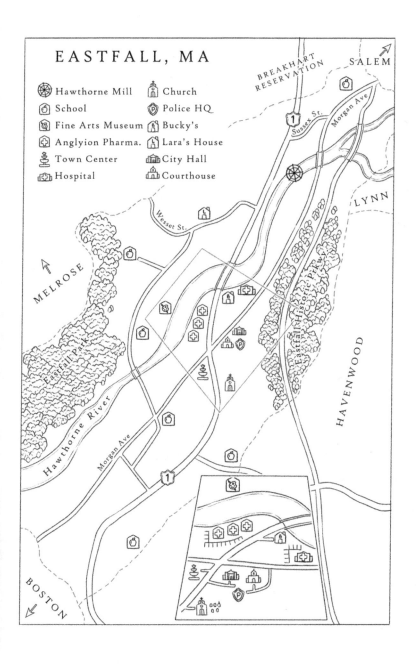

EASTFALL, MA

- ⊕ Hawthorne Mill
- ⌂ School
- 🏛 Fine Arts Museum
- ⊕ Anglyion Pharma.
- ⚱ Town Center
- 🏥 Hospital
- ⛪ Church
- Ⓟ Police HQ
- 🏠 Bucky's
- 🏠 Lara's House
- 🏛 City Hall
- 🏛 Courthouse

BREAKHART RESERVATION

SALEM

Sussex St.

Morgan Ave

LYNN

Wesset St.

MELROSE

Eastfall Park

Eastfall Historic Pkwy

HAVENWOOD

Hawthorne River

Morgan Ave

BOSTON

PROLOGUE

The quiet of the building settled around his ears as he sat behind his large, oaken desk. The historic center of Eastfall, Massachusetts loomed behind him, a scenic view through the floor-to-ceiling wall of windows. It had been hours since his secretary had gone home, but he still remained. It was no easy feat, his job. Neither was it easy leading a clandestine organization that had been in existence for hundreds of years.

Heavy lies the crown and all that...

A quiet tap came at the double-doored entrance of his office. Being CEO of a multinational corporation afforded one certain luxuries. A spacious and ornate workspace being one.

"Enter," he called toward the door.

In stepped another man who had once been the CEO's proudest recruit. Over the past five years, his protégé had grown too comfortable in his position. Too ambitious. The CEO would never admit that the fact others agreed with his protégé rather frightened him. It was a challenge to his authority.

He detested challenges to his authority.

"Evening, sir," his protégé greeted, stepping into the room and *crossing the distance between them. He stood before the CEO's desk, hands clasped at the small of his back.*

"Was there something I could help you with? I was unaware we had a meeting."

"We didn't. But I wanted to try again to convince you of my plan."

Ah yes, his protégé's plan. The foolhardy plan to complete a ritual that has not been verified or attempted ever in recorded history. That plan.

"There is nothing further to discuss," the CEO said. "You do not fully comprehend the powers that you are playing with. Not to mention the serious breach of secrecy it would cause..."

"Have we not spent long enough in the shadows, sir? Our forefathers bled and died for our cause. I sincerely doubt they would look favorably on us now, sitting behind our desks, hiding behind our masks of civility. The goals of this organization were clear from the onset. How can you keep us chained?"

It took everything for the CEO to stop himself rolling his eyes. His protégé always had had a flare for the dramatic.

"You are still very much a naive boy," the CEO began. "No matter how I found you. No matter how many years have gone by. You are still the same broken, hollow boy that I met a decade ago. There is still much for you to learn."

His protégé's hands shot from behind his back, and the CEO thought for a brief moment that the younger man would strike out at him. His protégé knew better, however, leaving his hands at his sides, but clenched in anger. The man had always been adept at shutting out emotions from his face. Too adept. The CEO was sure he'd never met a man so narcissistic, so power-starved, so unhinged.

"You are a fool," his protégé spat. "You'd see us stay under heel for all time? Weak?"

The CEO's eyebrows furrowed. "Watch your tone, boy."

His protégé, to the man's credit, leaned back.

"Listen...the type of ritual you wish to enact is not something even

I *have the authorization to greenlight. The copy you have, regardless, is incomplete. It would not work anyway."*

The fire returned to the younger man's dark eyes. "I beg to differ. It took me forever to find the copy I did. It is complete. All of my sources have confirmed."

"And I am telling you it is not," the CEO replied firmly.

Silence fell in the air between them, gazes locked.

"Why the fuck would you have brought me into The Order if not for me to reach my potential? Or was all the bullshit you spouted to me back in college just lies?" His protégé huffed through clenched teeth.

"You have and will always be my most promising recruit. As head of The Order, I am always afforded one acolyte at any given time. I chose you because of your quick intelligence and your drive. I have watched you grow, but lately, you've stretched in a direction that I did not anticipate you going. For that, I offer my sincerest apologies."

"Apologies? What for?" his protégé spat back.

"For failing you. I have clearly not done enough. Taught you enough, to understand our limitations."

His protégé shook his head furiously, the knuckles of his hands at his sides white now, and shaking.

"I am tired," the CEO spoke again. "That is enough for tonight. We can continue our discussion at a later time. Of my choosing."

The CEO watched his protégé wage a war within himself. His sense of duty urged him to leave, but his determination bade him to stay and fight. After a very long minute, the protégé nodded.

"As you wish, sir," his protégé said before spinning on his expensively shod heel, storming from the office.

Once the CEO was sure his protégé had gone, he let out a relieved sigh. Fingertips rubbed at graying temples. He had recognized so much of himself in his protégé, and now he feared that apprentice had outgrown master.

For the rest of the evening, the CEO could not shake a feeling of impending doom.

CHAPTER 1

I n life, the woman must have been beautiful.

But in death, she was a bloated, rotted perversion.

Grayed skin had begun to pull back around her face, causing her eyes to appear larger than what might have been normal. Maggots and flies swarmed and writhed in her gaping mouth, the orifice locked in the terror from her last moments alive, making the already gruesome scene more macabre.

The woman's body had been found in a secluded area, just off the beaten path of the city of Eastfall, Massachusetts. It was woodsy, overgrown, and halfway along the old Eastfall Historic Parkway, a stretch of exposed aggregate road connecting Eastfall with neighboring Havenwood, and ultimately, Salem. Not many trod this area of the historic parkway, only a few dedicated runners or teenagers out on a dare.

Police Lieutenant Lara Nadeau had witnessed murder scenes before in her ten years as a law enforcement officer, but none quite like this. In her beloved Boston, most deaths were gunshot wounds or stabbings. Dead bodies weren't a common occurrence in the New England town she'd been exiled to. The most violent crimes Eastfall had seen in the past two decades were an assault over a garden gnome, a few domestics, and drug-related offenses.

Murder came a long way from fighting over lawn decorations, but nevertheless, Eastfall was privileged to be one of a handful of agencies who could investigate homicides. Most of the time, that was the State Police's job.

It was late fall, and tendrils of winter had begun to take hold. A light blanket of snow fell last week, the first of the season, and tiny, half-melted piles remained as dirty predictions of a harsh winter. Ghostly clouds of warm breath hitting cool air floated around the uniformed officers and plainclothes investigators as they looked upon the scene.

One would think maggots couldn't cultivate in the godforsaken cold. But despite current frigid temperatures, a few warm spells had not only melted the errant snow, but also allowed for flies to land, to procreate. Only the coroner would be able to determine how long the body had been in the elements before discovery.

The dead woman, Lara knew only from word of mouth, had been an important figure in the Eastfall public school community.

"That's Ms. Rickerson. She's my kid's history teacher," muttered Lara's investigative partner and immediate supervisor, Captain Thomas Sharpe. "God, Lola's gonna be devastated. She loves her. Everyone loves her. Can't imagine why anyone would do something like this."

The crux of police work, the reason they had jobs to begin with, was the how, the who, and the why. Some people existed that didn't think like normal human beings. Their only goal was to hurt, to maim, to scratch a sadistic itch.

Someone assuredly scratched that itch with Lynn Rickerson.

The sound of an engine grew closer, and the city coroner's van pulled up between the police cruisers. The medical examiner, Doctor Stephanie Rogers, slid from the passenger seat, clutching her medical bag. She rounded the back of the van, joining her assistant in hauling out the stretcher.

"Gentlemen. Lieutenant," Doctor Rogers greeted, as she ducked under the crime scene tape, careful where she stepped.

A chorus of returned greetings sounded in the small clearing, as the examiner got right to work. After kneeling down next to the deceased teacher, she opened her medical kit and slapped on a fresh pair of latex gloves.

"Victim is female. Caucasian. Late twenties, early thirties," she began, dictating to her assistant as if making a grocery list. "Bruising around the neck might suggest strangulation." The doctor carefully pulled what little clothing was left aside. The killer had stripped her, ripped her clothing to shreds, to the point that what remained of her skirt bunched at her waist, and her chest was bare.

Lara jotted down these same notes on her own notepad. The official autopsy report would follow in a few days, but she liked to be thorough.

"Liver temperature and rigor mortis suggests time of death was between twenty-four and thirty hours ago. Victim is laid on her back, arms and legs spread out. Blood smears on the inside of her thighs might suggest sexual assault. More will be determined in the lab."

Lara had made these same observations, even made a note as to whether the position of the body had been deliberate. She had a feeling, despite the obvious violence, the entire scene was deliberate.

The doctor paused, taking a steadying breath before moving on to the most disturbing part of the crime scene.

"Victim's skull is sawed open..." Doctor Rogers said with practiced detachment and professionalism. She reached for the victim's blood-caked hair and carefully tugged. The piece of bone gave way to reveal an empty skull. The top portion of the woman's cranium had been sawed open and later put back in place, so as to appear whole. The brain sitting half a foot away said otherwise. "The brain was removed and placed apart from the body. It appears part of the frontal lobe was removed with some level of care."

"You ever see anything like this, Doc?" Lara asked.

"Can't say I have, Lieutenant. Especially these..."

Lara hadn't seen anything so gruesome. Not only had the brain been removed with a piece missing, but it had been carefully placed away from the body with meticulously drawn symbols etched in dirt surrounding the organ. It was a miracle the integrity of the symbols remained undisturbed.

"I don't know what this is," Doctor Rogers said, pointing a gloved finger at a scattered mess of plant greenery. It didn't appear naturally occurring. Lara had already instructed the crime scene technicians to collect a sample. "Neither can I think of significance for the blue paint, but I will be sure to send a sample to the lab."

As if everything done to the woman wasn't strange and brutal enough, a dark blue vertical line of paint or ink tracked from the bottom of Ms. Rickerson's nose down to her chin, crossing over lips nearly matching the color.

"This is unbelievable." Doctor Rogers sighed, standing, her preliminary work complete. "Ms. Rickerson was my son's World History teacher. She wrote a letter of recommendation for him to be in the National Honor Society this year."

"Unfortunately, murder doesn't discriminate, Doc," Tom Sharpe replied, idly tapping the tip of his pen on his notepad. Lara's fiery-haired superior looked green around the gills. This wasn't a frequent experience for him despite his tenure on the force.

As her assistant began to prepare for the transfer of the body into a body bag, Doctor Rogers said to Lara and Tom,

"We'll get her back to my office and do what we can. Some samples might need to be shipped to Boston for processing, but I'll get back to you with my findings as soon as possible."

Lara knew the good doctor from once upon a time, in her former life in Boston. Stephanie Rogers had been one of the top medical examiners in the capital, but had, at one point, decided to quasi-retire back where she'd been born and raised in Eastfall. Over their occasional clashing of cases, Lara had gotten to know the older woman and very much appreciated her skills and attention to detail.

"How's Eastfall treating you, Lieutenant?" Stephanie asked quietly, as a team of people transferred Ms. Rickerson into the body bag, and then onto the stretcher. The crime scene technicians had completed their photographs earlier, and now swooped in to collect more physical evidence.

"It's fine," Lara replied with a noncommittal shrug. "Quieter than the big city."

"I heard you're living in the old Morgan house." Stephanie stated, more a point of fact than a question. "It's a beautiful place."

"So everyone says."

Lara wasn't sure where the doctor was going with this idle small talk, but regardless, it made the lieutenant antsy. There was a time when she would have gladly fallen into the most mundane of conversations, but no more.

She wasn't the same person she'd once been.

"It's nice," Lara continued, voiced with the same indifference as before. "Suits my needs."

Rogers's assistant and uniforms loaded the woman into the back of the coroner's van.

"Well, I better get to work. I'll let you know when I'm finished," the doctor said, waving as she made her way back over to the vehicle.

Lara bid the doctor goodbye, as Tom followed to help

Stephanie up into the van, shutting the door behind her. The engine roared to life and trundled back out to the road, veering off into town.

"What d'you make of this?" Tom asked Lara, as they headed back to their beat-up unmarked.

Once back in the heated comfort of the car, she sighed.

"I'm not sure yet."

"Isn't that, like, your thing? Spidey senses and intuition that get cases solved?"

"I dunno what kind of bullshit you've heard," Lara replied, trying not to scoff. "I'm not a psychic. I use regular ol' deduction and reasoning to solve crimes, same as you. Ain't nothin' magical to it."

Tom sighed, fingertips kneading his forehead. Lara could relate. Her headaches were constant. Very rarely did she get a reprieve from the dull ache behind her temples. Doctors cited stress as the cause, and Lara felt inclined to agree. She'd been through a hell of a lot in the past three years. For Tom, in his thirty-plus years on the force, he'd never seen this kind of violent crime. Lara had seen murder, but nothing like this. She felt for him.

"Alright," Tom said with a resigned sigh. "Let's go tell her family. Shit, does she even have family nearby?"

CHAPTER 2

As it turned out, Lynn Rickerson did have family in Eastfall. Her mother, Gloria Ives, lived in a neighborhood of duplex homes north of the city center. The older woman had retired from Havenwood High School as a Biology teacher after twenty-five years. Her daughter had been the center of her universe. Lara could empathize, watching someone realize they had lost their anchor. Gloria was inconsolable at the news of her daughter's death, until shock kicked in and the tears ceased.

"I don't understand why someone would want to kill her," Gloria spoke, emotion crackling her voice. "Everyone loved her. All of her students, the administration, her friends, everyone."

"Are you positive, Ms. Ives, there's no one that would want to hurt her?" Lara asked, her own voice a picture of concern and kindness. She understood loss, but Ms. Ives wouldn't get closure from an investigator too emotionally invested.

"Yes!" Gloria exclaimed. After a pause, her eyebrows

pulled upward in thought. "Well, it didn't end well with her previous boyfriend."

It was the oldest song in the book, a man scorned and baited to murder.

"What's his name?" Lara urged, pen poised over her notepad where she had been scribbling notes nearly down the page.

Gloria looked to Tom, emotion heavy in her blue eyes.

"Lynn dated Zach Braddock for about six months before they broke up. She never told me the details, but she was pretty withdrawn for a while after."

It wasn't hard for Lara to miss the shock lining Tom's face. The name had meaning to him, and she could only guess Zach Braddock was likely connected to their chief of police, Henry Braddock.

"Thank you very much for your time, Ms. Ives," Tom said, shoving his notepad and pen into his jacket pocket, before getting to his feet. Confused, Lara followed suit. "I am so terribly sorry for your loss. If there is anything you need, please let us know. We'll get in touch with you when we know more." He handed Gloria one of his business cards.

"Thank you, Captain. My Lynnie is in good hands, I can see that."

Once back outside, Tom hurried to the driver's side of the unmarked. It was all Lara could do to keep up with his long-legged stride.

"Okay, Cap, what the hell's going on? I'm guessing Zach Braddock is related to the chief?"

"It's his son," Tom replied, folding his body behind the wheel. Lara scrambled into the passenger's side.

"This day just got interesting."

Here Lara thought nothing exciting happened in Eastfall.

As it turned out, Zachariah "Zach" Braddock was not just Chief Henry Braddock's son, but also a police sergeant in the Havenwood Police Department. It took no time for Lara to call up his personnel file from the onboard computer of their unmarked, and was not disappointed at the information she found.

Zach Braddock had been promoted to police detective three years ago. A year and a half ago, he was busted down to police sergeant, and given the school resource officer position at Eastfall High School. Lara assumed that's how he met Lynn Rickerson. Sergeant Braddock lasted only one school year before returning to patrol. The details of his demotion were not apparent in his personnel file. Lara found this odd. The information existed somewhere. No record like that could disappear.

It didn't take long to zip across city lines to Eastfall's neighbor, Havenwood. Lara, despite living in Eastfall for a handful of months, had yet to explore their twin city. Both towns were established in earlier colonial times by rival families opting to leave Plymouth. According to legend, the two families couldn't agree to much of anything, hence the separation. Eventually, in the early part of the twentieth century, the cities 'reconciled,' and declared themselves sister cities, occasionally referred to as the twin cities.

The police headquarters of Havenwood looked very much like Eastfall's—brand new (at least within five years), central location, and state of the art. Though law enforcement agencies followed the same laws and procedures, counterparts across the country were rarely identical. The lobby of Havenwood's headquarters was bustling, as uniformed and plainclothes officers alike went about their day-to-day business.

"Hey, Frank," Tom greeted the front desk sergeant with a small smile as they walked up.

Frank looked close to retirement, probably the reason he

manned the front desk. He'd not aged well, as his face resembled a bulldog's, all wrinkles and jowls. When he spoke, his voice betrayed him as a smoker, words gravelly and rusty.

"Tom Sharpe, how the hell are ya? How's the family?" Frank asked as the two men clapped palms.

"Doin' alright, Frank. Doin' alright, thanks for asking. Hey, any chance Sergeant Braddock's in?"

"As a matter of fact, yeah, he just came back from a call. Should be at his desk. Need to talk to him?"

"That would be grand, Frank, thanks."

Frank granted them access through the secured door that divided the public from the rest of the building. Tom, familiar with the building, led Lara down a hallway, then right down another, before the ceiling opened up into a desk farm.

Tom scanned the room for their primary suspect and found him quickly, because he began to stride down a row of desks. Lara scrambled to keep up.

Lara hadn't had a chance to take a long look at a photograph of the guy, so she didn't know what to expect. Sergeant Zach Braddock sat at his desk, seemingly entranced by paperwork and report writing. He looked much like his father, if his dad were twenty years younger. With broad shoulders and a torso that tapered into a narrow waist, Zach was massive. If he stood, he would no doubt stretch every bit of a six-foot frame. Dark-brown hair cascaded across his forehead, trimmed close to his skull on the sides with artfully unruly curls on top. A strong and linear jaw clenched as he concentrated, and his eyes were his father's same jade green. Zach Braddock ought to be a model rather than a cop.

"Hey, Zach," Tom greeted, tone cautious.

Zach looked up from his computer screen, surprise lighting in his eyes when he saw Tom and Lara. The sergeant rose from his desk chair and shook hands with Tom in greeting, a small smile crossing his face.

"Tom, hey, didn't think I'd get to see you twice in one month," Zach said, voice deep and pleasant.

"Funny how that happens," Tom replied, still guarded. "This is our new lieutenant, Lara Nadeau. L.T., this is Sergeant Braddock, the chief's oldest."

"It's nice to meet you," Lara replied, putting out her hand for a shake. Zach returned the sentiment, shaking her hand and nodding. She could tell by the glint of recognition in his eyes he'd heard her name before.

"Look, Zach," Tom cut in. "I'm not gonna beat around the bush with you, because we've known each other a long time. Lynn Rickerson is dead."

All emotion and color bled from Zach's face. His jaw clenched, eyes blinking quickly in attempt to ward away threatening tears.

"We're going to need you to come in," Tom continued.

Clutching a manila folder, Lara sucked in a deep breath before shouldering into Interview One. Her honeyed-chocolate eyes swept the room, immediately taking note of Tom's presence. He resided in the far corner, arms crossed over his chest, face schooled into complete but professional indifference. It had to be difficult for the captain. Zach seemed to be a favorite of most everyone in the Eastfall and Havenwood police departments, despite whatever transgression was in his past.

Lara's eyes ticked from Tom to the uniform sitting stoically in the chair. She had to admit Zach was an impressive sight. His presence was huge in such a tiny room. He kept his uniform well pressed, not a stray thread or chevron out of place, and his boots polished to a sleek shine. The stubble covering his face seemed just as well-kept as the rest of him.

Silently, Lara crossed to the table that sat dead center of the room. The chair slid metallically across the beat-up linoleum as she sat. Lara knew more eyes than Tom's and Zach's were watching her. The all-seeing eye of the surveillance camera loomed in a top corner of the room, despite the discreet size. This wasn't her first rodeo, but she suddenly felt that nervous itch she got the first time someone sat in her hot seat.

Lara took her time, setting the folder on the table, opening the folder, and leafing through the contents. At this point, there wasn't much to the case file. Prints of photographs taken at the scene had been waiting on her desk once they'd returned. Lara had studied them with what little time she'd had between arrival and stepping into this room.

Next, she took out her notepad, flipping it open to her notes from this morning. She often referred to them while in an interview, and took an extra set of notes for the case file. Though everything in the room was recorded, Lara pulled out her own recording device and engaged it, rattling off the time and date first before launching in.

"This interview is being conducted by Lieutenant Lara Nadeau, with Captain Thomas Sharpe present. Interviewee is Havenwood Police Sergeant Zachariah Braddock. Let the record show that Sergeant Braddock came in willingly. Sergeant Braddock is not under arrest. This is an exploratory interview to gather information. Let's get started so we don't take up too much more of your time." She directed the last statement to the man across the table.

"I wouldn't worry about *my* time, Lieutenant," Zach replied coolly. He sat ramrod straight in the uncomfortable chair, his arms resting on the table, fingers interlocked with each other. He didn't look nervous. There were no peculiar tics or a bouncing leg. His eyes were devoid of emotion, and locked on her own. "Don't think you need to be wasting too much more of your time on dead ends."

Lara nearly snorted. The guy had a set for sure. Zach may have come willingly, but he was not happy to be a suspect. However, as a former detective, the sergeant should know the drill. Any leads were better than none, and besides, after Lara's brief glance at his personnel file, she had to admit his close rate as an investigator had been quite impressive.

"Of course," she replied, finally allowing a terse smile. Glancing down to the table, Lara gingerly grabbed at the fresh, glossy photographs. Slowly, and with great care, she laid them out in front of him. "Do you know this woman?"

"Yes, that's Lynn Rickerson," Zach replied, betraying the slightest uptick in his voice. Seeing the photographs affected him, though he was trying hard not to show it.

"When was the last time you saw Ms. Rickerson?"

"I saw her last week at the grocery store. We crossed paths in the produce section."

"What was your relationship to Ms. Rickerson?"

"We worked in the same school, we dated, and then we broke up."

Lara paused, looking him over. His answers were just as short and curt as her questions. He didn't move once—no wavered tone, no muscle twitch, nothing.

"It's been mentioned that when your relationship with Ms. Rickerson ended, it didn't end well. Tell me more about that, Sergeant."

Finally, evidence emotion existed under that steel-like exterior. His jaw clenched, ever so subtly. A sore topic, even more so now that Lynn was dead.

"We disagreed about many things. We eventually decided it would be better for all parties involved if we ended it."

"I'm going to need more information than that, Sergeant," Lara replied.

"I honestly don't see how that is any of your business, Lieutenant."

"Ms. Rickerson is *dead*, Sergeant," Lara shot back, voice calm, but her fingers grasped at each other tightly, knuckles white. "A well-loved woman who seemingly has no enemies. The only thing questionable I've heard is you two had a volatile ending. How do you think that looks, Sergeant? Do you think it reflects well on you? It's why you're here. It's why you agreed to this interview. I can make it an interrogation, if you'd like, read you your Miranda."

Zach's shoulders rose and fell in a steadying breath.

"Where were you, Sergeant Braddock," Lara pressed on, "thirty hours ago?"

It takes too long for Zach to answer, only a second's hesitation, but it's enough for Lara to know not to believe what he was about to say next.

"I've been at home the past few nights. Watching television," was Zach's reply.

"Can anyone confirm that?"

"No, I live alone."

"Then you know if you can't give me something more solid, I can't rule you out, Sergeant. You'll be my number one person of interest. Do you understand that?"

Zach shrugged. "You've got to do what you've got to do, Lieutenant. But you're wasting your time."

"I don't see how if you can't give me a solid alibi," Lara shot back, annoyance slipping through. It wasn't that Lara wanted to slam the chief's son to the wall, in fact she wanted badly for him to be innocent, for the chief's sake. However, if the stubborn bastard couldn't give her more, there wasn't much else she could do for him. If she was honest, Lara's gut told her there was no way Zach murdered Lynn. Call it her freaky intuition or whatever Tom thought she had. He didn't seem the type to be that brutal, but for him to properly be taken out of the suspect pool, he needed to be more forthcoming. One thing Lara had learned in this job was you never knew what someone could be capable of.

When Zach remained quiet, Lara heaved a sigh before glancing over her shoulder at her captain. Tom's face was red, the expressive skin of a redhead. He was *pissed*. Turning around to Zach, Lara leaned back against the chair.

"All you've got on me is circumstantial at this point," Zach spoke. "There's not much else you can do right now."

"No, but the minute I find something, I'll nail your stubborn, arrogant ass to the wall," Lara growled.

CHAPTER 3

1 40 Wessex Street was once the ancestral home of the Morgans, a founding family of Eastfall. The first house on the property had been built in the late 1660s. Around 1750, the Morgans' eldest son built the existing house. The property remained in the family until the 1990s— a considerable time to keep in one family—when it was sold to the current mayor of Eastfall, Samuel Lothrop.

The house possessed as much of the original structure as modern code allowed and sat on five acres of attempted farmland. The building had been renovated over the years, but about sixty-five percent of the woodwork and frame were original. "History, plus a bit of modern charm" was how Mayor Lothrop had described it to Lara.

The house was Georgian style, with the exterior painted a deep blue. The style was all about symmetry. When a visitor entered, they stood in the main hallway that stretched to the back of the house where another door stood. Four rooms made up the downstairs, two on either side of the focal point. The front two rooms had once been the gentlemen and ladies' parlors. Today, they were an office and a formal dining room. At the back of the house sat the kitchen on one side and an informal living room on the other. Historically, the kitchen would have been a separate building on the property, but it burned down in the late nineteenth century, so the Morgan descendants heavily renovated a room. Today, the face-lift included modern appliances and ample room to cook and entertain.

If Lara ever cooked or entertained.

The informal living room squared off the remainder of the downstairs. Lara spent most of her evenings in that room. The master bedroom sat upstairs with an attached full bath, and three rooms to match their counterparts downstairs. Symmetry.

An attic space capped off the house.

It was plenty of space for a police lieutenant who never seemed to be home, nor owned many material things. However, when the mayor called you personally, offering Eastfall's newest police lieutenant affordable rent in a beautiful house, there was no option to turn it down. Besides, it was quiet, being back from the main road and far from downtown. While Lara had been used to the busyness and noise of Boston, it was good to have silence for a change.

Lara stumbled into the house, a six-pack of beer under one arm, and Chinese take-out under the other. As always, silence reigned except for the distant hum of the heating unit. An antique table stood to Lara's left, one of many pieces of furniture left for her use. She dropped her keys on the table and padded to the back of the house.

Lara, without fail, spent dinner in front of the television, a sports game or other show flickering across the screen. Tonight was no different. Setting the six-pack and brown bag on the coffee table, Lara fell into her nightly routine. First, off came the badge, clattering onto the table. Then, her sidearm and holster placed next to her badge. Lara shucked her suit jacket and threw it over the back of the ratty armchair she'd brought from Boston. It was her father's chair, and Lara didn't have the heart to leave it behind.

It was hockey season, and the Bruins currently skated circles around the Rangers. Lara half-heartedly watched the game, mind occupied by Lynn Rickerson. She wondered if her death was an isolated incident, or if something more sinister was at work. She hoped the autopsy and the crime scene revealed something about who could have committed this horrific act.

After Lara obliterated her beef and broccoli, she sat back with a contented sigh. She tipped up her third beer of the evening, the amber liquid of the Sam Adams disappearing smoothly from the bottle.

A few hours later, Lara blinked awake, realizing she had nodded off. The rest of the bottles in the six-pack covered the table. A couple littered the floor. Why she woke up, she wasn't sure, but could've sworn someone shouted her name. A remnant of a dream, perhaps.

The television sat black and blank from sleep mode kicking in. The lamp next to the couch still illuminated the room. The rest was silence, except for the ticktock of an old clock she inherited from her grandmother. Groaning, Lara sat up, neck twinging with pain from the odd angle she'd slept.

Lara tripped on a Sam Adams bottle as she left the room, heading for the staircase. Movement in the formal dining room caught her eye as her foot hit the first step. She paused, scrubbed at her eyes with her fingers, then turned.

Faint rays from an exterior light filtered through the closed blinds. There was nothing in the room but an antique dining room set, another heirloom from her grandmother. Nothing moved, nothing flashed. Lara could've sworn she'd seen a shadow moving past the doorway.

Chalking it up to exhaustion and beer, she continued up the stairs and collapsed into her bed, clothes and all.

The next morning, Lara woke in a haze. Sitting up, bones and cartilage crackling, she rubbed at her face, feeling the imprint of the creases of her pillow. Reaching out, Lara flailed her hand around for her phone. A brief press of the home button showed it was eight forty-six in the morning.

"Shit," Lara hissed, shooting up from the bed. Her head spun, along with the room. She pressed the heels of her palms into her eyes, waiting a moment or two for the dizziness to pass.

The hot spray of the shower helped combat the headache forming behind her temples. It also helped to get the blood flowing enough to remember she moved from the couch to her room in the wee hours of the morning. Her shoulder ached too, and she placed her palm over pale scar tissue to massage the stiffness. The injury got that way at times, a mild but annoying inconvenience. Sighing, Lara made quick work of getting clean and dressed in slacks, a blouse, and a fresh blazer. With a flourish, she knotted up her dark hair into a haphazard bun, then swiped a layer of mascara across her lashes.

Once downstairs, she grabbed her gun and badge, discarded where she'd left them last night, and positioned both at her waist. She had no time to brew her own coffee or make breakfast. As she made her way to the front door, she decided to hit up Dunkin Donuts en route to work. Her hand reached to the antique table for her keys. Fingertips hit air and smooth wood. Dark eyes searched the surface of the table, then the floor around it, but came up short.

Nothing.

Her keys were gone.

Eyebrows furrowed, Lara backtracked, looking first in the front two rooms, and then searched the back rooms. Eventually, Lara found the keys in the kitchen by a couple of rotten bananas.

Sighing, the lieutenant resisted the urge to crawl back in bed. Not a great start to the day. Deciding to brush it off as memory lapse, Lara headed back to the front door. Throwing it open, Lara gasped in surprise upon seeing an oddly paired couple about to swing the door knocker.

The man was average height and stocky build, though he dressed impeccably in a three-piece suit. He was balding, and whatever hair he did have remaining was mousy brown. Beady blue eyes looked across the threshold at her, and his fleshy face hung down, though it didn't look unkind. Perhaps in his youth the man had been handsome in a way, but age hadn't been his friend.

The woman might have stepped right off the runways of Milan or New York. Tall as Lara, perhaps an inch or so more than Lara, impeccably dressed, with long, shapely legs any woman would kill for, as well as the rest of her lithe but curvy form. Her long, blonde hair was styled carefully in flawless waves. Crystal-blue eyes looked almost mirthful but friendly in their tone, not to mention oddly timeless, as if holding the wisdom of the ages. Her face was delicately featured, and perhaps too perfect.

"I told you we should have called first, Sam!" the blonde woman exclaimed, her face morphing in horror upon noticing Lara's shocked expression.

Lara, eyes still adjusting to the godforsaken bright light of the early morning sun, blinked blearily at the two.

Definitely should've made the coffee.

"Um...can I help you?" she asked, voice rough from lack of use.

"I'm sorry, where are my manners? I'm Sam Lothrop, and this is my wife, Charlotte."

Lara's eyebrows furrowed in confusion for the briefest of moments before they shot up into her dark hairline.

"My God! Please...Please, come in!" Lara scrambled back, waving her arm furiously. "I'm so sorry, I was on my way to work, kinda running a little behind..."

"Which is exactly why I told him we needed to call first instead of just dropping in," the woman—Charlotte—replied. Her blue orbs looked Lara up and down, taking in the lieutenant's appearance. Self-consciousness struck Lara, all too aware of her rumpled clothes, with mismatched blouse and slacks, and hair haphazardly done.

Great first impression to make to one's landlords, not to mention the mayor of the city.

"My apologies. You can blame this venture on me," Sam chuckled. The inflection of his voice and his vocabulary hinted at a true New England businessman—someone constantly out to please people, but more importantly, make a pretty penny doing so. Which might explain his gorgeous, young wife. "I thought we would stop by on our way back into town. Check and make sure everything is in working order and you're settled. I've been a terrible landlord, not coming to welcome you sooner..."

"Oh, wow, I do appreciate that," Lara replied, trying to sound gracious. "Um...I'm Lara, by the way. Lara Nadeau. But, you already know that." After all, they had thoroughly vetted her and her finances before she'd been granted the opportunity to rent the house.

"We probably know more about you than you would like," joked Charlotte.

Lara laughed harder than necessary, perhaps due to the slight hangover or constant sleep deprivation.

"Um..." Lara intoned so eloquently, before scrubbing the

palm of her hand down her face. "C-Can I make you some coffee or somethin'?" Before they could answer, she continued.

"Let me just say, thank you for letting me stay here. This is such a beautiful home."

"We were happy you wanted to rent it. It's been vacant for far too long," the mayor replied.

"Vacant, huh?"

"Yeah, not many people wanting to move to or around Eastfall," Sam supplied. "We Eastfallians are content with what we have and are not much for change."

All three fell silent for an awkward beat, only broken by Lara's carefully hedged repeat question. "You sure I can't get you some coffee?"

"No, no, of course not, dear," Charlotte replied, despite the fact she couldn't be much younger or older than Lara. "We just wanted to pop in to make sure everything was in good shape and see if you needed anything."

"Everything's great, thank you so much. Again, you have a fantastic, beautiful home, and I'm grateful for the opportunity to live here."

"Of course! If you're ever interested in the history of the house, let me know. I have quite the collection of documents," said Sam with a chuckle. It was meant as a joke, considering he was the mayor, and therefore privy to the town's archives.

"When I have some spare time, I will definitely take you up on that," Lara replied, forcing sincerity. As long as she had running water, a Wi-Fi connection, and a bed, Lara was set. No need for further research, as research took over every other aspect of her life.

After she shooed the Lothrop couple away (in the most respectful way, of course), Lara waved as they backed out of the driveway and disappeared up Wessex Street toward Route

1. Letting out a breath she didn't know she'd been holding, the lieutenant ventured out to her unmarked. The air was crisp and cool again, only a few degrees colder than the trend over the past few days. The environment slowly turned from fall to winter, bringing a strange sense of serenity to the land.

CHAPTER 4

The sun glinted off the Hawthorne River as Lara drove over the Veterans Memorial Bridge, heading for midtown. Bucky's, the local cop watering hole, sped by as she followed the twists of Route 1. The old mill buildings, now the headquarters for Angylion Pharmaceuticals, loomed to her right as she crossed over Morgan Avenue, one of the main thoroughfares of the city. It wasn't long before Lara cut a left onto Police Plaza Boulevard and came to a screeching stop in a space designated for unmarked police vehicles.

Eastfall's Police Headquarters comprised three floors and a subterranean complex of holding cells, a rudimentary crime lab, and the city coroner's office. It was brand new within the last five years, courtesy of the mayor's business and budgeting savvy.

Lara used her key card to gain access through the back door. The hallways were empty, with a few other law enforcement officials trickling in. Her office sat on the second floor with the rest of her unit. The Investigative Division was made up of many specialty units, including homicide, robbery, special victims, and white-collar crimes. Since Lara had arrived six months ago, most of her cases had been robberies. Lynn Rickerson's death changed that.

"Hey, Tom," Lara greeted, as she passed the captain's office. Hers sat next door with her name and rank etched in the glass. The room wasn't anything spectacular. It was ten foot by ten foot, with a half wall of windows facing the front of the building and the town center, which included the courthouse and city hall. A simple desk stood inside, with a desktop computer and a couple of filing cabinets. It was stark and sterile, with white walls and even blander trimming. She had nothing hanging except past commendations and achievements from her time in Boston. Nothing personal had made it onto her desk either, except for one picture of her father in formal uniform.

When Lara transferred from Boston, it was with the promise of a promotion. She'd never been interested in the political side of things, and hated what came with being a lieutenant. To her, Tom Sharpe was her authority, though there were junior detectives that looked to her as their authority. It was bizarre, and surreal at times. Being a woman in a position of power, especially in a department not originally your own, was tougher than she could have ever imagined.

Lara barely sat and sipped her coffee before the front desk sergeant called. A woman named Jennifer Cassidy had come to request a moment with her to talk about Lynn Rickerson.

"I'll be right down," she replied, before replacing the phone back into the cradle, and headed for the public elevator.

The front lobby was empty except for a woman of similar age to Lara, with curly, auburn hair and green eyes. She was attractive, but not in the traditional sense. Her mouth was a smidge too big for her face, eyes a little too far apart, and a smattering of barely noticeable freckles adorned her nose. The woman seemed nervous, but above all sad.

"Hi, Jennifer Cassidy?" Lara asked, as she approached, holding out her hand. The woman nodded, sending her curls bouncing, as she shook Lara's hand firmly. "Lieutenant Lara Nadeau, nice to meet you."

"I don't mean to bother you, Lieutenant, but I wanted to talk about Lynn. Lynn Rickerson."

"I'm not at liberty to give any information about ongoing investigations, Ms. Cassidy—"

"No, no, I'm not here for that. I'm here to tell you about her," Jennifer interrupted.

Lara's eyebrow arched, arms crossing over her chest. "What's your relationship to Ms. Rickerson?"

"We're coworkers. Were coworkers..." Jennifer replied, green gaze dropping to the floor. "Our classrooms are—*were* next to each other."

"Let's step over here," Lara urged, unfolding her arms and motioning to a bench off to the side. They sat, and she pulled out her notebook and pencil from the pocket inside her blazer.

"How long have you known Ms. Rickerson?"

"About nine years. We started as first-year teachers together at Eastfall High. We're both alumnae, though we didn't run in the same circles in high school," Jennifer replied.

"Can you think of anyone that would want to hurt her? Old boyfriends?" Lara asked.

"No. People didn't want to hurt her, ever. She was one of the nicest people I've ever known. An amazing teacher. Truly dedicated to her students."

"What do you know about her and Zachariah Braddock's relationship?"

"They were cute together. Like, disgustingly cute. But

then something happened, and as you seem to know, it didn't end well. Lynn didn't want to talk about it, and I didn't want to push. She seemed to have gotten over him, though. That's why I came. A few weeks before you...you found her, she was like her old self again. Really happy and upbeat. She mentioned once, kind of an offhand comment, about a guy. I could only guess she'd recently started seeing someone new. But she was very, very close-lipped about him. I don't know why...but I figured I'd tell someone. It seemed the right thing to do. Maybe important."

"It could be, Ms. Cassidy. Thank you for coming to see me. I'm very sorry for the loss of your coworker. If you think of anything else, please let me know." Lara said with a kind smile.

All Jennifer could do was nod, blinking rapidly to bite back the tears. Lara knew it wasn't easy to lose someone you knew, no matter how close the connection. It always reminded you of your own mortality.

When Lara returned to her office, Tom was waiting for her.

"The chief wants to see us," he huffed.

A moment later, they stepped off the elevator on the third floor where the bigwigs had offices. The receptionist, Norma Simms, sat behind a high-top desk. The two investigators approached, cautious. Norma, having heard their approach, looked up with sharp, ice-blue eyes that harshly analyzed you anytime you interrupted her. Rectangular glasses sat near the tip of her shrewd nose. She was a prickly looking woman in her fifties with a shockingly white knot of hair tied severely at the crown of her head, so severe she belonged more in a library than a police department. Lara wasn't intimidated by many people, not after spending so many years in a male-dominated profession, but Ms. Simms was something else entirely. If the lieutenant ever had business on the third floor, she dreaded going through the Dragon Lady.

"May I help you, Captain?" she asked Tom in a clipped tone, always preferring to address the ranking officer of any group.

"Yeah, the chief called. Said he wanted to see us," Tom replied.

Ms. Simms said nothing, only waved her hand in the chief's direction, and turned back to the computer screen.

Lara wasn't proud of it, but she scurried away from that desk as fast as she could with Tom hot on her heels.

Eastfall's police chief was handsome for a man in his sixties. He had been on the job for forty-odd years, and the toll of it showed in the gunmetal gray of his hair and the tiredness in his light-green eyes.

Chief Henry Braddock hunched over his keyboard, ineffectively pecking away with two fingers. Lara and Tom stood in the doorway for a moment before Lara raised her hand to rap her knuckles against the door. The chief's head picked up. An odd twinge squeezed in her gut at how much Zachariah Braddock looked like his father.

"Tom, Lara, come on in," he motioned. "Close the door behind you."

Never a good thing to hear from one's boss.

Lara let the door click shut behind her, and the two sat stiffly in chairs situated in front of the chief's desk.

"Look, Chief—" Tom began, before Chief Braddock interrupted him.

"I get it. You're doing your jobs, which is exactly what I need you to do. I asked you up here for an update. I didn't ask you up here because I want you to ignore my son as a suspect."

Lara may not love her time in the distinguished police

department of Eastfall, but she respected the hell out of the chief—had since day one.

For the next ten minutes, Lara filled the chief in on the information they'd gathered thus far. She didn't leave anything out, not even the interview with Sergeant Braddock. The chief looked perturbed, but didn't comment. When Lara finished, ending with Jennifer Cassidy's new information, the chief nodded. He seemed tense, folded hands on the desk white from clutching tight. He'd never witnessed such a horrific crime as this. He'd seen the crime scene photographs, had been aghast at the details, even though he tried to hide his reactions.

"I don't have to tell you to make this top priority. And I know I don't have to ask for your discretion. Just be sure to keep me updated on developments as they come. I'd rather know things than be blindsided, and have to explain to a terrified city, you know?"

Lara and Tom nodded, feeling like they'd dodged a bullet.

"Alright," the chief continued. "Now get outta here. Go catch that psycho."

Out of the corner of her eye, Lara could tell Tom regretted eating lunch.

"Cause of death was strangulation," Doctor Stephanie Rogers declared. "There was petechial hemorrhaging and bruises around her throat. The vocal cords were crushed."

Between them lay Lynn Rickerson, the familiar Y incision slashed across her chest and torso. Lara had gotten the call that Dr. Rogers had completed her official report. Tom had insisted on going with her, but now regret splashed across his face.

"From what I can tell, your crime scene was your primary.

She wasn't dumped there. The murderer did the deed where we found her. He raped her first, no doubt choking her as he did. No semen was left behind, so he was smart enough to use a condom. The removal of the brain was post-mortem. Part of the frontal lobe is missing, as I noted preliminarily. Stomach contents are still being processed, but a toxicology screening showed nothing that shouldn't be there. No defensive wounds on her hands or anywhere else, which makes me think she knew her killer, and went willingly with him."

"Jesus," Tom hissed through his teeth.

"Anything else, Doc?" Lara asked, pencil poised over her notebook.

Dr. Rogers shook her head and sighed as she removed her glasses. They fell against her scrubs, dangling from her neck on a rose-gold chain. "Nothing. No foreign hairs, no bodily fluids, nothing I could find to link to a person other than our vic."

Lara's hopes of the presence of DNA fizzled. She remembered Locard's Principle from the academy. One always left behind some trace of their presence. This person couldn't have just appeared and disappeared without leaving a clue. There had to be something.

They thanked the medical examiner and headed out of the lab.

"What're you thinking?" Tom asked, stepping onto the elevator.

"I'm thinking we need to find out who this mystery guy is. I'm going to do my own sweep of Lynn's apartment, see if there's anything that went unnoticed by the techs."

"I'll come with you."

"No, you don't have to," Lara replied, stepping off the elevator and heading back toward her office. "Stay here, finish up the phone interviews with other EHS teachers. I'll go to her place."

"Are you sure?" Tom asked, walking in stride next to her.

"Yep. Don't worry, I'll be—"

Lara stopped dead. A familiar figure sat in an armchair in one of the alcoves dotting the hallway.

"Oh man, it's lover boy," Tom whispered, teasing.

The figure sat forward, face coming into view.

Oliver Bennett, Assistant District Attorney.

The man stood at their approach, looming at a cool six feet, two inches. Bennett was a few years older than Lara and handsome as the devil. If the devil had dark-brown eyes, always wore well-tailored suits covering a lean frame, and had dark hair carefully gelled. Lara wasn't sure how, but the man even had stubble down to an art form, putting Zach Braddock to shame. His fingernails were well manicured, and eyebrows carefully sculpted. This was a guy not afraid to do what was necessary to craft his appearance.

"Lieutenant!" Oliver greeted with a charming smile.

"Right. I'll, uh, talk to you later," Tom muttered. He sidled past her and immediately shut himself in his office.

Asshole.

"Hey, ADA Bennett," Lara said, with as much enthusiasm as she could muster. She reached for her keys and unlocked the door to her office.

"I was in the neighborhood, thought I'd stop by," Oliver said, as he leaned against the doorframe.

"Cracking skulls at the courthouse?"

"You know it," he replied, dark eyes watching as Lara roamed around the room, trying her hardest to look busy and unavailable.

It wasn't that she didn't like the guy. On the contrary, Lara very much liked ADA Oliver Bennett, both in the courtroom and out of the courtroom. Lara had met Oliver not long after arriving in Eastfall. They collaborated on a case, one thing led to another, and— they had an encounter. It had been one damn good encounter. Lara couldn't help but think the poor guy wanted something more. She wasn't one for relationships. Not anymore. But Lara didn't have the heart to tell him.

"Can we...uh...catch up another time?" Lara asked when she located her keys to her unmarked. "I've got this big case, and—"

"Say no more!" Oliver exclaimed, hands held outward, his palms facing her. "Like I said, I was close and wanted to say hi. I know you're busy, so maybe I'll catch you at Bucky's sometime. I owe you a drink."

Which was what they were supposed to have done, instead of *the encounter* as she'd taken to calling it.

Lara let a genuine smile form. It was small, but it was there. "Thanks. I'll hold you to that."

It wasn't until Lara was in her unmarked and driving away from headquarters that she glanced in the rearview mirror and saw she was blushing.

CHAPTER 5

Lynn Rickerson's living space was as Lara imagined—homey, mid-rent housing near Eastfall High School. The crime scene technicians already completed a sweep of the apartment yesterday after the discovery of the body, but had not caught anything out of the ordinary.

Upon her arrival, Lara commandeered the superintendent of the building, a squat, older man eager to help. The super sang Lynn Rickerson's praises—always paid rent on time, quiet, took care of her space. The man didn't hang around once the door swung open. He had other matters to attend to.

The apartment was uncluttered and tidy. A mixture of movie posters and cheap craft-store art hung on the wall space. There were plenty of personal photographs, a few of Lynn's mother and various other people. The kitchen was small, but fit the size of the apartment. Adjacent to the kitchen sat a closet and a small kitchen table with two chairs. Inside the closet, Lara found a stacked washer and dryer. One bedroom with a full bath and walk-in closet rounded out the place Lynn had called home.

After a cursory pass of the apartment, Lara saw nothing out of the ordinary. Once back in the living room, the lieutenant began her real work. A decent-sized flat-screen television perched on a low-slung table against one wall. On the opposite wall stood a well-loved and overstuffed couch. It was boxy around the edges but looked damn comfortable. A balcony and sliding glass door took up the majority of the third wall, and an armchair completed the remaining space with a couple of bookcases. Reaching into her jacket pocket, Lara pulled out a pair of latex gloves. She kept a baggie of them on her at all times but couldn't remember warm gloves to save her life.

Lara meticulously lifted the couch cushions, felt in the crevices, looked underneath the couch, and so on. This was perhaps Lara's favorite part, had always been, especially during her time in Boston. Alone, with no distractions and just her keen eyes, Lara loved leaving no stone unturned, so to speak. If there was something here to find, she would find it. Details were important in every case, and Lara enjoyed the details. Her attention to detail was what got her many commendations in her earlier years as a detective.

Once she searched the couch and armchair, Lara moved to the kitchen, opting to leave the bookcases for last. The kitchen yielded nothing of importance, and neither did the full bath.

The distant hum of a heater kicked on as Lara swept through Lynn's bedroom. She searched the closet and every pocket of Lynn's clothing, then the dresser, under the bed, under the mattress, in the sheets, all to no avail. Inside the nightstand drawer, Lara found a picture of Lynn with Zach Braddock. The ex-couple were at Boston Common, in front of the Make Way for Ducklings statue. They both grinned up at Lara, happy and smitten. It surprised Lara to find this vestige of Lynn and Zach's relationship. Though the breakup had been volatile, Lynn still harbored feelings for him.

With the picture in hand, Lara returned to the living room to comb through the bookcases. She pulled out every book and flipped through the pages.

Nothing.

Sighing, Lara placed the last book back in its slot, and headed for the door. On her way, something muted-green caught her eye. It was another book, resting on the breakfast nook of the kitchen. In her focus, Lara had looked over it.

A book out and within easy reach was a book in progress.

Padding back to the kitchen, Lara grabbed the tattered copy of *Persuasion*. A piece of paper fluttered out and fell to the floor. Peering down, Lara swept it up between her fingers and unfolded it.

She skimmed the contents. It was a letter offering Lynn an opportunity to join a clinical trial for a new drug to treat high blood pressure. Lara recalled the toxicology report, and Dr. Rogers's careful note that Lynn Rickerson had been taking medicine for hypertension. According to the brochure, Angylion Pharmaceuticals offered the clinical trial of the experiment. Lara recognized the logo of an infinity symbol formed by feathery wings. Could the mystery man Lynn had been seeing work at Angylion? Or perhaps another potential candidate for the same clinical experiment?

The sun began its descent into the afternoon hours as Lara headed back to the center of town. The Angylion Pharmaceuticals corporate complex teemed with workers and vehicles, but eventually Lara squeezed the unmarked into an empty parking space.

The once-booming business of Eastfall's textile mill had

been the main employer of the city for years. In fact, when the mill opened in the middle years of the nineteenth century, the town had still been about the size and population it was at its foundation. Now, because people had moved to the area for work at the mill, the town had become a thriving city. When the mill closed at the end of World War II, the fledgling medicine company of Angylion took over one of the vacant buildings. Angylion now sprawled to include the entire campus and was a successful business venture that employed many of the citizens of Eastfall with skilled and unskilled jobs.

Three large buildings once comprised the Willoughby & Company Textile Mill. Today, Angylion had repurposed them. One of the buildings housed the administrative hand of the company. Another building was for research and development, and the third was the factory and shipping center. Lara headed for the administration building, which was blessedly warm inside, chasing away the chill of the afternoon. Plush armchairs scattered the waiting area for those with appointments to meet the higher-ups, and a long receptionist counter served to block access to the rest of the building. The opulent decor held Lara's attention immediately, from the Art Deco lighting fixtures to the parquet floors to the steadily trickling fountain dead center of the large space. The statuary of the fountain unsettled Lara, not overtly, but enough to make her stomach twist. It depicted an angel, his wings curled around a sphere easily recognizable as the Earth. The angel's expression, though meant to be serene and comforting, looked menacing.

Lara stepped rapidly around the fountain and up to the desk, wanting to shake the gaze of the angel. A young woman sat behind the high counter, wearing a headset. She masterfully fielded phone calls, transferring them with a flourish.

When she noticed Lara, the blonde gave a wide, but not at all genuine smile.

"Welcome to Angylion Pharmaceuticals, how can I assist you today?"

"Yeah, uh, hi," Lara began, reaching for her badge and flashing her shield. "My name is Lieutenant Lara Nadeau with Eastfall Police. I was wondering if there was someone I could talk to that works on clinical trials?"

The blonde looked startled to see the badge, but to her credit, her blue eyes were critical as she examined the shield and Lara's ID.

"May I ask what this pertains to?" she asked, as her fingers worked effortlessly at the keypad of the phone.

"A police investigation," was all Lara supplied.

The blonde nodded, silent, listening to the ringing on the other end of the line. After a few murmured words, she hung up and gave Lara the same fake smile as before.

"Dr. Gibbons will be over shortly. He is our assistant director of Research and Development."

"Great, thank you," Lara replied, forcing her mouth into the exact smile the receptionist had given her.

She stepped away from the counter and shoved her hands in her jacket pockets. Lara did not have to wait long.

"Lieutenant?"

Turning, Lara's gaze met with a pleasant looking gentleman. He was as tall as he was round, and wore a fitted three-piece suit.

"Yes, Lieutenant Lara Nadeau. And you are Dr. Gibbons?"

"Correct. I am Dr. Robert Gibbons, Assistant Director of Research and Development here at Angylion. How can I be of help?" His speech revealed a crisp, refined English accent.

"I'm investigating a wrongful death and found a brochure that suggested she was considering a clinical trial for blood pressure medication. I was wondering if I could talk to you about that?"

"Lieutenant, I hope you are not implying our drugs killed her?" Dr. Gibbons asked, immediately on the defensive.

"Not at all, doctor. My apologies if it seemed I was. I'm looking for connections between my victim and others involved in the clinical trial. Just gathering some information."

"Ah, I see," the man said, visibly relaxing. "I will do what I can. Let us go over to the R&D building to see what we can find."

It was a brief walk to the research and development building. Dr. Gibbons led Lara to a door and swiped his keycard. They traveled through a hallway and a glass connector to another building. Scientists in lab coats scurried around, clipboards or biohazard containers in hand, going about their day-to-day.

Lara wordlessly followed Dr. Gibbons through labyrinthian corridors, passing through the sterile environment uneasily. The starkness reminded her of hospitals, and she hated hospitals ever since having her appendix removed as a teenager. There were tons of laboratories with names Lara couldn't begin to understand. She gleaned that there were various departments, and each department had its own slew of offices and labs.

Eventually, Dr. Gibbons came to a halt in front of a glass door proclaiming the clinical trials department lay beyond. An overhead bell chimed as they stepped inside the office space. On cue, a middle-aged, dark-haired woman appeared, lab coat crisp and stark white.

"Dr. Gibbons," the woman greeted, surprised by the visit from her superior.

"Dr. Michaelson," Dr. Gibbons nodded. "Lieutenant

Nadeau has some questions for you regarding a potential patient for the *Gwaed* clinical trials."

"I am limited in what I am allowed to tell you, Lieutenant, due to privacy," Dr. Michaelson replied, not unkindly.

"I will be grateful for whatever information you can offer," Lara replied.

Dr. Michaelson motioned for her to follow, and they stepped around a corner and into an office. The woman's name was on the door along with her credentials. A lot of stuff about biochemistry, and even more words and abbreviations Lara didn't comprehend. Dr. Gibbons followed closely behind Lara, and both made themselves comfortable in the proffered chairs.

"What is the patient's name?" Dr. Michaelson asked, logging in to her computer.

"Lynn Rickerson," Lara replied.

"Oh yes," Dr. Michaelson said with a smile, typing in the familiar name. "What a doll. Funny as all get out."

"Yes, well, unfortunately, she's dead."

That brought down the mood in the room. Dr. Michaelson's eyes misted over, eyebrows scrunched. Lara wasn't often known for her tact during an investigation. She didn't mince words, because there wasn't time to do so. She'd left guilt at the door a long time ago, allowing for curtness to speak for itself.

"That's awful," Dr. Michaelson murmured, eyes misty as she trained them on the computer screen.

"As I was searching her apartment, I found this letter," Lara pressed on, producing the folded letter encased in an evidence bag.

Dr. Michaelson took the bag carefully, and skimmed over the words, nodding in recognition.

"Yes, this is the initial interest letter we send. We get referrals from primary care physicians. Ms. Rickerson came to several of the introductory meetings where we explain the finer points of the drug, what to expect from the process...that sort of thing. She hadn't officially signed on for the trial. Patients have until the end of the month to decide."

"Were you present at these meetings, doctor?" Lara asked.

"I run all of the meetings myself, yes."

"Did you notice Ms. Rickerson conversing with many people at these meetings?"

"She talked to everyone, Lieutenant. I only met with her a handful of times, but you were just...drawn to her, you know? She was magnetic and so personable."

"There wasn't anyone she seemed particularly friendly with?"

Dr. Michaelson sat in thought for a moment, eyes moving as if searching for an answer in the air.

"She did seem rather close to a male patient, and Jeff, who's a member of my research team."

"I don't suppose I could get the name of that male patient?" Lara asked, knowing the answer but figuring she would try anyway.

"I can't," Dr. Michaelson replied regretfully, though she would have no doubt produced the name in a heartbeat if not for privacy agreements.

"Can I speak with Jeff, then?"

"Of course, but unfortunately, Jeff isn't here today. He requested the day off."

Lara nodded, reaching into her jacket pocket for her notebook. "Could I have Jeff's full name?"

"His name is Jeffrey McMullens. You don't think..."

"I need to follow every lead I can, Dr. Michaelson."

CHAPTER 6

J effrey McMullens did not answer his phone, nor did he answer the door when Lara drove by on the roundabout way back to her office. She filed McMullens's contact information away for later.

When she returned to HQ, Tom had finished interviewing Lynn Rickerson's coworkers with no solid results. Tests had yet to be returned from the crime scene techs, though they had retrieved Lynn Rickerson's financials. The report waited in her email inbox, which Lara mulled over until her eyes crossed. Nothing out of the ordinary—crappy teacher salary, normal bills every month, savings accounts, and retirement accounts. Nothing that screamed entanglement with a sadistic killer.

Midmorning hit, and Oliver Bennett ducked his head in on his way to discuss an upcoming case with the chief. He smiled and waved from the doorway. Lara smiled and waved in return, a giddy sensation wriggling in her belly.

"Next time I come back around like this, I'll make sure to bring food," Oliver joked, before bidding her goodbye and disappearing to have his meeting with Chief Braddock.

In the early afternoon slump, Lara escaped her desk and took the stairs to the first floor. The coffee was always better downstairs with patrol, and she desperately needed a caffeine jolt. Sidling up to the coffeepot, Lara took the urn and poured the liquid into her mug. It had been a Christmas gift from her dad, not long after she'd made it through her probationary period as a patrol officer. Emblazoned on one side of the mug were the words: WOW, LOOK AT YOU BECOMING A POLICE OFFICER AND SHIT. On the other side was a cartoon police cruiser and her name.

"Seems kind of ironic."

Lara turned, meeting the hazel gaze of Sierra Fitzgerald, another of Eastfall's finest patrol officers.

Shame Sierra didn't have quite the same respect as Lara held for her.

"What does?" Lara asked, not wanting to bite, but doing it anyway.

"Your mug. It's ironic, considering I'd hardly call you a police officer," Fitzgerald replied. Sierra stood tall, her body athletic, with brown hair held tightly in a bun and hazel eyes that always leveled Lara with untold scrutiny. Sierra was proud of her job and proud of her department. To her, Lara was an outsider, no better than a pest invading a warm and beloved home. They worked together on several previous cases, and from the get-go Sierra had been thorny.

"Congratulations on your commendation and Medal of Valor," Lara said, choosing instead to highlight a recent major achievement, rather than fall into another barbed conversation. "Saving that mother and daughter from a fire...awfully heroic of you."

Fitzgerald seemed surprised at the praise.

"Thanks. I did what anyone would have done."

"I can't say anyone would have run into a burning apartment. At least anyone not a trained firefighter."

Sierra shuffled from foot to foot, heated gaze softer and now rooted to the floor.

"I was just happy to help," she murmured.

Lara recognized much of herself in Sierra. There was an ambition in the patrol officer that could not be matched. Lara remembered those early days, the drive to be something great, to protect and save as many people as possible. If this was any other universe or life, Lara would have gladly been Sierra's mentor, but the disdain that existed in the younger woman could not be surmounted. Why it was there, Lara could not say. The chief had assured her no one knew her past, but she knew how gossip got around in police stations. Sierra probably knew and didn't much like having someone like Lara around. Especially someone that came from the outside.

"Right, well, you have yourself a great day, Officer," Lara said, injecting a hint of snideness.

"You too, Lieutenant. Enjoy it up in your ivory tower, while all the real police work gets done down here."

And there was the parting shot.

Lara, having already made it to the elevator, stepped in as the door opened, acting as though she had not heard the remark.

More than anything, Lara wished to be accepted in the new place she called home. It had been the same back in Boston. Forced to fight for respect and acceptance, Lara busted her ass to prove she could police as well as any other. What she learned along the way had been a valuable lesson. Who gives a shit what others think? As long as you did your job, and did it well, no sly comments could touch you. This quick realization hit hard, but times came when it still jabbed her in the belly. Especially in Eastfall, where she knew practically no one, and most people had been just shy of antagonistic to her since she walked through the door.

A few hours later, Tom poked his head in her office.

"Hey, let's get out of here. First round's on me."

Bucky's Bar and Grill was an Eastfall staple since 1983. The owner, Bucky, had been an Eastfall police officer up until 2003, in which he retired to spend the rest of his days running the restaurant full time. The decor screamed American sports bar with sports memorabilia, antique items probably taken straight out of a junkyard, and a beat-up old jukebox. The jukebox didn't work, its existence merely for aesthetics. The tables were dark wood, crudely shaped, and the surfaces lacquered to within an inch of their lives.

It was a cop bar, a step above a dive, but the atmosphere was surprisingly pleasant. Lara loved it. The place reminded her of an old watering hole back in Boston, Alfredo's. It was also a cop bar, a few streets removed from Beacon Hill. She used to stop in once a week or so, mostly whatever day was her Friday. As a patrol officer, that could have been any day of the week, depending on the schedule. Her father had also frequented Alfredo's, even in retirement. It'd been a great commiserating spot with her Field Training Officer and beat partner, and a great place to meet up with her father.

When Tom and Lara ambled in, business had already kicked up as uniforms ended their shifts. Lara immediately spotted Captain Amelia Shepherd, head of the Cyber Security division, and the only other high-ranking woman in the entire department. The two locked eyes and Amelia's chocolate eyes lit up with a smile as she waved them over to the table she'd commandeered. Amelia was happily married to her high school sweetheart, Armand. Together, they had three children, ages ranging from six to twelve. One of the first things Lara learned about Amelia was how fiercely she loved her family. Lara admired, and envied, that. Amelia was a beautiful woman in her late forties, with light-brown skin and dark, tight curls.

"Started without us, huh?" Tom chuckled, as he sat in the chair across from her. Lara followed, sliding into the seat next to Amelia.

"Unlike you Investigative types, I keep decent hours," Amelia joked, eyes sparkling with mirth, as she took a sip of her beer. "Speaking of...your dead body is all the talk at HQ."

"Yeah," Lara sighed.

"Everyone that knows anything is being tight-lipped. That bad?"

Before either could answer, a waitress appeared at their side with frosted beer glasses filled with Sam Adams, Lara and Tom's favorite.

"Thanks, Tiff," they both said as the woman set down the glasses. Tiffany winked and scooted away.

"I've never seen anything like it," Tom replied gravely.

Amelia knew not to press.

The three companions lapsed into idle conversation, enjoying the precious downtime, until the front entrance swung open, letting in a draft of cold air and Sergeant Zach Braddock.

Lara and the sergeant locked eyes immediately, to her chagrin. A look passed over his handsome features, one she couldn't quite define, as he turned and moved toward the bar. It wasn't as if it was her fault he'd been pegged as a murder suspect. Why such coolness and hostility? Surely he couldn't fault her for doing her job. Lara glanced over at Tom, who also noticed Zach's entrance. They both turned, looking down at the table.

"I heard about that too," Amelia said, polishing off her pint.

Police officers were worse than old ladies at their weekly trip to the salon.

"I guess he couldn't go to a bar in Havenwood and save us the trouble," Lara murmured.

"Stubborn bastard," Tom huffed.

"If he'd just tell us where he was..."

Another beer later, and Amelia bowed out to get home to her family. Tom followed her out, and Lara opted to leave as well, not wanting to risk a confrontation with Sergeant Braddock. Taking a roundabout way home, Lara stopped at a gas station for a six-pack and finished the rest of the drive home with her stomach grumbling for food and her mind preoccupied by Lynn Rickerson.

The fading light of the sun dipped below the horizon as Lara turned down her street. When she got closer, she noticed, through the trees, a sleek, white BMW parked in the driveway. Pulling in beside the car, she saw a flash of familiar, perfectly styled blonde hair sitting in the driver's seat.

The mayor's wife, Charlotte.

"I know we keep imposing on you," the young woman greeted cheerfully, getting out of the car at the same time as Lara. "I swear we don't normally visit our tenants this much. In fact, I avoid this place as much as possible. I just figured you as a hard-working career woman who probably didn't have time to cook much so...I made you a casserole."

"That's way too kind of you, Mrs. Lothrop. I appreciate it." But not the painful reminder she still had yet to go to the grocery store. "Will you come in?"

"Sure! And, please, call me Charlotte. I promise I won't stay long—I know you must be tired."

The blonde carried the casserole into the kitchen and set it down on empty counter space. It smelled heavenly, and Lara's mouth began to water. She hadn't had lunch that day. Or breakfast, for that matter.

"We appreciate you keeping up with the house. It truly is a treasure to the city."

"It's no problem. I clean regularly. Probably too regularly. It's a...a quirk of mine."

More like a coping mechanism suggested by a psychologist, as a way to occupy her mind and keep a clean, calm space.

"Well, I have all the time in the world to do both." Was that resentment laced in Charlotte's tone? It must get boring being the trophy wife of some rich, older man.

Mr. Lothrop owned a marketing firm in Boston and often worked from his office at city hall. Charlotte had to have had ambitions at one point, and they couldn't have included being an out-of-work, stay-at-home wife.

"However," Charlotte began again. "I don't have enough time to garden. You should see my garden at the house. It's so overgrown. It's almost winter so it's all pretty much dead anyway."

Lara grimaced. "Sorry, I'm a city girl. I don't believe in gardens. I tried keeping a cactus alive once, but somehow managed to kill it."

Charlotte laughed, a musical sound. "Good to know. I'll make sure to have someone come over in the future to tend to the garden out back."

"I don't mind cutting grass. Pulling weeds and remembering to water? Yeah, that's not gonna happen."

"Fair. Well, I best be going. I hope you have a good night. Anything you need, don't hesitate to call. You have both our numbers, correct?"

"Yes, ma'am." Lara paused. "Um, would you like to stay and enjoy some of your hard work? Or is Mr. Lothrop waiting for you?"

Charlotte hesitated, pondering. "I think I could stay and have a plate."

Lara couldn't remember the last time she'd had a truly enjoyable, companionable experience with a woman her own age. They sat in front of the television, munching on the delicious casserole and watching Jeopardy, shouting out answers.

"You said outside you tried to avoid this place as much as possible. Why is that?" Lara asked, curious, not having missed the offhand comment from earlier in the driveway.

Charlotte laughed delicately around a mouthful of the casserole, waving her hand. "Forgive me, I shouldn't have said that. I just...I do tend to avoid coming here by myself is all."

"Should I be concerned?" Lara asked, feigning a humorous tone, but was indeed now wary.

"Oh, God, no. Not if you don't get creeped out easily."

"Why would I get creeped out?"

"I don't know how you feel about haunted houses, but I'm pretty sure this place is one."

The serious way in which Charlotte delivered that statement surprised Lara a little. She'd grown up Catholic, with a very Catholic family, and with that came talk of certain superstitions of the mystical and otherworldly. Lara never bought into it.

"I've never felt creeped out here." That wasn't entirely true.

"Oh, then you're fine. It's probably just my imagination, and Sam's stories that he spins." Charlotte laughed it off.

"So how long have you lived in Eastfall?" Lara asked, quickly changing the subject. She popped another forkful of casserole into her mouth. It truly was a thing of beauty, a culinary masterpiece. Or maybe it was just the fact that it was the first home-cooked meal she'd had in a while.

"As long as I've been married to Sam, so about four years. He's my first husband, and I'm his first wife."

That surprised Lara, considering Sam Lothrop had to be at least thirteen years Charlotte's senior.

"Are you from Massachusetts originally?"

"Maine, actually. From a town called Falmouth. It's in the southeastern part of the state."

Lara learned Charlotte had attended college, studying literature, in Boston. The blonde was an aspiring writer, though she hadn't ever finished a piece in her life. She had worked as an English teacher in Eastfall, when she met Mr. Lothrop. The way Charlotte spoke of Sam Lothrop, however, could only be described as fond. Despite what Lara had thought about Charlotte leading a dull life as a trophy wife, Charlotte spoke so highly of the mayor, and about how she very much enjoyed being part of the community. Lara considered herself a good judge of motives and someone's character, but she'd completely misread Charlotte Lothrop. She was far from some vapid, rich woman, and proved to be quite intelligent. It was easy to judge, to want to think of Charlotte as a gold digger. Why else would she be with a much older, rich man? Despite her initial judgement, Lara would bet her police pension Charlotte genuinely loved her husband.

Another hour later, Charlotte insisted she leave. They made loose plans to try and have another social evening in the future. It surprised her how much she'd actually enjoyed the other woman's company. Lara stood at the front door and waved as Charlotte drove off, the BMW quickly disappearing into the night.

As Lara rinsed dishes to be put into the dishwasher, a soft but resounding creak echoed from somewhere above her head. Her eyes drifted to the ceiling, waiting for the noise to repeat, thinking maybe it was the house settling. After a brief moment of silence, however, the steady cadence of what sounded like heavy footfalls came. Swallowing thickly, Lara turned off the sink. Maybe it was something in the plumbing?

Another beat of silence later, and the rhythmic thuds began again.

Thud. Thud. Thud. Thud.

Maybe an animal had gotten in through the attic?

With Charlotte's earlier comments racing through her mind, Lara reached for the ankle holster she had yet to take off. Palming the familiar grip of the Sig Sauer, she cautiously and quietly made her way toward the stairs. Lara had been there long enough to learn which floorboards and which steps creaked, and avoided them now. With her back to the wall, she advanced, carefully making her way up the staircase. The noises came again, heavy and deliberate. At the top of the stairs, Lara peered around the corner, looking either way.

The sounds ceased.

There was no one, no shadow of movement, no creak. Nothing.

Lara moved to the left down the hall, testing the attic door first to find it secured. She continued room to room, finding nothing that could be a source. When she crept into the last room, her bedroom, her heart leapt into her throat. The curtains at the window fluttered for a millisecond, then stopped. Her fingers went for the light switch, illuminating the room. Nothing revealed the cause of the disturbance. Perhaps it had been a draft? Or the heat flowing from a duct?

Scrubbing her palm down her face, Lara heaved a sigh.

The movement of the curtains was a trick of the light from the outside streetlamp. The sounds had been the house creaking, perhaps water running through the pipes.

She would keep track of these occurrences, and let the Lothrops know if it persisted.

Trudging back down the stairs to the living room, Lara finished the six-pack she'd brought home and passed out on the couch. Several hours later she awoke and, in her alcohol-induced slumber, could not tell if the faint pacing of footsteps upstairs was real or in her dream.

CHAPTER 7

After her father's death and the incident that followed, Lara's dreams were constant triggers—memories she loathed to relive over and over, like a broken record. When she drank, those dreams, nightmares rather, became muted. Lara eventually got to the point where she didn't remember much of her dreams, if she dreamed at all.

But this one...

This dream was unlike any she had experienced before.

She was a spectator, a voyeur on a meeting she was not meant to see. The room was dark except for tendrils of light emanating from wall sconces, illuminating the hexagonal shape of the room. Silence reigned, until broken by muffled voices from dark figures seated in the center of the room. One stood in front of a long table filled with other shrouded shapes, a humanoid figure, as far as Lara could tell with the dim lighting.

The others were nightmarish creatures. Though they appeared humanoid, horns sprouted from several of the figures' heads. One appeared to have a long, barbed tail that swayed back and forth. Another had a single eye in the middle of its forehead. Yet another had too many eyes to count.

The speech patterns were off, even from the lone figure in the center, the only human in the room. Their face was shrouded by a hood, while the rest of the cloak shielded Lara from discerning other distinguishing features.

They weren't speaking English.

Nor did they speak any language Lara recognized.

The very sound of the syllables and intonations sent shivers of dread down Lara's spine. Raw evil permeated the space, falling heavy across Lara's shoulders.

None in the room noticed Lara's presence, of which she was grateful. A thought flitted through her subconscious—she shouldn't be here, it was forbidden, she shouldn't be privy to the content of the meeting.

A shrill sound echoed through the room. Lara pressed her palms to her ears, trying to drown it out. Her hands didn't muffle the noise. At first she couldn't tell the origins of the sound. Dread curled in her stomach—perhaps the sound came from one of the horrific creatures.

Lara's eyes flew open as she sucked in a deep breath.

The piercing shrill was her cellphone ringtone.

Hands lowered, reaching for the device, only briefly acknowledging she had been clutching her palms to her ears in reality as well as in the nightmare-scape.

"H-Hello?" Lara croaked, nearly rolling right off the couch in her haste to grab the phone.

A quick glance at the cable box underneath the television told her it was 7:45 a.m.

"Lieutenant? This is Jeffrey McMullens. You've been trying to reach me?"

After a quick change of clothes, Lara pushed her way into Grimm Brothers' Bakery. The shop sat in the historic district of Eastfall, a town staple for nearly one hundred years. The theme was, of course, the Grimm Brothers' fairy tales. Products ranged from coffee to freshly baked bread to any other pastry under the sun, all with a name matching the theme. The wall decor comprised hand-painted trees to represent the numerous stories of kids getting lost in the woods. On one wall, a candied house loomed, with two children following a path to the front door. On another wall, a tall tower held a fair maiden, golden hair hanging from the window with a prince at the bottom, asking to climb up. Grimm theme aside, it was a quaint little shop, and Lara enjoyed their cannoli and eclairs.

Jeffrey McMullens sat in a back corner, foot tapping a mile a minute against the scuffed linoleum, fingers idly drumming against a coffee mug. When she spotted him, the only other customer, Lara motioned toward the front counter and held up a finger.

No way this interview would happen without coffee first.

With a piping-hot mug of black coffee in one hand and a plate with a "Granny's Apple Cruller" in the other, Lara finally situated herself across from McMullens.

"Morning. Lieutenant Nadeau," she said shortly, by way of greeting.

"Jeff McMullens," he replied.

Jeffrey McMullens was the stereotypical "nerd." He wore glasses, high-waisted pants, loafers, and a checked shirt with matching bow tie. His ash-blond hair was cropped short, and blue eyes held sharp intelligence. He wasn't classically handsome, but no doubt turned a head or two.

Lara didn't immediately jump into her questions. First, she enjoyed a few, deep sips from the mug and a couple large bites of the delicious confection. Crullers reminded her of her father, as they had been one of his favorites.

"Okay," she said after another sip, feeling the liquid ambrosia settling in her belly, warming her limbs, and more importantly, chasing away the fog. "Thank you for meeting with me, Mr. McMullens."

"I felt I didn't have much of a choice. Not when the police want to talk to you."

Ignoring the subtle jibe, Lara pressed on.

"What can you tell me about Lynn Rickerson? She was a potential participant in your blood pressure medicine clinical trial, correct?"

Jeff McMullens's face phased between confusion and recognition.

"Lynn? What about Lynn?"

"What was your impression of her? Your relationship to her?"

McMullens didn't like the implication of the last question. Sitting up, back straight, he leaned in.

"I met Lynn Rickerson a few times at informational meetings for the clinical trial. She was extremely nice, hilarious, and a patient."

"Mmhmm..." Lara hummed, almost absently, as she ripped off another bite of the cruller.

"And you had no contact with her, whatsoever, outside of the clinical environment?"

"No," said Jeff, vehemently. "It is unethical and could mean experiment tampering."

"But you wanted to?"

The question caught him off guard again.

"What's this about, Lieutenant?"

"Can you please just answer the question, Mr. McMullens? A simple 'yes' or 'no' would suffice."

Jeff fell silent. Lara saw the gears turning, realization of how his defensiveness must look. He let out a defeated sigh.

"Yes, I wanted to. I really liked her. A lot. But I never followed through, would never have followed through. My work is too important to me."

"Is there anyone else she seemed close to in the meetings?" Lara pressed.

"Besides everyone else?"

Lara fought back a sigh.

"Anyone in particular?"

"There was one other potential candidate for the trial she seemed close with." There was a hint of jealousy in McMullens's voice.

"Who?"

"I can't tell you that, Lieutenant."

Lara couldn't contain a sigh. "Look, I get it, Mr. McMullens. It's a HIPAA thing, a nondisclosure, whatever, but Lynn Rickerson is dead."

A herd of elephants could have traipsed through the bakery then, and Jeff McMullens wouldn't have been more shocked.

"Wh-What? She's dead?"

"Yes. And considering that everyone loved her, I'm finding it hard to drum up suspects and motive. So, I get it. You can't legally tell me anything." Lara was nothing if not a by-the- book investigator. One of the first things learned in the academy is that evidence obtained through improper channels would not be admissible in a court of law.

Jeff grew silent, looking analytically across the small square table at Lara. He was weighing options. She could see it in the pull of his face.

Lara may be a stickler for the book, but sometimes, you had to bend the rules to move forward. Swallowing thickly, a decision reached, Jeff stood, looking down his long nose at Lara.

"I can't help you, Lieutenant. I'm sorry."

Well, it had been worth a shot.

"I need your alibi then, Mr. McMullens."

"For when?"

After Lara rattled off the time frame, he thought for a moment. "I was working late in the lab that night. I'll email security footage and keycard access logs if you like."

Lara stood, feeling less vulnerable at eye level. She held out a business card. "Please. That would be fine."

Jeff nodded and stalked from the bakery.

Shame. Lara had believed she could get something out of him. Sitting back down, she made quick work of the rest of her cruller and coffee, and then headed out to her unmarked. A blast of a chilly breeze kicked up, biting at the exposed bits of her skin, and nearly dislodged a piece of paper wedged underneath the windshield wipers.

Surging forward, Lara grabbed the paper.

Brooks Mayfield.

Just that. First and last name, written in surprisingly elegant handwriting. Lara grinned, knowing McMullens put it there.

Or rather, an anonymous tipper.

Brooks Mayfield was a career criminal, according to police records.

The guy had sealed juvenile records, but it didn't matter because his adult records were astounding—public intoxication, aggravated assault, assault and battery, drug possession, breaking and entering, robbery, and the pièce de résistance: sexual assault.

Mayfield lived in a low-income housing area of downtown, not far from Route 1. There had been attempts in the past to revitalize this area of town, but to no avail. The funding just wasn't there. Once upon a time, it had been a popular part of town, back when the mill still operated. The death of the mill caused the death of parts of Eastfall. It had spread, like a sickness affecting certain organs, but not all. Angylion was the attempted cure but couldn't provide as many jobs as the mill once had.

Patrol officers hated this part of town. Lara should have asked Tom to tag along, but she had seen worse in Boston.

Angling the unmarked into a spot, Lara shuffled out of the car and hunched in on herself.

She shoved her hands into her pockets, but made sure she could access her gun, if needed. Fortunately, it was too cold for hecklers to be out on front stoops, so, with some relief, Lara scrambled quickly along the sidewalk.

This particular set of row houses had seen better days. Paint chipped away before her eyes, front porches sagged nearly to the ground, siding had disappeared, and broken windows were boarded up.

It didn't take long for Lara to locate Mayfield's apartment. Fist raised, she tapped her knuckles against the door. After a few beats, it creaked open, and a pair of beady brown eyes peered out. A bedraggled woman, muddy-brown hair a rat's nest, stood in the doorway.

"Yeah?"

"Hi, I was wondering if Brooks Mayfield was home?"

"Who's askin'?" The woman said, Massachusetts accent deep, and voice roughened by a life filled with cigarettes.

Lara held up her badge. "Lieutenant Lara Nadeau with EPD. I just need to ask him a couple of questions."

"What'd he do now?"

"Nothing I know of. Just need to talk to him."

The woman looked skeptically at Lara, sizing her up, no doubt having had her own fair share of run-ins with law enforcement.

"Come on in," she eventually responded, stepping aside and opening the door wider.

The inside of the house was surprisingly well-kept, considering the condition of the exterior. The sound of a television trickled forward from the back.

"Brooksy!" The woman shouted, catching Lara off guard for a second. "Someone here to see you!"

A loud bang followed with muffled cursing, then the soft thuds of someone moving around upstairs. The sounds grew closer, and Brooks Mayfield appeared, padding down the stairs.

The thought had occurred to Lara, as she drove past old row house after old row house, what interest Lynn Rickerson would have had in a man like Brooks Mayfield.

He was handsome. Clean him up a little and put him in clothing not ripped or moth-eaten, and he could've ended up the male version of Eliza Doolittle in *My Fair Lady*. Thick blond hair fell nearly to his shoulders, framing elfin features. The guy looked like he should've had a successful modeling career, and not be the poster child for criminals.

When Mayfield spotted Lara, he stopped dead. He'd been around law enforcement enough to spot them a mile off. He knew, without needing to see her badge, Lara was a cop. Despite the deer-in-headlights look, he didn't run.

"Mr. Mayfield? Do you mind if I ask you a few questions?"

A couple minutes later, Lara found herself seated on a patio set that had seen better days.

Why they had to sit outside in the chill of early winter, she didn't know, but Lara suspected it had to do with

Mayfield's comfort. He had already smoked three cigarettes in the span it had taken Lara to explain the situation.

"I can't believe she's dead," he let out on a breath, the vapor and cigarette smoke swirling into a cloud before dissipating. One leg bounced against the table, causing it to shake. The cigarette shook with his fingers, and his eyes roamed everywhere but Lara.

"Yeah, murder and death tend to create disbelief," Lara deadpanned, waving away an errant cloud of smoke. It had taken her a damn near act of God to get her father to quit smoking. She hated the habit. "An anonymous tip pointed me in your direction. How did you know Lynn Rickerson?"

Brooks Mayfield lifted one shoulder in a shrug. "We were in the same selection pool for a clinical trial at Angylion. We saw each other a couple of times."

"What was the nature of your acquaintance?"

"Are you asking if we dated? No. Though we talked about going for a coffee."

"Ms. Rickerson was sexually assaulted before she was brutally murdered, Mr. Mayfield. You understand, with your record, why I'm here, right?"

Brooks froze, finally, eyebrows scrunched.

"You think I killed her?" he asked, voice surprisingly even.

"I'm not thinking anything, Mr. Mayfield. I'm just telling you how it looks. Sexual assault, aggravated assault... Your criminal record is something we would've studied at the academy. A guy with your rap sheet is bound to graduate to murder. You're a butcher by trade, aren't you?"

Mayfield sat up, crushing the end of his cigarette in an ashtray heaped with used butts. The line of his shoulders and the color in his cheeks betrayed his ire.

"Look, I'm trying to get straight, okay? Haven't done coke in months, haven't touched a drop of alcohol in double that. I have a steady job. The clinical trial was a way for me to keep myself accountable to stay clean. They test for that shit, you know? Why would I kill one of the sweetest ladies I have ever met in my life?"

"Why does anyone kill?" Lara replied with a loose shrug. She wasn't buying this schtick. Recidivism rates were terrible in America. Lara didn't believe a career criminal could ever truly go straight. It was just her cynical nature, built over the entirety of her career as a police officer. She wished she wasn't some days, but it was the nature of all that she'd seen on the job. "Can you tell me where you were four nights ago?"

"I was here. Watching TV."

"Can your girlfriend corroborate that?" Lara asked.

"Linda? She's my sister. And no, she wasn't here."

By the looks of it, and the circles Linda ran in, Lara wouldn't be surprised if the woman had been out, neck deep in Johns that night.

"No one can place you here?"

"No."

Lara sighed. Two people with shaky alibis. She couldn't get a read on Mayfield, her gut not pointing one way or another. She stood, rubbing the palms of her hands together and stomping her feet to get the blood pumping again.

"Do me a favor, Mr. Mayfield. Don't leave town. I may need to ask you more questions."

CHAPTER 8

A few days later, Lara found herself in the same predicament as the moment Lynn Rickerson's body had been found, namely, square one. No leads, few suspects, and all the physical evidence collected by the crime scene techs resulted in nothing. No foreign hairs left behind, no foreign fibers, and no foreign bodily fluids. The theory of Locard's Principle conjectured that the perpetrator of a crime always left something behind at the scene, *always*. It didn't matter how microscopic. Lara couldn't recall one case she had worked where something hadn't been left behind, ultimately leading to the culprit.

This one was different. Lara felt it in the very marrow of her bones, in the depths of her psyche. Something wasn't right. She'd be damned if she'd let it become a cold case, locked away in some storage facility, never to be investigated again.

The view from her office window at headquarters currently served as a distraction. Lara sat in her chair, staring out toward the courthouse, not focused on anything in particular. Her mind whirled with the few facts of the case she knew.

"Knock, knock," a smooth voice said behind her. Lara spun, coming face to face with Oliver Bennett.

"Hi," she said, heart hammering this side of too fast from the startle he'd caused.

"Lieutenant," the dark-haired man greeted her with a wide smile, moving to make himself comfortable in one of her office chairs. With a flick of his fingers, he unbuttoned his suit jacket to sit with ease. He crossed his legs, ankle resting on the opposite knee.

"ADA," Lara replied, using her feet to propel herself and her chair back to the desk.

"You okay? You don't take me as the type to stare out the window and daydream," Oliver teased.

"Oh. Yeah," she said, waving her hand. "Just thinking. Definitely not daydreaming."

"What a shame. I would've asked if you were daydreaming about me."

And damn if that didn't make Lara smile with a snort, no matter how much she didn't want to acknowledge that sorry excuse for flirting. Once, Lara would've given as good as she got.

"You're a real riot, Bennett," she said instead.

The dimming of the normal twinkle in his eyes revealed his disappointment, and for a moment something else took its place. An emotion Lara couldn't identify. Oliver had hoped for a return serve, an effortless lob back into his court. Lara wouldn't, and couldn't, give him that.

Busying herself, Lara began to fold up the local paper to be recycled. Her eyes landed on the section that housed the daily crossword puzzle and zodiac forecast.

"You wanna know what your horoscope says today?" Lara joked, having already read hers. She didn't make it a habit but would sometimes indulge just for the shits and giggles. When she did, she'd read Tom's his and anyone else that came by her office.

Oliver scoffed. "Yeah, no. But thanks."

"What? Don't believe in it?" Lara teased.

"Hell no. Why should I? We make our own destinies. Us, not some *cosmic* force, or whatever," Oliver replied.

"Wow, deep, Mr. ADA."

Oliver grinned.

A commotion outside her door preceded several SWAT team members racing past the open office door. Eyebrows crinkled, Lara jumped from her chair in a flash to investigate. Looking down the hallway, she saw the disappearing forms of the three men dressed in tactical gear.

Next door, Tom popped his head out of his office, curious as to the origin of the disturbance.

Captain Homer Lacey appeared at the other end of the hallway. The head of SWAT was an imposing man—tall, built, salt-and-pepper hair buzzed to a crew cut. He had been in the military for a time before retiring and joining the force. He was a shrewd leader, at least according to the gossip Lara had heard. From her brief interactions with him, when the guy wasn't all business, he was a teddy bear.

"Lieutenant," Captain Lacey greeted as he strode past, combat boots thumping on the floor as he went.

"Captain," she replied. "What's the hurry?"

Captain Lacey never hurried to anything, his gait always purposeful, and somehow, he still arrived before the men he'd dispatched, like the tortoise in his race with the hare. Or the eighties slasher-film villain, who always seemed to get the running teenager despite the fact he stalked them.

"My boys just got a call," he replied gruffly, pausing and turning to address her and give a nod in greeting to Tom. The tone in which Captain Lacey spoke said he could be casually discussing the weather, and not a code red situation.

"All hands on deck, huh?" Lara asked, stepping into the hallway as Oliver came to stand next to her.

"Hostage situation."

Lara tensed, as though someone had splashed a bucket of ice over her head. No two words could send her into a tailspin as those Captain Lacey had just uttered.

Hostage situation.

"Oh, Jesus," Tom muttered, arms crossed and leaning against the door frame. "How bad is it?"

"Eastfall Credit Union. Couple idiots thinkin' they can make a quick buck. No one's been hurt. From what I understand from dispatch, they're rookies tryin' to be Pretty Boy Floyd or somethin'. Probably watchin' too much TV or playin' too many video games." Captain Lacey made a sound that could have been a chuckle, or what passed as a laugh for the mountain of a man.

The words echoed around Lara, processing slowly.

At her side, her hands shook and her palms grew damp. Lara tried to take a few deep breaths, but to no avail. Fingers curled tightly into her palm in an effort to stop the tremors. Fingernails dug into flesh, pressing half-moon divots into her skin, causing droplets of blood to well.

Lara didn't notice. Didn't feel the pain.

"Well, better go make sure my boys get things covered. Catch ya at Bucky's later?" Captain Lacey's voice trickled through the rush of white noise roaring in Lara's ears.

"Yeah, we'll see you there," Tom answered, clapping palms briefly with the SWAT commander before they both disappeared, getting back to their respective jobs.

Lara was frozen, feet rooted.

"Lieutenant?" came Oliver's voice, cutting through the raging din only Lara could hear.

"Uh, yeah, I'm gonna...I'm gonna go...work from home for the rest of the day."

Stumbling into her office, she quickly slung on her jacket and grabbed her bag before shooing Oliver out of her office.

"Are you okay?" Oliver asked, concern filling the space between them.

"Yep. Fine. Totally fine. Just going home. Work from there." It didn't matter if she repeated herself. Her hand fumbled slightly with the key as she slid it home, locking things up tightly. "Talk to you later?"

Before she could get an answer, not that she was looking for one, Lara rushed down the hallway in the direction Captain Lacey had gone, heading for her car.

Lara broke about five traffic and moving violations in her rush to get home. She knew, because she counted as she committed them. The temptation had been there to flip on the siren and lights of her unmarked, but ultimately she decided against it. The misuse of police equipment was not on her list of acceptable rules to bend.

Thankfully, for occasions such as this, Lara had an emergency stash.

She brought her unmarked to a halt in the driveway, tires squealing, and nearly fell out in her haste to get inside. The white noise crackled louder, ears and head ringing with it. She couldn't unlock the door fast enough, and the walk to the kitchen felt like miles. Her hands trembled so much it was difficult to get the cabinets open. But Lara managed, and pulled down a bottle of clear liquid from a high shelf.

It was another full thirty seconds before Lara could get the cap unscrewed. When she finally did, she didn't even bother with a cup and instead took a deep swig of vodka straight from the bottle. Lara grimaced as the liquid scorched down her throat, nearly doubling over the counter from the effects.

The change was instant.

As soon as the vodka slipped down and settled in her gut, the white noise quieted. Taking another pull, Lara set the bottle on the counter, misjudging the placement, and nearly let it topple onto the floor. Luckily, she caught it, saving the precious liquid.

By then, the second swallow had settled and taken root, her brain quieting further until the noise was a dim buzz, like bees busy at work in a garden.

"Fuck," she breathed, fingers curling around the lip of the countertop, holding on for dear life. "Un, deux, trois, quatre, cinq, six, sept, huit, neuf..." As she counted upwards in French, a memory of her Mémère Nadeau's New England/French Canadian accent swept through her, blanketing her in warmth and comfort. She could hear her grandmother scolding her father in that long-suffering but not genuinely angry way mothers spoke to their adult sons.

"T'ick, ma! I want it t'ick!"

"I'm gonna hurt my wrist, Steven! You'll get it as t'ick as I can!"

They had a monthly tradition of eating breakfast over at her grandparents' house. Here mémère's specialty was crepes, the paper-thin confections often a staple of French cuisine. Lara's father had always eaten his crepes thicker than one should be, which was a source of contention between mother and son. Lara had always laughed. It was a memory of happier times. Simpler times. And one she would always lean on in moments like these.

"'Your mémère always knows how to make it just right,'" Lara whispered into the silence of the kitchen, a quote her father would say when he leaned away from an empty, maple syrup stained plate, rubbing his belly.

Curling her fingers around the neck of the bottle, Lara took another deep pull and screwed the cap back on. Her hands had ceased shaking.

After placing the bottle back on its high shelf, she scuffed into the living room and collapsed on the couch.

Three taps on the door jolted her from unconsciousness, not realizing she had fallen asleep. It was dusk out—the sun dipped in the sky and created a bluish-purple tint to the land outside her windows.

Sitting up with a groan, she scrubbed the palm of her hand along her chin, wiping up drool. The taps came again, and through her sleep-addled mind, she realized someone was at the door.

Lara banged her shin into the coffee table in her haste to get up, and nearly tripped over the jacket she didn't remember shedding, on her way to the front of the house.

"Hey," Oliver Bennett greeted softly when Lara opened the door. He stood on the front stoop, in his tailored three-piece suit, clutching a six-pack of beer in one hand and a brown paper bag in the other.

"ADA?" Lara said, voice husky from sleep.

"I, uh...I was a little worried about your hasty exit today, so I thought I'd bring dinner after I finished court for the day."

Of course, he remembered where she lived. They'd opted to come here after an outing at Bucky's that ended rather... heatedly. It happened months ago, not long after Lara had arrived in Eastfall. To Lara, it was a means of stress relief, a means of forgetting, readily available from a willing partner. Since the first instance, they'd clashed a few more times, though it always ended with one of them tiptoeing out not long after the finale.

Oliver's gesture was entirely too sweet, and the implications of it made Lara want to slam the door in his face and run up to her room. This was supposed to be purely physical. Providing food said otherwise. No matter how much she wanted to get rid of Oliver, her grandmother's voice in her head fussed that she would not approve of such behavior.

"Right...Um...Thank you? Come in." Lara stepped back, and Oliver entered with a small, pleased smile.

———————

There were times when Lara wished she had better self-control and resolve.

Once more, she found herself lying in bed with a softly snoring and very naked Oliver Bennett next to her. Oliver had been a complete gentleman the entire evening, to his credit. He even offered to leave before Lara practically attacked him.

The sex was good. It was a release she needed after the panic from earlier, but it hadn't meant anything. Lust with zero desire for attachment, at least on her part. The man wanted to be with her, poor guy.

Lara lay awake well into the early hours of the morning, a thin blanket the only thing keeping the cool air from her naked body. Giving up on sleep happening, Lara gingerly rolled from the bed, pulled on sweatpants and a T-shirt, and quietly stepped into the hallway.

The old wooden floorboards creaked beneath her weight as Lara headed for the stairs.

If it hadn't been for moonlight peeking through the sheer curtains in the windows of the hallway, Lara would've missed the door to the attic standing wide open.

CHAPTER 9

H*ours earlier...*

The rush from the first kill still lingered in his veins, rushing and humming like the sweetest kind of drug. He had never thought it could feel like that, taking a human life, watching the light leave the iris. The high school teacher had proved an easy target, still hung up over a breakup with her cop ex-boyfriend, vulnerable and easy to mold. All it took were a few sanguine words, a couple of dinner dates, and she'd been eating out of the palm of his hand.

He would admit he'd been nervous. A ritual of this magnitude needed to be carried out as an exact science. The herbs needed to be placed correctly. The sigils drawn perfectly. The colored paint.

The removal of the organ had proven to be the most challenging, but he was an intelligent man. He did a bit of Internet searching of the art of animal butchering, and voilà!

Perhaps the sweetest part of it all was the utter terror in the teacher's eyes as he overpowered her, ripped her clothes, and violated her in the most primordial way a man could violate a woman. The release had been the sweetest he'd ever had, and now that he had a taste, he craved more.

He was hooked.

Luckily, he had three more to go, and already he could feel the raw power of a completed step surging within him. It was only a matter of time before he could claim this cosmic dominance as his own. And only then could he show his master he had been right all along.

This next kill would be tricky. The woman, by nature, distrusted him, as his next intended target had worked with him on many occasions. He would have to be very careful in his reasoning for her to meet him somewhere, but he had already pondered the idea and knew exactly what to do.

He also had the bolt cutters ready and could feel the growing anticipation of the crack of bone beneath his hand.

This hadn't been his first taste of blood, though the first death he'd caused, well before the teacher, had been an accident.

The violation hadn't been his first rodeo either. Undergraduate school had been the best playground for a man like him. Young coeds never knew what had hit them, and none ever attempted to report him. Not that the university would have done much. The higher education system was not equipped with the know-how to bring justice for raped young women.

As he packed his duffel bag for his next victim, the thought didn't even occur to him that he could be caught. He was fucking smart and prepared. And there was nothing and no one that could stop him. Not The Order. Not the police. Not his own conscience.

Hell, he probably had never had one of those.

Smoothing back his hair, he stopped to examine himself in his hallway mirror. It should probably alarm him how at ease he looked. As if bound for the river to partake in some leisurely fishing.

If he were a normal man, he'd be concerned.

But he was far from a normal man. And very soon, he would be an *extraordinary* man.

CHAPTER 10

Heart in her throat, Lara returned to the bedroom, grabbing her cell phone and her Sig Sauer ankle piece she stored in her nightstand. Armed with phone and gun, she paused as she stood at the side of the bed.

Oliver lay there, dead to the world, and took that moment to turn over and away from her. A million thoughts ran through Lara's head in the span of seconds.

What good was a lawyer to help her, a police officer, if an intruder was in the attic?

If she woke him, Oliver would no doubt act all posturing alpha male and try to push her aside in favor of investigating for himself.

No. That wasn't her. That wasn't Lara Nadeau.

Let the man sleep. She had everything she needed in her hands anyway. Besides, it could be nothing. The attic door probably sat on old hinges that tended to expand and contract, causing the door to open.

At least, that's what Lara wanted to believe.

With resolve, she turned and crept back into the hallway.

iPhone gripped in one hand, flashlight on, Sig Sauer P238

in her other, finger near the trigger, Lara crossed them at the wrists, right over left, and advanced down the hallway. She cringed with every step that creaked beneath her weight but pushed onward.

Oliver's comments from earlier returned. Something about cosmic forces at work, and how he didn't believe them? Yeah, she didn't want to either. Lara never considered herself a particularly religious or superstitious person. Her father and grandparents raised her in the Catholic church, and she dutifully made her way through the childhood sacraments. Now, she attended Mass rarely. In fact, she hadn't been to church since her father's funeral. The beliefs of the Catholic church, religion in general, did not gel with her. They never had. Lara was a logical person, a concrete thinker who believed in what she experienced and perceived with her five senses.

To Lara, there should be no one else in the house besides her and Oliver Bennet.

It hadn't been a trick of the light or her imagination, it turned out. The attic door indeed stood open. The thing had been solidly shut the last time she happened to glance this direction, which, granted, had been yesterday. Lara had been otherwise occupied when she and Oliver made the journey upstairs earlier.

Arms up, gun muzzle pointed right at the dark opening of the door, Lara continued forward, bare feet shuffling mutely against the floor.

Wasn't this an inciting incident of every horror movie? Lara couldn't help but ponder.

Much to her horror, the door creaked open further. Right in front of her. As if inviting her in.

Lara couldn't move, couldn't scream, couldn't think to form words. That simple movement seemed to have caused her heart to stop.

She didn't know what she was expecting to see on the

other side of that door. Once the shock wore off enough for voluntary movement to return, she stepped closer. Empty air and the darkness of the stairs leading upward was all that met her.

Ears tuned up, she listened to every single minute sound the house made. Lara couldn't discern whether the utter silence relieved her or not.

Surging forward, Lara quickly snaked her hand inside the doorway, and flipped the light switch, illuminating the stairway and the attic space above. The light revealed nothing.

Pulling back the safety on her Sig and sucking in a deep breath, Lara hesitantly ascended the stairs.

As soon as her line of sight crested over the staircase, she stopped, cautious, tense, and poised. Lifting her arms higher, she pointed her gun into the giant, seemingly empty space, sweeping back and forth.

Nothing.

The lighting of the attic was frustratingly dim, creating many shadows that didn't sway or undulate to give away the presence of someone (or something).

Just silence.

Silence, and a lot of stuff.

A lot of junk.

Quickly and deftly taking the rest of the stairs, she paused at the top, arms still up and achingly tensed, expecting an attack.

Nothing.

Eyes adjusted to the room, Lara saw antiques everywhere —oval mirrors, desks, settees, and a chaise lounge. Not to mention trunks and boxes and broken-down bed frames. Some of the older items were covered with white sheets, though they looked gray and blackened by thick layers of dust.

Keeping the Sig up, finger rested on the side of the muzzle, Lara swept the phone flashlight to illuminate more darkness. Her shoulder ached from holding this position, but Lara willed herself to ignore it.

The space spanned the entire length and breadth of the house and was entirely full of what she assumed were Mr. Lothrop's things. Possibly Charlotte's. Lara couldn't imagine why he would leave all this stuff here. Certainly, he could afford a climate-controlled storage unit? Not to mention some of this, if sold, could garner a pretty penny.

Her feet propelled her deeper into the attic, away from the stairs.

There was no discernible organization to the chaos, though rows and aisles had been formed for ease of access. There were interesting items for sure—old hat boxes with moth-eaten contents, an IBM computer from the 1980s, and what looked like a Victorian vanity complete with a ratty stool.

Anyone could be hiding amongst the piles; anyone could jump out at her and take her down. But no one could remain this still and silent, especially when the old, wooden floor-boards creaked with every step Lara took.

As she rounded another grouping of antiques, a clang sounded to her left, yet deeper in the maze of the attic. Startled, Lara jumped, gun flying to point into the darkness from where the noise had come, heart thumping.

Though the sound had been muffled, to Lara's ears it seemed like a bomb blast. After all of her experience and all the training she had received, it frustrated her to no end there were things that still affected her. She'd once prided herself on being cool and collected in high stress situations.

But no more.

As any idiot in a horror movie, Lara stepped toward the noise and possibly toward impending danger.

Lara finally reached the west facing wall of the attic, the end of the road. Something was off.

There was no one in this attic, and no room for an intruder to double back without her seeing or hearing them.

A chill snaked down her spine, and the hairs on the back of her neck stood.

There was something in this attic either playing with her or trying to tell her something. She knew she had heard it. This time, she'd consumed far more takeout than alcohol, so she wasn't delusional. Lara recalled the night she had trudged up to bed and saw something move in the dining room. She remembered the clear sound of footsteps that, after investigation, had also yielded nothing.

Though she considered herself a logical thinker, Lara couldn't deny what her senses had picked up. Lara reluctantly let her thoughts wander to a possible solution.

Growing up and even now, Lara had been ambivalent about things strange and unusual. Dare she say...supernatural? Though human beings had existed for millennia, many things still remained hidden and unexplained. There was always room to doubt—room to be proven wrong. Wasn't that what the scientific process was about?

Lara shifted and froze when a piece of flooring made a different sound beneath her.

It was hollow. She tapped her toes against the board in question, suspicions further confirmed.

Dropping to her knees, Lara carefully set down her Sig and scrambled to get her fingertips purchased between the floorboards. It took maneuvering, but she managed to pry it up, phone shoved into her mouth, flashlight illuminating the exposed compartment.

There was something inside.

Slowly, Lara reached in, careful to not let her hands

wander, lest she cut herself on rusted nails or rotten pieces of wood.

Fingers found purchase on a smooth, cool surface. Grasping at the object, she pulled out a wooden box with brass hinges. In elegant, flowing script there were initials inlaid in mother-of-pearl atop the lid of the box.

A.B.

Lara could only guess at the age of the box. It was in good condition, despite (or perhaps because of) hiding beneath the floor. The container was the size of a cigar box, but three times the depth. There was no lock. Lara's fingers pressed against the latch, intending to open and reveal the contents, but the shrill ring of her phone startled her.

Letting out a yelp, the lieutenant fell back onto her backside, palm clutched to her sternum where her heart threatened to race out of her rib cage.

"Nadeau," she gasped in greeting, breathless from the scare.

"Hey," came the gruff voice of Tom from the other end. "We've got another one..."

CHAPTER 11

Lara opted to leave Oliver sleeping peacefully in her bed in the interest of avoiding an awkward goodbye. She even did the cliché thing and left a note for him on her pillow.

The body had been discovered in a small but densely wooded area behind the Morgan Street Apartments, not a handful of blocks from Brooks Mayfield's residence, where Lara had been mere days ago. As she drove the unmarked car through quiet streets, it occurred to her the location seemed oddly timely.

Despite the early hour, there were a number of spectators gathered around the police tape that formed a horseshoe, blocking an opening into a patch of trees. This being downtown, there were more patrol officers on hand to act as crowd control. The real downtown area of Eastfall, the one no one mentioned in tourism guides, had seen higher heydays. Poverty dripped in the streets, a once-proud area now ramshackle and gang-ridden. Eastfall had gangs, national and local. Any other time, finding a body might be solved as rival gangs settling a score. But the moment Tom's weary voice filtered over the phone line, Lara knew this wasn't gang related.

She nosed her car into a makeshift parking space next to another unmarked. Tom stood by it, elbow braced on the roof of the car. The drawn look to his brow could only be a mirror of her own.

"Hi, Tom," Lara greeted, coming around the back of her car to stand next to him. Even in the dim light of the early morning, the auburn shade of his hair shone as his head tipped in her direction.

"Hey," he replied quietly.

Lara led the way to the barrier where uniformed officers stood with their fingers looped in their gun belts, eyes piercing and alert as they scanned the area.

After Lara flashed her badge, an officer lifted the tape for her and Tom. They ducked under and stepped toward a copse of trees where more uniforms stood.

The miniscule light from the early morning rays of the sun disappeared when the lieutenant and captain entered the tree line, only to be replaced by the artificial light of portable lamps. They circled the spot where the body lay, just a few feet ahead of them. Dr. Rogers had already begun her preliminary examination.

Patrol Officer Sierra Fitzgerald had not been afforded a dignified death. It took all Lara had to not visibly react to the state of the poor young woman, a sight so different from her dignified indifference to Lara back at the precinct. Lara had just seen her the other day, been on the receiving end of a bit of Sierra's disdain. Now, Lara would never hear it again.

Sierra had been laid out on the ground, arms splayed to the sides, uniform shirt ripped open. Nothing could have prepared Lara for the shock of seeing one of her own like this. The crime scene technicians had already marked the places on the ground where the buttons of the shirt had fallen. Officer Fitzgerald's bra had been torn, her sternum cut open and bloodied. Even in the lighting from the portable lamps, Lara could tell bone and tissue were cracked open. A bloody hole remained. The heart was absent from the cavity. One half of the essential organ, cut vertically, lay to the left of Sierra's chest, just under her outstretched arm. The remaining half was gone.

The organ appeared blackened in the meager light, but there was no mistaking the strange symbols etched in the dirt, and the presence of a sprinkled herb.

Whoever killed Lynn Rickerson also killed Sierra Fitzgerald.

"Lieutenant... Captain..." Dr. Rogers greeted them as she stepped over. Her assistant and the crime scene technicians clicked away with their cameras, flashes lighting up the darkness surrounding them. "My preliminary guess for TOD would be somewhere between ten to twelve hours ago. Signs of bruising around her neck would suggest strangulation as COD. Also, there are signs of...," the doctor paused, glancing over at the mangled body and Lara followed her gaze, noting the officer's lower half stripped bare, legs splayed outward, "... sexual assault."

"Christ," Tom breathed, raking a hand through his hair. Lara had already brought out her notepad, jotting down notes from what she saw and from Dr. Rogers's summations. Tom looked more green around the gills than he had for Lynn. Then again, this hit closer to home.

"Anything different you notice here, doc, compared to Lynn Rickerson?" Lara asked.

The older woman shook her head, wisps of blonde hair faded to white escaping from the doctor's haphazard ponytail. "Not much that I've seen so far. Though, you know how Ms. Rickerson had blue paint drawn across her lips? The killer drew a red line across Officer Fitzgerald's wound."

"It's not blood?"

"No. Not the same consistency. I'd say paint or ink. I would also bet forensic tests will report it's the same type of paint found on Ms. Rickerson."

"Thanks for coming out, Doc," Lara said.

"One body's bad enough. Now there are two," Dr. Rogers lamented, turning to watch her assistant as he got the body bag ready to transfer Officer Fitzgerald. "One being one of our own. Three would make a troubling pattern."

The widely accepted body count number to identify a serial killer was three, though the FBI might make an argument for two. In all of her father's years on the force, he'd never encountered one. Neither had Lara. The idea such atrocities could occur on her watch? It scared her.

"So fuckin' young," Tom murmured, as he shuffled down the line at the closest Dunkin Donuts. By the time they wrapped up at the scene, the regular workday drew near. They opted to grab coffee on their way back to police head-quarters. Now, they stood with the rest of the morning rush crowd, having decided to skip the drive-thru because of the ridiculously long line. The inside line did not move any faster.

"I talked to her the other day," Lara said softly, though their interaction could be considered far from completely civil.

"She *just* earned a commendation and medal of valor," Tom replied. "Went to the damn ceremony. She busted into a burning apartment building and dragged out a mother and her two kids. Plus the damn dog. And this is how she meets her maker? I can't...I'll never be able to get the sight of her out of my head. Fuckin' awful."

Sierra had her whole life and career ahead. She'd already been well on her way to great things. Lara didn't let on, but she simultaneously ached for the young officer's death and worried about how it could have been her. Maybe not now, but when she was younger, fresh out of the academy with an ax to grind. The world had been her oyster—had been Sierra's too. Now it had been taken from her. As they moved forward in the line again, Lara noticed her hands shook in her coat pockets, and not because of the arctic air outside.

As soon as Lara situated herself behind her desk, she called up Patrol Officer Sierra Fitzgerald's personnel file. Lara read over the commendation and story of how she'd earned it. She read Sierra's field training records from the beginning of her career in Eastfall. Lara skimmed over Sierra's personal information, too, her heart squeezing to see the names of the parents she predeceased.

No immediate and obvious connection in the file put her in the same sphere as Lynn Rickerson, but that didn't mean anything. If there was a connection, Lara would find it.

As it turned out, she didn't have to find it. An hour later, Tom rushed in from next door, face ghost white.

"We might have a problem."

"What?" Lara asked, alert.

"Guess who graduated the academy with Fitzgerald?"

Lara's jaw clenched, heart sinking in her chest. "Sergeant Braddock?"

Once again, Lara found herself facing Zachariah Braddock in an interview room. And once again, he sat as still as a statue, arms braced on the table with hands folded together. His handsome face didn't give much away, and neither did his pretty mouth give helpful answers.

"Come on, Zach, don't be an idiot," Tom hissed, more active in this interview than the last. His palms braced on the scuffed table, face red, upper body leaning in, a classic method of intimidation. Too bad it didn't work on Braddock.

"I told you, Captain," Zach replied in an even tone. "I was at home, and I can't give you names of anyone to confirm. Yes, I did go to the academy with Officer Fitzgerald, but I haven't seen her since. The connection is there, sure, but it's a flimsy connection to make. I thought you were better at this. Coming from Boston and all. Or," he paused menacingly, "maybe not."

He directed that last comment at Lara, who sat up straighter in the uncomfortable chair, hackles securely ruffled. She was really fucking tired of people pulling the 'outsider' card on her. She'd been there for six months. In no time, it'll be a year. But, she supposed this was what small town living and policing was. Everyone knew everyone else, and everyone else's business.

As much as Lara hated to admit it, Braddock was right. If they went to a judge with their meager evidence in order to obtain a warrant to search Braddock's living space, the judge would laugh in their faces. That was true of Eastfall, and that was true of Boston.

The law didn't differ.

Zach leaned in, mimicking Tom's stance. "I know the pressure's on here, and the chief's expecting you to nail someone's balls to the table really soon, but you're barking up the wrong tree."

"You need to worry about your own problems right now, Sergeant," Lara said, scooting closer to the table in a subconscious way of showing her own intimidation. "Like why you're connected to two women who are now dead."

A heavy sigh passed Zach's lips. He sat back in the chair, his back hitting the wood with a thunk. It was his day off, evidenced by the jeans, heavy black boots, T-shirt, and peacoat he wore. The casual look worked for him as much as the uniform.

"I thought you Eastfall cops were supposed to be good," Zach said, ice in his words. "And like I said, I expect better from a city cop."

Lara despised that he kept lobbing cheap shots at her.

"You don't know shit about me, Braddock," she sneered, teeth clenched so tightly her jaw ached. "So cut it out."

"Yeah, and you don't know shit about me," he shot back.

The door to the interview room flew open and Chief Braddock entered.

"This interview isn't going anywhere," the chief said, annoyance etched across his face. He had been watching from the observation room. "Sergeant Braddock knows he is a person of interest in two murders. He'll not go anywhere in case you need to ask him further questions. Isn't that right, Sergeant Braddock?"

Lara could tell by the line of his shoulders and the expression on Zach's face he didn't like nor appreciate his father coming to rescue him. There was no way in hell she would've wanted her father to do the same for her.

Zach stood, glancing from Lara to his father. "That is correct, sir."

"You're free to go, Sergeant," Chief Braddock said, stepping aside to give Zach space to squeeze past and out the door.

When the sergeant disappeared down the hallway, the chief looked back over at his two Investigation leads. The man looked bone tired, like he held a world-weariness Lara could never imagine.

"I've looked over all of the reports from Rickerson, and what you've got for Fitzgerald so far. I know there isn't concrete evidence to lead anywhere. Keep trying. You're bound to catch this fucker in a mistake."

Then the chief disappeared.

Lara glanced to Tom.

"What're we going to do?" he asked, stance sagging from the stress.

Standing, she shoved her notebook back into her pocket.

"There's someone else we can talk to...."

Lara pulled into the same parking space as her first meeting with Brooks Mayfield ten minutes later.

"Jesus, this guy sounds like a piece of work," Tom commented on the drive over. He had perused the light reading material of Brooks Mayfield's criminal record.

"According to him, he's going straight," Lara had replied.

Now, they both stood in the familiar dingy alley, and knocked on the same beaten-up door.

Linda answered the door again, annoyed, reminding Lara it was still early in the morning for most people. The woman stood before them nearly naked under her grubby robe. Must have been a busy night.

"You want Brooks again?" she asked when she recognized Lara. "He's at work."

Something in Linda's eyes and the curt way in which she spoke cued Lara into the falseness of that information.

A few thunks sounded from the back of the apartment. Scuffling, the tell-tale sounds of the pitter-patter of running feet. Lara took off like a shot into the apartment, nearly bowling Linda over in her attempt to get to the backyard. The sliding glass door stood ajar, and through the streaked glass, Lara could see Brooks Mayfield attempting to hop the back fence.

Surging forward, Lara shoved open the door as quickly as she could, enough to squeeze out, before feet pounded across the lawn. It was lucky Brooks Mayfield was a crappy climber. She reached him before he scaled the fence. Grabbing hold of the back of his shirt, Lara wrenched him down with all her might. She nearly fell to the ground with him, but in a flash, she had her gun unholstered and trained on him. Her shoulder had pulled a little—Lara had felt the strain—but she'd be okay.

"Don't. Move," she hissed.

Brooks, wide-eyed and hands raised with palms out, looked like he was about to piss his pants.

"You didn't have to end up here," Lara said to Brooks, as she once more settled in Interview Room One for the second time in over an hour. "But you made me run. I don't like running."

"I didn't do anything!" Brooks exclaimed, his wrists cuffed to the metal loop on the table.

"Then why'd you run?" Lara huffed. Tom stood in the observation booth this time. She wanted to go for this guy herself.

Brooks's pupils were so dilated, she could barely make out the color of the iris. He was definitely on something.

So much for staying clean.

"I need to know your whereabouts yesterday. Walk me through your day."

Mayfield pursed his lips, defiant.

"You're gonna be like that, huh? What happened to the guy I talked to the other day, the one going straight? He disappear somewhere?"

After another moment of fierce resolve, Mayfield hung his

head. "I went to work early, left around two p.m. I didn't want to go home."

"Where did you go?"

Swallowing thickly, Mayfield paused, then pressed on. "*Provocateurs*."

Provocateurs was the seedy gentlemen's club downtown. Lara never had the pleasure of visiting, but its reputation preceded it. It wasn't just a mere strip joint, but also a drug hub, and God knew what else.

"How long were you there?"

Mayfield's eyes glanced everywhere but Lara, shame set in his shoulders.

"How long?" She repeated.

"Until closing. About three a.m."

If his story was indeed true, he would've been at the club for nearly twelve hours, during the window Dr. Rogers gave for Sierra's time of death.

Lara continued her questions.

A few minutes later, Tom knocked on the two-way mirror behind her. Glancing over her shoulder, she looked back at Mayfield for a moment before getting up and leaving the room.

Tom met her in the hallway.

"Took the liberty of calling *Provocateurs*. They're already open for their breakfast buffet special."

"Oh wow, how entrepreneurial of them," Lara replied wryly.

"Yeah. Kid's story checks out. The owner said they almost kicked him out for getting too handsy. In a roundabout way, guy said Mayfield's nose accidentally tripped into some cocaine, and he was out of it for most of the evening and early morning."

"Fuck," Lara hissed.

Back to square one.

CHAPTER 12

The next morning, Lara received the phone call not many investigators relished—someone had leaked details of the murders to the local news stations. At first, she thought it was some sort of alcohol-laced fever dream.

If only.

Chief Braddock was on the other end of the connection, cursing and raving about the "fuckery" of some of the police officers under his command. Lara rolled out of bed and winced as her feet touched the coolness of the hardwood floors. The chief rambled on for another few minutes about "PR nightmares" and "blood-sucking reporters" before he barked one final command.

"Press conference at noon. Be there."

Then hung up.

Holding the mobile device away from her ear, Lara blinked sleepily at the thing, before tossing it behind her onto her bed.

One freezing cold shower and a new set of clothes later,

Lara pulled out of her driveway and into the nearest drive-thru Dunkin.

No amount of coffee in the world could prepare her for the harrowing ahead. As a cop in Boston, she had given a few statements to the press over the years but had never been at the head of a full-blown press conference. Those were always reserved for the higher-ups, above her pay grade, and the like. In Eastfall, she *was* a higher-up. There were times she forgot this.

When Lara stepped off the elevator heading toward her office, she stopped in her tracks at the sight of Oliver. They hadn't spoken since their previous encounter—something Lara was grateful for, especially since she'd left him in her bed and hadn't returned home right away.

Oliver looked as impeccable and well-kept as ever. The well-tailored suit hugged his tall, lithe body. He looked damn sharp, down to the Louboutin shoes on his feet. His dark features were right out of anyone's fantasies. And to top it all off, he held two cups of coffee in his hand, one clearly meant for her.

Lara's heart should flutter, swoon, or whatever happens in those crappy romance novels.

But the muscle didn't move, didn't so much as twitch. And because of that, guilt ate at her. Oliver Bennett was a means to an end for her. A release, a substitution for when alcohol just wasn't cutting it.

He was such a nice guy. A great guy. But Lara felt nothing.

"I heard about...well, God, that's awful. You're working on the case, aren't you?"

Lara unlocked the door to her office and stepped in, deftly flipping on the lights. She didn't respond to his question, didn't feel like she needed to.

Oliver took the hint, because he didn't press, merely stepped into the room and set down the extra coffee.

"Thanks," she said softly, setting the cup she'd just bought next to it. Oliver didn't comment, only folded his tall body into one of the chairs by her desk. It irked her a little. She hadn't invited him to stay, yet here he was, making himself comfortable.

"What can I do to help?"

Lara followed suit and sat down heavily in her desk chair, scrubbing a hand across her face as though she could banish the vestiges of her exhaustion.

"Nothin'," she replied. "But thanks for the offer."

"You know you don't have to do this alone."

"I'm not alone. I've got Tom."

"I love Captain Sharpe as much as the next person, but let's face the facts—he doesn't have as much experience investigating homicides as you."

"That's not necessarily a bad thing," Lara grumbled, pressing the button to boot up her desktop computer.

"But I can't imagine it's very helpful to a woman of your prowess. More of a hindrance, probably."

Lara glanced over, eyebrow arched. She wasn't sure she liked Oliver's tone.

"Tom's a good cop. He's all the help I need, but thanks anyway."

With that, she turned to face the home screen on her computer, hoping Oliver would take that as dismissal. When he didn't move, Lara thought she'd have to be more explicit. A second later, though, he stood. She could feel his dark eyes on her, attempting to read her. When he didn't find what he was looking for, Oliver turned and left.

Lara let out the relieved breath she hadn't realized she was holding.

After a few beats more, letting Oliver carry himself as far from her as possible, Lara pulled up her Outlook inbox. Her eyes zeroed in immediately on an email from Jeff McMullens. It was the email she'd been waiting for, with his where-abouts on the night of Lynn Rickerson's murder. He had attached logs of key card entries and snippets of security footage. Sure enough, he'd been there during the estimated time of death.

Lara couldn't shake the feeling there was something else Jeff McMullens could tell her. Reaching over for her office phone, Lara picked up the receiver and dialed the number from her notes. The phone rang and rang, and then Jeff's voicemail initiated. Figures. Lara left a brief message thanking him for the email and rattled off her cell phone number for him to call at his earliest convenience.

She'd keep trying.

"You ready, Cap?"

"I've never had to do this in my life...of course I'm not ready."

"You'll be fine, Tom. Just read what the departmental publicist wrote on the notecards and say 'no comment' to every question you're asked."

"Gee, thanks. You make it sound so simple."

"You kiddin' me? So simple. And just think what Jason's gonna say when he sees you lookin' fine on the local news."

"You're buying the first round tonight, Nadeau."

"You got it, sir."

Since the title "Captain" came before his name, the chief tasked Tom with briefing the local media. He would give as few details as possible, but enough to stoke the media's curiosity (who was she kidding, that would never happen). As the head of the Investigations Unit, it was the captain's duty to carry out the arduous task. Lara was just glad it wasn't her. She hated public speaking, especially to the media. They always took words out of context and twisted them any way they wanted.

Tom would address a crowd of reporters for a live conference during the midday news. Currently, Doctor Rogers worked overtime to finish up Officer Fitzgerald's autopsy report, just as the forensics team was down in their lab running whatever they could.

"Don't go off script," the police department publicist commented on his way past where Tom and Lara stood. "Just read what you have on the cards. No more, no less."

"Got it. I ain't dumb," Tom mumbled to the publicist's retreating back. Lara snorted.

"Didn't realize this would be in the job description, huh?" she asked him with an attempt at a reassuring smile.

"Hell, no, I didn't," Tom grumbled, just as Captain Amelia Shepherd came striding up to them, tight curls bouncing.

"Any leads?" she asked curiously but gleaned the answer from the looks on her colleagues' faces. "Dammit. I'm not gonna let my kids leave the house ever again. They'll be there until they turn sixty."

"We're doing the best we can," Lara consoled. "But we don't have much to work with."

"So I've heard."

Silence came over the sea of people in the largest conference room city hall could offer, as Mayor Lothrop stepped up on the dais. He settled in behind the podium, the seal of the city of Eastfall emblazoned on the wood, and behind him sat the city flag next to the American flag and Massachusetts state flag. The reporters sat in the press section at the front of the audience, while a myriad of police officers sat and stood toward the back of the room and off to the sides. It was crowded, standing room only.

"Good afternoon, ladies and gentlemen," Sam Lothrop began, voice serious and down to business. Charlotte had made an appearance as well, standing off to the side as a show of support. The blonde had waved at Lara upon first taking up her perch. Chief Braddock stood to the right of the mayor.

"We have called this press conference for the express purpose of informing the citizens of Eastfall of the terrible events that have befallen our great city. Without further ado, I would like to call forward Police Chief Henry Braddock to the podium. Chief?"

The mayor stepped out of the way as the chief stepped up to the microphone. The members of the press were waiting with bated breath, pencil or pens poised over notepads, or recorders clutched tightly in their fingers. The blinking light of the news cameras flashed from the back of the room.

"Good afternoon," the chief began with an even tone. "The body of Ms. Lynn Rickerson, a Social Studies teacher from Eastfall High School, was discovered in the woods near Eastfall Colonial Parkway. Earlier yesterday, the body of Eastfall Police Officer Sierra Fitzgerald was found downtown. Preliminary reports deem these two deaths connected. This investigation is ongoing, and as chief of police for the city of Eastfall, I want to reassure our residents every resource within our power is being put toward bringing the killer to justice. The men and women of our Investigations Unit are working tirelessly to interpret the evidence to determine a suspect.

"I also would like to encourage everyone to be mindful of leaving your houses during the evening hours. Do not go alone, or do not leave unless you absolutely need to. There is no apparent cause for alarm—just be safe, be aware of your surroundings, and use common sense to make decisions. Our amazing force of police officers will continue to protect and serve this city. If you have any concerns, please do not hesitate to inform us.

"At this time I would like to bring forward the head of the Investigations Unit, Captain Thomas Sharpe, to give a few more details on the progress of the case."

The chief turned, looking over at the captain to signal it was his turn.

Tom made his way to the dais, easily taking the two steps up to the platform, and over to the podium.

"Good afternoon," Tom cleared his throat, glancing down at the cue cards he'd been given earlier. "As Chief Braddock said, I am Captain Tom Sharpe, head of the Investigations Unit. It's my job to reassure everyone that everything is being done at this time to apprehend the perpetrator of the murders of Lynn Rickerson and Sierra Fitzgerald. I cannot release specific details about an ongoing investigation, but I can say we have been conducting interviews to gather all the information we can in order to create a list of suspects. I have the privilege of working with a fantastic investigative team, especially my second-in-command, who is a seasoned detective formerly of the Boston Police Department.

"Ms. Rickerson and Ms. Fitzgerald were both Caucasian women between the ages of thirty and thirty-five. There are no other apparent connections between the two victims other than the murderer, but we urge everyone to take caution. Do not be out alone, especially during the nighttime hours. Use good judgement, as I know the citizens of Eastfall possess.

"In closing, be assured we will not stop until the perpetrator is arrested and until we know for sure the people of the city of Eastfall are not in immediate danger. Thank you."

As soon as Tom finished his prepared statement, the members of the media erupted in a fit of questions, surging from their chairs with their arms raised high in the air, waving back and forth. The chief stepped up to the podium with Tom to help field a couple of questions. Judging by the tension in the chief's shoulders, he wouldn't take many.

"Chief, is it true the young women were in some kind of cult?" a reporter from the Eastfall Daily newspaper asked.

"That is not something that's been confirmed nor denied at this time," was the chief's simple answer.

"Captain, are you sure you want a disgraced Boston police detective to be co-lead on such a high profile case?" asked another reporter, one whose credentials weren't clear.

Lara sucked in a breath, teeth clenched.

The man implied she was unfit to do her job.

She hated being unable to speak up. She especially hated thinking she wasn't sure he might not be right. Lara looked out into the crowd at the reporter who had asked. His eyes weren't on Tom—they were on her, waiting to see her react. Lara would be damned if she gave him the satisfaction. How much did he know about what had happened? His gaze said he knew enough.

"Lieutenant Nadeau is one of the finest investigators I've ever seen. She is working as hard and as efficiently as she can to solve this. Implying anything else would be a grievous insult to her and her abilities," Tom jumped in, defending her. It made her heart swell for a moment with an emotion she hadn't felt in a long time.

A few more questions about details on the case were hurled around, and of course, no one was at liberty to divulge information. The mayor called the press conference to a close after the chief bade anyone with information pertaining to the case to call the police hotline number. Everyone dispersed from the dais and left the room.

Lara remained standing with Amelia, arms crossed over her chest as she watched the media file out of the room.

"Well, that went well," Amelia said sarcastically when Tom rejoined the group.

"Seriously, fuck them." Amelia pointed the neck of the beer bottle at Lara for emphasis. "Always gotta find something to make a scandal about. Like the murders of two innocent women aren't enough."

Lara had already polished off three beers at this point, and the alcohol did nothing to curb the edge of panic and anxiety.

"Reporters never know what the hell they're talkin' about," Tom tossed in for good measure. The comment he'd made on camera had been enough to shut down other comments, and it heartened Lara to know he had her back. The guy had only known her for six months.

Tom's husband, Jason, had joined them at Bucky's for a nightcap. He, too, had something to say.

"I went to high school with the asshat that asked that question. He's always been a sleaze. I wouldn't worry much about it, Frenchie."

Jason was a few years younger than Tom. He had a mop of jet-black curls, piercing blue eyes, naturally tanned skin, and a sharp, white smile. He owned the local bookstore that managed to stay open by some continued miracle. Out of everyone in Eastfall Lara had met so far, she liked Jason the most. Plus, Jason and Tom had the cutest adopted daughter, Lola. Not that children, or teenagers rather, were much of Lara's thing.

"Thanks," Lara muttered, before taking a pull at her fourth beer of the evening. There was a warmth in her stomach not attributed to the beer. "Frenchie" was Jason's pet name for her, a nod to her French-Canadian heritage. Nicknames like that always made her feel like she belonged. Even when she didn't belong.

They sat in an amiable silence for the rest of their drinks, sprinkling in idle chatter. Eventually, they dispersed, just in time for Bucky's to become too crowded for Lara's comfort. The din of the bar and restaurant had started a headache behind her right eye and straining to see in the dim lighting didn't help.

As she drove back to her house, an urge overtook her to yank the wheel and send the car and herself careening off the road into a ditch. These unbidden thoughts came to mind rarely. They would pop into her head and disappear quickly, like fireworks on the Fourth of July. They were fleeting, as was the urge to fulfill them. The last time she'd had even a passing thought like this one had been the day Captain Lacey rushed by on his way to the bank robbery.

Instead, Lara pushed on and soon pulled into her driveway, just in time for the heater to catch up and finally do its job.

For a brief moment, Lara sat, the car running, gazing out the windshield at the front of the colonial and the surrounding woods.

It truly would be the perfect place to settle a family. A shame she wasn't family material. Though she'd had a loving father, Lara had grown up without a mother. Perhaps she wasn't hardwired for a family, or functioning, normal romantic relationships. Her mother had walked out on them when she was a toddler, leaving Lara with knowing nothing about her but what she looked like—a single photograph her father had kept hidden in a drawer in his room. As she grew older, she would sneak in to steal peeks at the picture, making up wild stories in her head as to where her mother was at that moment.

Once, her mother was an astronaut, training to make the journey to Mars. Another time, her mother was a rock star, touring constantly. Her mother was a great and powerful witch, off protecting the innocent. Her mother was an actress, not wanting her family to get caught in the limelight. The list went on...

Lara sighed, the words of the reporter echoing through her head.

Are you sure you want a disgraced Boston police detective to be co-lead on such a high profile case?

The palm of her right hand came down harshly on the unmarked's steering wheel, feeling the sting vibrating through her fingers. Lara brought her hand down on the wheel again, and again, feeling fury and helplessness eating away at her. Hot tears pricked her eyes as she sat in the dark of her car, sobbing, chest aching.

So wrapped in her emotions, Lara missed the rustle and flutter of the curtains in her bedroom, moving and dancing from a nonexistent wind.

CHAPTER 13

The weather was crisp and dry the morning of the Sister Cities Harvest Festival. The long-running event was an annual ordeal put on by the Parks, Recreation, and Tourism Departments of both Eastfall and Havenwood. Normally, the festival would have occurred the previous month, but a rash of horrible thunderstorms had forced organizers to push it back.

Peppered throughout the winding trails of Eastfall Park were dozens of tents with crafts and tradespeople hawking their wares. In a large clearing that made up a substantial picnic area, food truck upon food truck had staked in. The smell of kettle corn, lobster rolls, and fried goods wafted all the way to the Eastfall Police Department's booth where Lara sat. To the left was the Havenwood Police Department booth and to the right were Tourism departments for both cities. The friendly marketing specialists had been doling out brochures and offering a spin of the prize wheel to passersby. One of the workers, a tall, lithe blonde woman, had already visited, gifting Lara a bottle hugger with the Eastfall city logo emblazoned across the polyester-neoprene material.

Honestly, that was all Lara needed, a device to unintentionally enable.

A chilly breeze kicked up, scooting multicolored leaves along the pathway. Lara scrambled to grasp at the pamphlets before they whipped up into a maelstrom. Sighing, she sat back down in the stiff, plastic chair. How had she been awarded such an honor as manning this booth?

Next to her sat a uniformed sergeant. The middle-aged man was a part of the community relations group within the department, the guy whose job it was to actually be at functions like this one. His uniform was crisp, whereas Lara's navy-blue polo and khakis were rumpled. She would have preferred to wear her usual work uniform—however, Chief Braddock had been particular about dress. She hated tucking in her shirt.

"It's a beautiful day, eh, Lieutenant?" Sergeant Stevens commented as he sat on one of the plastic foldable chairs they'd been given. It sagged slightly into the damp ground beneath his weight.

"Yeah, real beautiful," Lara muttered in reply.

The festival opened to the public an hour ago, and people trickled down the path in front of them, but none stopped. Visitors to the table were few and far between, only stopping to see if they had any freebies. The chief had been adamant they take plenty of Eastfall Police Department pens, cheap little things people loved picking up at events.

Mayor Lothrop and Charlotte even paid a visit to the booth.

"Lieutenant, good to see you," the mayor greeted. Lara stood, shaking hands with the guy then his wife.

"Pleasure to see you, sir."

"How's the house?"

Lara hesitated. "Just fine."

"It really is a gem, you know? A piece of history. The offer still stands if you ever want to see the documents I have on it."

"Thank you, that's much appreciated," Lara replied. She had half a mind to take him up on the offer. To see if anything might reveal what was happening and who *AB* might be. She didn't want to bring it up to the mayor, as Lara didn't want to have to give up the box she had discovered.

The mayor and Charlotte stayed for another minute before moving on to the rest of the crafters.

"I'm going to grab something to eat," Lara said, glancing over at her booth partner. "Want anything?"

"One of those craft beers they've got on tap would be nice right about now," Sergeant Stevens joked, his substantial belly shaking with laughter.

"You and me both, Sarge," she replied, before stepping out from around the table and making her way to the food vendor area. Kids ran by, screaming and carrying on, while harried parents attempted to catch them. As she walked, Lara took in the fall décor—hay bales and scarecrows and pumpkins. They were everywhere. Fall had been Lara's most favored time of the year. Now, it was simply another season, further rotations of the earth.

The combination of kettle corn, funnel cakes, and fried food cloyed at Lara's nose, stealing the air from her lungs for a moment. Fair food was about as unhealthy as could be, and expensive, but damn, was it good. Lara settled on a lobster roll and some fries. As she ate, she couldn't help but stare longingly at the area cordoned off for the alcohol vendors.

"Didn't take you for the festival type, Lieutenant," Zach Braddock greeted from behind her. Rolling her eyes and sucking in a discreet breath, Lara turned, caught off guard by the presence of the sergeant. Zach wore a pair of well-fitting jeans, black high-top Converse, and a button-up plaid shirt with the sleeves rolled to his elbows. His dark hair was perfectly coiffed, as it always was, forelock hanging artfully against his forehead.

"I'm not," Lara replied, casually dumping her food container in the nearby trash can. "I'm on duty."

"Ah," he said with a slight smile. "That's unfortunate. This festival is always the highlight for Eastfall and Havenwood. They've got dance troupes, pumpkin-carving contests, pumpkin growing contests...all the good stuff."

Lara wasn't sure how this man could stand in front of her and have an idle conversation. He was still a person of interest in a murder case she was investigating.

"That's nice," Lara replied, before turning on her heel and heading back to the booth. Zach had other ideas.

"I saw the press conference the other day," he called to her as he scurried to catch up.

"Good for you," Lara replied, as Sergeant Stevens's rotund figure came into view.

"Why are you like this?" Zach pressed. "I'm trying to make friendly conversation." The tone in which he spoke was far from friendly, more mocking than anything. It vaguely reminded her of all the men that had ever told her to smile because she'd "look prettier."

"Me?" Lara stopped, twirling around, just shy of the Eastfall police booth. "Why am I like this? You're a murder suspect, Braddock. I can't socialize with you. Don't you know jack all about investigation? Oh wait, I forgot, you got shitcanned back to uniform for fucking up on the job. My mistake."

Zach's dark eyebrows furrowed.

"You're right. We can't all fuck up in the line of duty and get Goddamn promotions."

It took every ounce of strength in Lara's body not to lash out, not to wipe the self-satisfied smirk right off of his angelic face. Before the lieutenant could make another biting remark, a familiar face entered her periphery. The handsome visage of Oliver Bennett came into view, smiling genuinely over Zach's shoulder.

"Lieutenant, nice to see you," Oliver greeted.

"Bennett," Lara offered in terse greeting, before sidestepping around Zach. The man let out a disgusted scoff and went on his way. Lara glanced over her shoulder, watching Zach's retreating form for a moment before turning back to the attorney.

"Such great weather we're having, am I right?" Oliver asked, hands casually ensconced in his jeans pockets. "In past years, we've had hellish weather…really unpleasant."

"Must've brought the good weather with me," Lara replied, allowing herself a little grin. "I should get back to the booth, wouldn't want to leave Sergeant Stevens by himself."

"Of course…always working, even when you're not, huh?"

"It's a curse, really. Nice to see you."

Oliver paused for a moment, his face looking expectant, as though he thought she might say something more. When he didn't hear what he wanted, he flashed a blazing smile.

"I'll see you later." And with a tip of his head, he too was off, disappearing into the crowd.

Lara returned to the police booth, allowing Sergeant Stevens a bathroom break and a chance to walk around. Plopping down in one of the chairs, something pressed against her thigh through the pocket of her khakis. Rolling to the opposite side, Lara reached in. Fingertips glanced against smooth, solid metal. With eyebrows cranked down in confusion, she pulled the object from her pocket and nearly dropped it.

It was her father's wedding ring, lying casually in the palm of her hand.

The early afternoon light glinted off the simple gold band. The mere sight of it caused her chest cavity to constrict, the agonizing ache of loss returning.

After her father's funeral and subsequent interment, she had shoved this piece of jewelry into a box, and then shoved that box into the far corners of a dresser drawer. The dresser in question now sat in the guest bedroom of the colonial.

Or at least, it's where the ring *had* been.

Jewelry wasn't something she indulged in often, preferring not to run the risk of injuries on the job. How the ring had gotten into her pocket was her current worry, the metal warm from being wedged against her body. Another chilling gust of wind picked up around her, ripping through her jacket and police department polo, sending a chill down her spine. Fingers curled tightly around the ring as she shoved her hand back into her pocket, making a mental note to put the thing back where it was supposed to be.

That was when she saw her.

The woman was young, no older than Lara herself. Her hair was black and tucked into a cap. Her clothes were early colonial, making the woman appear as though she had stepped right off the Mayflower. The woman smiled softly, knowingly, at Lara.

A noise caused Lara's concentration to break. For a second, Lara's head turned to the source of the sound—a particularly overzealous scream of a child who had hit big on the prize wheel of the tourism booth. When Lara looked back, the woman was gone, and after craning her neck, Lara didn't spot her in the crowd.

A moment later, Sergeant Stevens returned, sitting down with a grunt, a loaded hot dog in one hand and a giant soft drink in the other.

"You okay? You look pale," he asked, having caught Lara's expression.

"Y-Yeah, I'm fine. Hey, do people normally dress up for this festival?"

"What do you mean? Like in costumes? Mostly the kids."

"No, like, period clothing? From old Salem or something?"

Sergeant Stevens sat for a moment, chewing a bite of hot dog as he contemplated.

"Can't say I've heard such a thing. Mostly you see Native peoples in their full regalia on the way to their dance demonstration."

"No one dresses up like Puritans?" Lara asked, incredulous.

Sergeant Stevens shook his head. "Nope, generally not. That's not the thing to do around here." He chuckled.

Lara turned again to scan the crowd but didn't see the woman.

Sergeant Stevens continued to eat his hot dog and suck at the soda in silence, leaving Lara to contemplate.

It was odd. The woman had looked at Lara as though she knew her, but Lara had never seen the woman before. The woman's gaze had bored into Lara's, as if reading her very soul. The smile had been familiar, somehow.

With one final look around, Lara brushed the event from her mind, just in time for a family to come up and ask about the citizens' police academy for Eastfall.

Lara was glad to see the park in her rear-view mirror as she headed home, taking time to marvel at the blasts of bright yellow and vibrant red of the leaves along the back roads. This part of the city was more rural than urban, evoking a memory of the woods of Maine where she and her father would camp over the summers. It made her remember the strange appearance of her father's wedding band.

The only explanation that came to mind was that she must've pulled it out at some point. Though, it had been a spell since she held something of her father's, something she used to do to feel closer to him.

Dinner that evening consisted of a bag of Ruffles chips and Sam Adams. It felt nice to lie out on the couch, to relax and take some time to busy her mind with something other than murder. It only worked for so long before the wheels started to crank and grind again.

Once the Bruins hockey game ended, Lara got to her feet to stretch, swaying a little from the rush of blood to her head and the effects of the five beers she'd consumed. Slowly, she shuffled her way to the front of the house, becoming more wide-eyed and alert with every step.

The light was jarring when she flipped the switch in her home office, but her eyes soon adjusted. It wasn't much of an office—a simple desk from Ikea complete with matching chair, an Apple laptop, and a printer. Propped against one of the walls was a cork board. She had meant to hang it to use for investigations, but she'd become preoccupied with other matters.

On the desk, looking as innocuous as it could, was the box from the attic. Lara had almost forgotten it. The murder of a fellow police officer, the press conference, and the harvest festival had pushed the box to the back of her mind. Now, she slumped down in her chair and scooted forward to take a closer look.

The box didn't have an obvious latch or lock. It appeared to be fused shut. Reaching forward, Lara tried to dig her fingers into the seam and tug. The lid of the box didn't budge. Huffing, Lara tried again. When it still didn't open, annoyance began to bubble. She loved a challenge and did not meet something she couldn't figure out.

Despite the fact the box had been under floorboards for an indeterminate amount of time, there was no evidence of rust anywhere or signs of water damage, and the mother-of-pearl *AB* appeared as though it had been freshly made.

Picking up the box, Lara turned it this way and that, analyzing the outside for trick latches or hidden buttons.

Nothing.

Setting the box down, Lara idly brushed her palm across the mother-of-pearl initials. For a brief moment, she thought she felt the box vibrate, but dismissed the sensation.

Lara pushed away from her desk, abandoning the idea she would get anything accomplished that evening. As she exited the room and turned to make for the stairs, she heard scratching and a faint creak.

Feet froze, her hand hovering over the wooden banister. Slowly, she turned, eyes sweeping the hallway for the source of the noise. When she didn't find anything, she went back to her office.

Peeking around the corner, the cause became immediately apparent.

The lid of the box stood open.

Swallowing thickly, Lara waffled between running from the room or investigating further. Being the curious soul she was, a strength and a weakness, she couldn't help but carry out the latter. Stepping back into the room, she cautiously approached her desk. Nothing jumped at her, nothing grabbed her from behind, the box didn't launch itself at her.

It was just silence.

Silence, and the box all but calling for her to slake her curiosity and discover the contents.

Sitting down on her desk chair, Lara slowly reached for the box, fingers shakily bringing it closer.

Nestled inside was a thick book, a bundle of herbs, and a pale-yellow flower with deeper yellow in the center. Reaching inside, she gingerly grasped the bundle of herbs, thinking that age should have made them disintegrate years ago.

But they were as fresh as if put in the box yesterday.

Tentatively, she brought the bundle beneath her nose. It gave off a sweet smell—pleasant, almost soothing. Setting it aside, she pulled out the yellow flower to do the same.

The book was a thick tome, and near as long as the box itself. It was bound in dark brown leather with a simple gold border. Eyebrows furrowed, Lara delicately held it in her hands and opened the book.

It was blank.

The pages were as empty and crisp as the first day it had been bound.

Sighing, she put the book back in the box, and replaced the herbs and flower. Closing the lid, she set the box aside for later inspection. She left the room again, only to freeze once more in the same spot, having heard the familiar scratch of wood and creak.

Quickly, Lara ducked back into the doorway, as if she would catch the culprit. The box stood where she had left it, opened now, room empty.

"What do you want from me?" She found herself whispering to the stillness of the room, as if truly expecting an answer in return.

There was no response, of course.

Crossing the room with a quick stride, she ripped the contents out of the box. Again, no words in the book, just empty pages and a slightly pungent combined scent of the yellow flower and the herbs. Instead of putting them back in the box, she set them on her desk. Lara then left the room hurriedly and didn't stop until she was up the stairs and slamming the door to her room. Her heart hammered against her rib cage.

She was afraid.

Afraid she had finally hit the wall of insanity she so feared running into.

Not bothering to shuck her clothes, Lara hopped onto her bed and burrowed beneath the covers.

She didn't know what was with this box. It had to be a trip mechanism of some sort. Maybe she would get the forensics team to look at it, sweep it for prints or DNA or other physical evidence.

It wasn't long until she blissfully fell asleep, dreaming of police officers punching annoying reporters.

CHAPTER 14

The next morning didn't offer any clarity about the box. Of course, Lara would never admit she certainly couldn't get clarity from fifteen feet away, the minimum distance she kept between the box and herself at all times.

Monday morning dawned, finding Eastfall recovering from the high of the harvest festival. Denizens made their sleepy morning commute to work, with Lara right there in it, though traffic could never be as bad as Boston's.

Once situated in her office with an extra-large cup of Dunkin, Lara began skimming back over the case files as well as her notes. Reports had come in from Dr. Rogers and the forensics team. Dr. Rogers's conclusions were the same as Lynn Rickerson's case, and forensics had found nothing.

Lara, back to square one, embraced the square.

Sometimes, she did her best thinking by starting over. Lara examined the crime scene photos from Lynn Rickerson, taking in even the most minute detail.

For good measure, Lara attempted to give Jeff McMullens a call, but was met with his voicemail again. She left the same message she had before. A thread she would keep pulling at until it unraveled.

Her cell phone buzzed on the desk near her elbow. It was a text message from Oliver Bennett, confirming that she would be testifying in a couple of cases coming up in the next few weeks. Lara shot off a quick reply text, reassuring him that she would indeed be there. His reply was instant—a smiling emoji and the thumbs-up emoji. If nothing else, it made Lara smile.

"Good morning, Sunshine," Tom greeted, poking his head in. The morning hellos had started as a means to keep an eye on her, to report unusual behavior to the chief, though she knew Tom would never admit to it. Now, it was genuine.

"Morning, Cap," Lara greeted with a halfhearted wave and a deep sip from her coffee.

From around Tom's shoulder popped Jason's familiar dark curls.

"Hey, Frenchie," Jason said with a grin as he muscled his way around his husband and made himself comfortable in one of Lara's chairs. Lara couldn't help the small smile.

"Did you leave Lola somewhere?"

"At school, where any young person should be," Jason replied. Lara snorted.

"Did you come here just to harass us?"

"I don't think of it as harassment. I think of it as—I dunno—motivation. I'm motivating you to get your work done."

"Yeah, because police work is actual work," Tom growled from the doorway, though no real malice existed in his words. It was an ongoing joke between the couple that Tom did the real work and Jason got to sit and read all day. No matter that Jason had owned the bookstore well before they met, and actually turned a decent profit for a century where online shopping and bigger corporations reigned supreme.

"Darling, why don't you go sit down and enjoy your coffee. I'll be there in a minute," Jason soothed, waving Tom off with a flick of his wrist. Tom huffed and slouched out of view. Jason turned back to Lara with a wide grin.

"You're going to nag him into an early grave," Lara mused, hiding her wry smile behind her coffee.

"Nah, he'll live longer *because* I harass him so much. He loves it."

Lara laughed.

"How are you doing, Frenchie? That press conference the other day...brutal..."

"I'm fine," Lara muttered, unable to hold back an eyeroll. "Nothing I can't handle."

"Mhm," Jason hummed, his eyes boring into her, picking her apart in a way that made her a little uncomfortable. He'd had a knack for reading her ever since she came to Eastfall. It was a little unnerving to have the tables turned on you, to have someone else pick apart your minute reactions. After a beat, his gaze dipped down to the pictures she had strewn across. Before she could scramble to hide them, Jason reached forward, plucking one of the glossy, high-resolution horrors in his fingers.

"I've seen these before," he mused.

The picture he held was from Lynn Rickerson's crime scene, a close-up of the peculiar symbols etched into the dirt around her body. Lara had run a cursory search on the databases she had access to, but no luck. Now, though, her heart raced with the hope Jason knew something.

"You have?" she pressed, leaning closer.

"As you might know, I have a small, but decent, rare book selection at my store. I've seen these in one of them."

Lara stepped into the store with Jason in front of her and Tom behind. At its inception, the place had been called The Book Store, but now had been rebranded, lovingly, into Lola's Books. As a younger child, Lola had wanted to spend every waking moment in the store, having been a voracious reader from an early age. The teen was wicked smart, and well on her way to being valedictorian of her class. It wouldn't surprise Lara if she ended up at Harvard in a couple of years.

"The rare books are in the back. Need to keep them safe and in a temperature-controlled environment. It pays to know someone with good security connections," Jason said, shooting a fond smile at Tom.

Lola's Books took up prime corner shop space, no more than a quarter of a football field in length and width. There were shelves upon shelves of new and repurposed books. Jason accepted trade-ins and resold them. He even had a small section for journals and stationery. The place was well lit and easy to maneuver, which Lara did now, heading straight for the back room. The scent of new and old books lay thick in the air. It reminded her of time spent at the Boylston Street branch of the Boston Public Library.

"Do you remember which book?" she asked, getting right down to business, while Jason took his time to hang up his jacket and put away his lunch.

"I don't. I just know I've seen the symbols before...," Jason replied, stepping into the back room, hands on hips, "somewhere in here."

That was both a relief and a disappointment.

"Any idea where to start?" Lara asked.

"Uno momento, Frenchie," Jason said, before stepping up to one of his shelving units. His blue eyes skimmed over the spines. The smell of old books hung stronger here, almost overpowering. Some of the tomes were worn and frayed, while others looked damn near brand new. Lara wasn't sure she wanted to handle any of them, lest they lose their value.

Jason turned away from the bookshelf with a stack of books in his arms and set them on a nearby square table.

"Here...if you want to help, leaf through these."

"Are you sure you want me touchin' these?" Lara asked, skeptically.

"Yeah, it's fine. Just, you know, be careful."

"I don't need gloves or anything?"

"No. As I said, it'll be fine. Just...handle with care."

For the next hour, the three companions leafed through the volumes, some from the nineteenth century and some a little more recent. There were large tomes and skinny tomes. One book was an entire list of recipes for herbal remedies, and others were occult writings about summoning demons. Lara took the opportunity to read some of the works written in English. The language was beautiful, perhaps too flowery at times, but elegant just the same.

When Lara's eyes began to cross from the strain, she sat back, digging her fingertips into her eyes.

"I'm sorry," Jason said with a frustrated sigh. "I was sure I'd seen those symbols before in a book I had. At this point, it's like we're searching for a needle in a haystack."

"It's okay," Tom replied, reaching over to cover Jason's hand with his own.

"I'll keep looking," Jason assured them. "I thought for sure I could help."

"Don't worry. We'll find something," Lara replied.

Getting up, she found a piece of scrap paper on the counter near the cash register and grabbed a pencil. Quickly, she sketched the symbols, the few she'd committed to memory.

"Here you go, just in case you find something." Lara set the piece of paper down on the table.

In her pocket, her cell phone began to vibrate. She checked the caller ID. It was the chief. Lara's heart leapt into her throat.

"Hi, Chief," she greeted.

"Hi, Lieutenant. I need you back at the station."

Ten minutes later, Tom and Lara stepped off the elevator heading for their offices.

Turning the corner, they spotted the chief talking to someone standing in the doorway of Tom's office. For a moment, Lara couldn't see who the person was, but the chief appeared serious and animated.

As they got closer, however, a horrible thought occurred to her. A bad feeling roiled and wiggled in her gut, causing her to stop dead. Swallowing thickly, she let out a shaky breath.

The chief shifted his weight and revealed the visitor.

It took all her willpower to keep from spinning on her heels and beat feet out of the building.

Needless to say, things between her and her ex-girlfriend, Natalia de Benedetto, had not ended on the best of terms.

For either of them.

Mostly because of Lara.

Okay, entirely because of Lara.

"Ah, Lieutenant, Captain, meet—"

"Hey, Nat," Lara greeted, trying to keep her face and tone even, emotionless, eyes unable to meet Natalia's dark-brown gaze.

"Lara," Natalia said, face schooled, no emotion whatsoever. She'd always been better at that.

"I guess I don't need to make introductions then," the chief replied, surprised.

Natalia, however, did step forward with her hand outstretched to Tom.

"FBI Special Agent Natalia de Benedetto, pleasure to meet you."

Tom looked as if someone had switched his favorite toothpaste for shaving cream. No one could have looked more surprised.

"Captain Tom Sharpe, nice to meet you," Tom replied, sliding his palm against Natalia's and shaking firmly.

"I imagine Special Agent de Benedetto is here to do what the FBI does best...butt in on someone else's investigation," Lara blurted once the pleasantries had passed. The chief looked taken aback at Lara's forward comment.

Natalia rolled her eyes, crossing her arms over her chest. She was a tick taller than Lara, and lithe but muscular, like a ballerina. She had the olive skin tone of her Italian ancestry, long, thick dark hair, and dark eyes of the rest of her Mediterranean ancestors.

Natalia de Benedetto was beautiful, smart, determined, and a complete hard-ass. They were—or rather had been—of similar minds, and perhaps that had been their downfall.

"I think the lieutenant here knows very well that's not what the Bureau does," Natalia responded coolly.

"Isn't it?" Lara replied, eyebrow arched. "The first time we met, you booted me off the case, pulling rank and higher jurisdiction."

The agent sighed again, stance tall and straight, body tense. She had to have come prepared for a fight from Lara.

"Look, why don't we—" the chief began, before Lara cut him off.

"We have things well in hand here, agent. You can go back to Boston and tell the rest of the feds the locals have it handled. No need to stick your noses where they're not wanted—"

"Lieutenant!" the chief shouted, ire splashed across his face. Lara had never seen him anything but calm and collected, and perhaps this wasn't the best time to test that.

"It's alright, Chief Braddock. I expect this behavior from Lieutenant Nadeau."

The chief looked like he didn't know how to handle this situation. In his experience, the FBI and Eastfall had been nothing but cooperative. But those FBI agents and those Eastfall cops weren't Natalia and Lara.

"How about we step into your office, Captain," the chief said, giving a pointed look to Tom as though he hoped for backup. "And we'll have a civilized conversation."

"Yes, sir," Lara replied. The chief's tone said he wasn't fucking around.

Her feet moved, closing the distance, and as Lara brushed past Natalia, she couldn't help but recognize the familiar scent of body wash, shampoo, and something purely Nat. This was not a trip down memory lane Lara wanted.

The chief allowed Tom to sit behind his desk, even after Tom had offered. The chief brushed him off and instead stood next to Tom as he sat. Natalia grabbed a visitor chair, back ramrod straight and sitting forward, all business. Lara chose not to sit and instead hovered in the doorway.

"For the record, Lieutenant, I asked the FBI to come. It wasn't because I wanted them to take over the investigation, but to pool our resources. There's only so much we have access to in Eastfall, as you well know."

The chief might be able to swallow his pride and ask for help, but Lara and most other cops certainly weren't.

"I am more than willing to be cooperative," Natalia spoke up, her tone utterly professional. "And I will be happy to help in this investigation, or take on an advisory role, if the lieutenant can handle that?"

Lara's jaw clenched. Natalia certainly knew how to play to

Lara's sense of propriety and tact. There was no way she could say no, especially not in front of two superior officers. Sucking in a breath, Lara nodded.

"Yes, I can handle it."

"Great. I trust you will get Agent de Benedetto up to speed on what you've gotten so far?" The chief uncrossed his arms, tone and body language acting as if everything would be fine now.

Things were far from fine for Lara.

CHAPTER 15

It took the rest of the morning and part of the early afternoon to fill Natalia in on their findings, complete with a tour of the station. Their conversations were stilted but remained professional. The entire time, Tom shot Lara confused looks over Natalia's shoulder. Lara would just shrug.

To say a shroud of awkwardness hung over them would be an understatement. It'd been a year or more since Lara had last seen Natalia, and they didn't part on the best of terms. The bad taste still lingered in both of their mouths, though Natalia's was more justified than Lara's.

"Quittin' time for me," Tom said, when the sun had started to dip low on the horizon. "It's my turn to cook tonight."

They'd been sitting in a conference room for the past hour, poring over the crime scene photographs and reports from Dr. Rogers. Lara had hoped Natalia's fresh eyes might immediately uncover something she'd missed.

No such luck.

"Give Lola a hug for me," Lara murmured, looking up to give Tom a soft smile.

"Will do. Agent de Benedetto, I'll see you tomorrow. Hope the Bureau's put you up in a decent place."

"Please, you can call me Natalia, Captain Sharpe. And yes, the little bed and breakfast close by? The Ancient Mariner?"

"Oh wow, fancy," Tom hummed. "They're pulling out all the stops for you. The Ancient Mariner is the poshest thing we've got to offer in Eastfall. Also, it's one of the oldest buildings in town. Used to be the local watering hole and an inn. Some people say it's haunted."

Natalia laughed. An all too familiar and all too musical sound. It was different, though. Lara couldn't put her finger on how. Was it less happy? Less carefree? More guarded?

"I'll keep you posted, but I'm not really worried about things that go bump in the night," Natalia replied. "More worried about the monsters that hide in plain sight."

"How poetic," Tom replied, thoroughly charmed.

Lara couldn't even be mad. Natalia was everything—beauty, brains, courage.

And Lara had all but dragged Nat down into her dark hole.

With a final goodbye, Tom disappeared, leaving the two women alone. It'd been fine for most of the day, as there was always a third person around. Now, Lara felt her heart kick up in her chest again, anxiety and nervousness gnawing. She didn't want a continuation of their last face-to-face.

"Well, uh..." Lara began, so eloquently, "...there's really not much else we can do for today, so we can call it quits. I'll see you tomorrow." Before Lara could get the hell out of the conference room, Natalia's next words stopped her.

"Why don't we grab a bite? Catch up? It's been a while since we've seen each other."

"I don't know if that's such a good idea, Nat," Lara replied, looking anywhere but Natalia's eyes. In the deep-brown depths, Lara had never been able to keep the truth hidden from her.

"Oh, come on. We can't eat together? Or have you replaced all food groups with Jim, Jack, and Jose?"

Yikes. Okay. Lara deserved that.

"Of course I eat," she replied lamely.

"Okay, good," Natalia said curtly, getting to her feet. "I'm feeling Italian."

The woman always had a way of bending Lara to her will. Not in all things, of course, but in the little things—where they would eat, who would get control of the remote, which side of the bed she would sleep on....

But Natalia had never been able to help Lara better herself, and that's what had driven in the biggest wedge.

———

"Shit, shit, shit," Lara muttered, frustrated, as the unmarked clinked over a deep apron. She swung the huge chunk of metal into a tight parking space and cursed some more when she nearly banged the driver's side door into the car parked next to her. Boots hit the ground, hustling as she made her way to the front door of the only good Italian restaurant in Eastfall.

She was late.

How she could be late was beyond her. Before they'd left the police station, they agreed to meet back at the restaurant in an hour, after they had some time to take a break, wind down. Unable to bring herself to make the drive home, Lara had stayed in her office, pacing back and forth. She had come really close to texting Natalia—did she even have the same number?—to cancel.

Lara was a fucking coward, and she would admit it to the heavens if it meant getting out of this meal.

Natalia stood inside the entrance in the toasty warmth, aimlessly thumbing through her phone. Her dark head, hair coiled into a tight braid, lifted upon hearing the tinkling of the bell over the door. Lara slid inside, bringing a gust of cold air with her. How fitting. Almost immediately, she pulled her dark peacoat tighter around herself.

"I'm so sorry," Lara muttered. Natalia's impeccably manicured eyebrow gave the barest twitch, but otherwise her face was steel. She didn't look surprised at Lara's tardiness.

Together, they approached the harried-looking hostess, who greeted them, nevertheless, with a welcoming smile. She looked not much older than eighteen, probably a high school student in her very first job. Both women followed close behind the young girl and thanked her when they were seated in their booth.

Bello Italiano was Eastfall's premier Italian restaurant, and in Lara's opinion, the best one from Havenwood up to Salem. To one side, there was a rather massive fireplace that held a crackling fire, perfect to fight the chill outside. The ceilings were high, and the lighting dim.

A young, blonde woman, probably in her early twenties, sidled up to their table. Her greeting was tempered with a thick Russian accent.

"Good evening, what can I get you to drink?"

"I will take water with lemon, please," Natalia replied, jumping right in as always. The waitress looked expectantly at Lara.

"Uh...a cappuccino, please?"

The young woman nodded, scribbled their drink orders on her notepad, and whisked away.

Lara wanted very much to say something in that following moment, to fill the awkward void of silence. Instead, because she was a coward, she remained silent. Her hands began traveling around the table—adjusting the position of her silverware, pulling the salt and pepper shakers closer, and then flicking at a packet of sugar braced between her fingertip and the table. Lara had never been this twitchy and uncomfortable around Natalia. Maybe she was making it awkward, more awkward than it needed to be.

The waitress soon reappeared, to Lara's relief, without a word having passed between them. A serving tray solidly balanced on the palm of her hand, the young woman gingerly plopped their drinks in front of them, as well as a basket of bread knots glistening with olive oil, garlic, and parmesan cheese. Lara's mouth began to water, and realization dawned that she hadn't eaten lunch.

"Are you ready to order?" the waitress asked.

With a tight nod, Natalia listed off her meal choice. It was exactly the kind of meal Lara expected Natalia to order—healthier fare, more vegetables than meat, and practically no pasta.

Yet another box Lara had never been able to check. Even before the incident and their subsequent break-up, eating healthily had never been Lara's strong suit. She loved food.

When Natalia finished dictating her order, ending with tacking on some ridiculous, gluten-free item, the waitress turned to Lara.

"Um…I'll take the baked spaghetti with meat sauce, please."

Natalia gave the waitress another tight-lipped smile as the younger woman collected their menus, as if trying to excuse Lara's awkwardness.

"So, how's life?" Lara asked, when the silence got to be too much.

"Life's great," Natalia replied, with no hint of falsehood.

"That's good. Real good."

"Yeah. How are you liking Eastfall?"

Lara shrugged, then reached forward to grab one of the piping hot garlic knots. Absently, she ripped it in two, then tore off a smaller bite and popped it into her mouth.

"It's fine," she said, trying her best to focus on how delicious the bread tasted and not how much she wanted to run from the table.

"Of course it is," Natalia said, unable to keep the bitterness from her voice. Her fingers reached into the basket and grabbed a garlic knot. It caught Lara off guard. In times past, Natalia rarely partook of any bread.

"What does that mean?" Lara asked, hackles rising.

"Nothing. It just means nothing's changed. You haven't changed."

"Really, you want to do this here? Now?" Lara gritted through clenched teeth.

"No. No, I don't. Sorry."

Silence reigned supreme for the next five minutes. Enough time for the waitress to come back around to check on them. Lara noticed when Natalia elected to take another garlic knot.

How things had changed in the year since she'd seen her...

"How's the Bureau? You on track to that promotion?" Lara asked, offering an olive branch.

"In theory," Natalia replied, relieved to have this change of conversation. "There's a couple other people in line for it."

"Let me guess...men?"

"You know it."

Lara scoffed, grabbing up her third garlic knot. She was just getting started.

"So, Lynn Rickerson—" she began, but Natalia cut her off.

"Come on, Lara. We always agreed to never talk case specifics outside work hours. Did you forget?"

Apparently, she had. Swallowing thickly, Lara fell silent. It had always been a rule for them to never talk shop. It was part of Natalia's efforts to have some sort of a life outside of her job. Lara had never understood.

It took a couple more tries, but they finally fell into companionable conversation. Lara had to admit—by the time they were through with their entrees, she was actually enjoying herself. It was like old times, like riding a bike, like falling back into habits.

"Can I get you ladies dessert?" the waitress asked as she cleared away their plates to box up the leftover food.

"Oh no, I can't," Natalia said, not unkindly.

"Come on, Nat, live a little," Lara ribbed her. "We'll take tiramisu. Two forks, please."

The waitress nodded with a smile and left.

"Still don't indulge in dessert, huh?"

"No. You know I don't eat sweets."

"I know, but you eat them at least once a year," Lara teased. "Let this be your one time, huh?"

Natalia smiled. An honest to God smile. "Alright, fine. I'll have a few bites."

They ate their dessert, and soon came the fight for the check. Natalia eventually won, using the excuse that the Bureau would shoulder the expense. Lara couldn't argue with that logic.

With the check squared away, Lara and Natalia braved the cold. The wind played off the water of Hawthorne River, bringing a biting chill. Both women were used to the harsh climes of the northeast, and without meaning to, they huddled together for warmth.

"This was nice," Natalia commented as she hit the key fob to unlock the stereotypical governmental black SUV. Lara nodded, hands crunched down deep in her pockets.

"Definitely. It's...it's good to see you, Nat. It really is."

Natalia smiled softly. "It's good to see you too. You seem more at ease here. I'm glad."

Lara didn't know about that. She missed Boston. Missed big city policing. Missed the unreliability of the T. Missed the culture and the restaurants.

"Yeah. So, uh, I'll see you tomorrow morning, then."

"Definitely," Natalia said.

Neither moved, their eyes met and held. Those feelings Lara believed long buried came crashing back. The memories of their time together, the shit they went through together. More Lara's shit than Natalia's. Lara could never blame Natalia for breaking up with her. Lara had been like poison, any longer together and Lara would have ruined her. But God, had she loved Natalia.

Without realizing, Lara leaned in, driven by the memory of Natalia's soft, plush lips.

"Wh-What are you doing?" Natalia jerked back, nearly flush against the SUV.

"Jesus...fuck, I'm...I'm so sorry. I don't...I'm sorry."

Lara, completely embarrassed at her moment of weakness, turned and rushed to the unmarked. She didn't hesitate or look back until she found herself parked in her driveway, both hands gripping the steering wheel.

"Goddamned idiot," Lara muttered over and over as she banged her forehead against the wheel.

After another moment of berating, she got out of her car. It was tunnel vision all the way to the refrigerator. She couldn't get a grip on a bottle of beer on the first attempt. Eventually, she grabbed hold of a long neck, and twisted the cap off, guzzling the amber liquid until it was half gone. Sucking in a breath, Lara doubled over the island, finding some solace in the coolness of the counter on her forehead.

God, she was a Grade A Fuckup.

CHAPTER 16

The rest of the night passed in a beer haze. She couldn't stop herself. Beer after beer, until she passed out on the couch with old reruns of *The Golden Girls* playing. Bottles littered the coffee table and the floor.

It didn't matter though. Nothing mattered in that moment. Nothing ever did when she got low, except the numbness. Not feeling the emotions she couldn't seem to control. Didn't even want to control.

Lara wasn't sure the hour, but as she teetered on that line between sleep and awake, she was certain she heard someone say her name. The voice was far away, and it echoed as though she were in a cavern. There were moments in the past she had imagined hearing her father, hearing his voice and the way he used to say her name. But this time it was a woman's voice she heard.

She shifted on the couch, eyes blearily blinking in the dim living room. The only light the flickering television, lit up by Blanche and one of her bright, flamboyant outfits. With groans and creaking bones, Lara sat up, peering over the back of the couch.

She saw darkness and nothing else.

Stumbling to her feet, Lara shuffled to the downstairs bathroom. Once finished, Lara collapsed back on the couch and remembered nothing more until morning light shone through the blinds.

It was rough making it to work, but Lara had the power of coffee and Tylenol on her side. She managed to avoid Natalia for a time, who was somewhere in the building. Thankfully, she hadn't been waiting in Lara's office. Lara wasn't ready to face the music on that mistake.

"Morning," Tom said, standing in her office doorway.

"Hey," Lara croaked, wincing. The inside of her skull rattled from the effort. Behind her, she kept the blinds closed to keep out the bright morning sun.

"How did it go last night?" Tom asked, fishing for something. No doubt he was dying to know the history between Lara and Natalia. That's not a chapter in her life she was ready to reveal to anyone, let alone someone she'd only known for six months.

"Fine," Lara replied. "We finished discussing the case, had dinner, and called it a night."

The look on Tom's face revealed pure disappointment, like he'd been waiting for hot gossip.

"Good morning, Captain," came the familiar, musical voice of Natalia de Benedetto, her face appearing behind Tom. The man in question looked shaken, as if he were the kid sticking his hand in the cookie jar.

"Er, morning, Special Agent," Tom greeted, turning to her with a forced smile.

Natalia stepped inside Lara's office, careful not to make eye contact with the police lieutenant.

"So, I was thinking last night. I think we should bring in,"—here Natalia referenced the notepad clutched in her hand—"Sergeant Zach Braddock. He's the chief's son, I know, but we've got to try and break him. He's the only known person connected to both victims, and he has a shaky alibi."

"It's not him, Nat," Lara sighed, fingers massaging at her right temple where the hangover headache clustered.

"How do you know that?" Natalia asked, skeptical. "Another one of your feelings?"

Lara cringed at how judgmental that sounded. It'd been a mistake to tell Natalia, so long ago, the bursts of intuition she felt at times. Natalia, though she had also been raised Catholic, broke from those bonds when she attended college. She only understood what she could process with her five senses. Science was more her language. Logic.

"Yes, Scully," Lara shot back, becoming more and more irritable as the seconds ticked past. "He's not our guy."

"I don't see you with any other leads or solid suspects. We need to bring him in. He'll talk to me."

That was one thing that had attracted Lara to Natalia so long ago—her confidence. Natalia was a damn good investigator. She made the FBI proud to call her one of their own. But she was calculating and too logical. She rarely used her instincts and didn't pay much attention to her gut.

"Fine. Whatever's gonna make you happy," Lara caved.

Natalia bristled, those plush lips parted as though about to start arguing. The fact Tom was there, lurking in the background, saved Lara's ass.

"I'll call him in," Natalia continued, back straightening, guarded. She turned on her heel and disappeared down the hallway to the conference room that had become her temporary office.

"Yikes. The temperature went down in here," Tom mused, disappearing back over to his office.

Lara heaved a heavy sigh and cradled her head in her hands.

No amount of coffee and Tylenol could prepare her for the day ahead.

"I was wondering when the FBI would get involved."

Zach Braddock looked as cool as a cucumber sitting across the table from Natalia, his arms crossed over his powerful chest, meeting Natalia's stare with an equally intense gaze. Lara stood off in a corner, holding up the wall with her shoulder, watching this unfold like she was watching a daytime drama.

"I can't tell if you're relieved or worried," Natalia responded.

"Of course I'm relieved," Zach replied, sitting back in the chair. Lara couldn't tell whether the chair was minuscule or whether his body was just that large.

Seeing the two of them squaring off across an interview table was a prime example of Lara's bisexuality.

Hyperbole, of course.

"Relief? Interesting," Natalia mused, her hands folded atop the unopened manila case file. She looked completely at ease sitting at the table, not shaken or nervous, just ready. Ready to nail someone to the wall. Because Natalia was Natalia, she'd already memorized the entire contents of their findings thus far, from the autopsy reports to the crime scene photographs.

"Why wouldn't I be relieved? You're here to help the

incompetent lieutenant my father mistakenly decided to take in out of the goodness of his heart."

Natalia visibly blanched, surprised by the obvious insult not to herself, but to Lara. The line of Natalia's shoulders tensed.

"From what I hear about you, Sergeant, you've no room to talk about incompetence."

That struck a nerve.

Both times Lara had Zach in that exact same chair, he'd been like a statue—not giving away any emotion, not even a telling twitch of an eyebrow or lip. This time, though, Lara could see the muscles of Zach's jaw working as he tried to hide the fact he clenched his jaw.

"Let's talk about that, actually," Natalia continued, pulling out a file from the bag that sat at her feet. This was off script, not something Natalia had discussed with Lara. The agent had done her own homework.

"I don't see how that's got anything to do with the two dead women," Zach gritted out.

"Doesn't it have everything to do with the murders? Or at least motive?"

Silence. Deafening silence, with not even the sound of breathing to break it.

"I didn't kill those women," Zach said, breaking the long silence.

"I hear you, yet you can't seem to give us a solid alibi. You're connected to both women. One you had an intimate relationship with, and another you went to the academy with. Who knows, you could've had a romantic relationship with Officer Fitzgerald, and we don't know."

"Officer Fitzgerald and I had nothing but a professional relationship," Zach replied, irritation seeping into his voice. "We were close friends. That's it. We leaned on each other for support in the academy. The last time I talked to her was her commendation ceremony, and it was just to congratulate her."

"Still, that wasn't that long ago," Natalia pointed out. With a little bit more dramatic flair than Lara was used to seeing from the FBI agent, Natalia flipped open the file containing documents she must have dug up on Zach.

"Is there a point to all of this, Agent de Benedetto, or are you just going to waste more of my time?"

"No, Sergeant, that's not my intention. Since you won't talk about what got you demoted from detective to patrol, I will." Pause for dramatic effect. This, Lara was used to seeing.

When Zach didn't say anything in return, Natalia powered on.

"So, Sergeant Braddock, you were investigated and even brought to a disciplinary hearing because of a case you worked on," Natalia said, painting the picture. "You were a police detective for Havenwood, correct?"

"Yes," Zach replied.

"And your last case as a detective was of a domestic dispute between a woman and her husband, correct?"

"Yes."

In her little corner of the room, Lara's heart began to beat a little faster. An anxiety that wasn't her own pulsed through her veins and spread to every point in her body. Her heart hammered quicker, and a cold sweat broke out across her forehead, her upper lip, and down the line of her spine.

What the fuck was going on? She wasn't the one being interrogated.

"Is it true during this investigation the woman placed a call to you in the middle of the night, asking you to come protect her from her husband?"

"Yes."

Fear. That's what it was. Fear crawled across Lara's skin,

made itself at home in her stomach, in her head. She had nothing to do with the proceedings happening in front of her, yet it was as if she was tapping into Zach Braddock's emotions. It scared Lara, thinking that's what this was. The last time she believed she'd felt someone else's emotions was with her father the night he died. There were memories of other times through her life, but she'd always brushed them off. However, with the strangeness of her house and this case, Lara couldn't help but wonder....

"The woman and her husband were alive when you arrived, correct?"

"Yes."

"But the woman was dead when police back-up arrived later to the scene?"

"...Yes."

"Interesting. Your statement, and the statement from the husband, are shaky and contradictory, at best. Yet all evidence was circumstantial and hearsay. There was nothing concrete to prove who exactly it was that killed this woman."

Zach didn't reply. He didn't need to, as it had been more of a statement than a question.

It was the kid.

Lara's shoulder slid off the wall out of surprise as the thought popped into her head. Where it came from, she didn't know, but had an unbelievable guess.

"This couple...they had one child, right? Isaac, aged ten at the time," Natalia trudged on, glancing down at the notes in the file.

"Yes."

"And Isaac was there that night as well, though he'd been upstairs during the altercation. He couldn't give a solid statement either. But then again, because he wasn't in the room, his testimony wasn't easy to corroborate or give validity to."

Again, nothing from Zach. He saw no point. It was all statements of fact.

"Cause of death for Mrs. Roxanna Crow was exsanguination from a gunshot wound. The round came from a firearm registered to Mr. Donald Crow. Oddly enough, there were no viable fingerprints recovered from the pistol."

Lara's heart practically burst from her chest. Her stomach roiled, bile rising in her throat. Her muscles ached, and her vision and thoughts grew foggy.

Where in the hell was this coming from?

"So...there's no solid explanation as to the events that occurred that night. I have notes from the investigator of the case. They don't shine a very good light on you, Sergeant. He said you were borderline obsessed with this family. That you might have even been harassing Mrs. Crow. I'll be honest, all the evidence, no matter how circumstantial, does not look good for you, Sergeant Braddock. Yet here you are, not in jail, still a police officer, in fact. The only thing you received was a slap on the wrist and a demotion. Pays to have parents in high places, doesn't it?"

"This is bullshit," Zach hissed out, getting to his feet so quickly the chair nearly toppled over. "I'm not on trial for Roxanna's murder, Agent. That investigation's in the past. Why in the fuck are you bringing this up now?"

"Look, Sergeant Braddock, I'm just trying to follow all angles here. You can't blame me for doing my job," Natalia replied, not even the least bit shaken she had a seething, hulk of a man standing over her.

Lara leaned in on herself, clutching at her stomach from the sheer panic, hopelessness, and helplessness she felt. She couldn't explain how or why, but she knew whatever happened that night at the Crow residence was not as it appeared in the official record.

Staggering forward, Lara slumped into the chair next to

Natalia, and laid her upper body across the table to reach for one of Zach's braced hands.

"Hey," Lara said softly. "Take a deep breath. Sit down for me, hm?"

Inexplicably, some of the panic and fear leached from her, enough that she felt she could think clearer. Surprisingly, Zach did as she requested. He shakily sat down, fear and sadness pooled in those staggering blue eyes.

"Talk us through what actually happened. It's been long enough, Zach. Tell us what really went down that night," Lara said. Where the informal use of his name came from, she wasn't sure, but it did the trick. The guy had been so freaking tight-lipped since all this started. All of a sudden, he seemed to cave under the weight of what he'd hidden.

"Roxanna was a girl I knew from high school. And no, we didn't date, we were just friends," Zach began. "She'd married Don young. They were high school sweethearts, the kind that made you sick from how lovey they were. Don started to change, though, not long after Isaac turned eight. Don would come home from his shift in the Angylion factory, already a few beers deep, drinking with his buddies. He'd have a few more when he got home, and he'd...he'd just get mad. He'd get so mad, he beat her. She took the hits for Isaac on more than one occasion."

Lara listened intently, thankfully experiencing her own emotions once again. Natalia, the stone sentinel at her side, listened as well.

"I tried to get Roxanna to file charges, but she wouldn't. I kept pushing and pushing and didn't realize until it was too late that my hanging around made everything worse. Don would accuse her of...of sleeping around, particularly with me. Called her every name in the book.

"One night, I got a phone call from Roxanna. She was fucking terrified. Saying Don was worse than she'd ever seen him. Like he had the Devil in him, was how she described him. So, I rushed over there as fast as I could. When I got there, Roxanna and Isaac had barricaded themselves in her bedroom, and Don was literally taking an ax to it like he was Jack Torrance in *The* fucking *Shining*..."

Zach stopped, taking a moment to gather his thoughts. He seemed defeated. Those broad shoulders appeared half as wide, hunched forward as he was then. His youthful face looked ten years older. A lot of the piss and vinegar was gone, and Lara had the feeling they were finally seeing the real Zachariah Braddock.

Police work was hard. There were some things her father wouldn't ever discuss with her, not even when she became a cop herself, things he'd seen on the job.

"I was able to talk Don down enough to give up the ax and got Isaac and Roxanne out of the room. I'd never seen Don like that. It was like he did have something inside of him, driving him to do those things. His eyes were...they were dead. Like there was no one human behind them. It was the scariest fucking thing I'd ever seen."

"What happened next?"

"I called for backup while I took Roxanna and Isaac out of the house. Rookie fucking mistake. I hadn't restrained Don. He came charging out of the house, like a switch had flipped. He'd gone crazy again, gunning for Roxanna like he'd take her head off with his bare hands. I put myself in his path to try and stop him, braced for impact and everything, and that's when it happened...the gunshot. Don stopped dead in his tracks, and in that moment, I knew he'd been the one hit. It was like the gunshot flipped the switch again, and he was Don."

"But he wasn't the one that had been hit?" Lara asked, though she knew the answer.

"No. Isaac...he...Isaac knew Don owned a handgun. It was

registered, but not secured. Isaac had grabbed it from his parents' bedroom and put it in the pocket of his sweatpants. When he saw his dad running toward them...he pulled it out. But the kid hit his mom instead...."

Genuine tears rolled from Zach's eyes, his body hunched over the table as he finally released the truth he'd guarded for so long. "He'd accidentally shot her instead of his dad," he clarified. He hadn't needed to, Lara knew. "She bled out in Don's arms. It was like...like the old Don had finally come back. The one from high school that had believed Roxanna hung the moon. The Don we always counted on for a laugh. The reason Don couldn't give a straight statement is because he claimed he couldn't remember anything that happened that night. He claimed he wasn't in control of his body. I just wanted to protect the kid, and so did Don. So, I made up some vague statement about how I couldn't say for sure what had happened because it was dark, and everything went so quickly. Don said the same."

Reaching up, Zach brushed away the line of tears that streamed down his cheeks.

"There was no real evidence to hash out the truth, so I let it lie, and Don couldn't forgive himself, so he took the blame. The investigator made his own notes and assumptions, and the next thing I knew I was busted down to patrol sergeant. But if that's what it took to protect Isaac...Christ."

"Sergeant Braddock," Lara began, voice softer than she'd ever heard from herself, "where were you when Lynn Rickerson and Sierra Fitzgerald were murdered?"

Zach sucked in a deep breath, sat up straight, shoulders wide once again. "I do under-the-table handyman work for one of the women's shelters in Salem. I do it...well, shit, I don't know why I do it. Maybe because I feel like I could save Roxanna that way? I was fixing a pipe leak when Lynn was killed and was installing a new refrigerator and oven when Sierra was killed."

"You could've told me before," Lara pointed out. "You wouldn't have had to tell me the why of it."

"I dunno. I don't advertise what I do for the shelter. I don't want anything happening to those women. I thought maybe if I said something about it, the truth would get out. And it has anyway."

The truth always revealed itself.

CHAPTER 17

Natalia calmly put the documents back into the correct folders while Lara sat, watching the man across the table, watching the way he fidgeted and sat uncomfortably in the chair.

"Quite the tale," Lara murmured. "I don't see any reason why Isaac Crow needs to be brought in for further questioning, as the night was dark and everything happened so quickly. Do you agree, Agent de Benedetto?"

Natalia paused, hesitating over her response. For a moment, Lara thought she would try to push this.

"No. I think Isaac's been through enough."

What hadn't been mentioned was that Isaac had been taken from Don Crow's custody and transferred to Roxanna's sister's. They had moved to Virginia a few months back. There was no reason to drag the kid through the wringer again. It was bad enough he would have to live through the guilt of having accidentally killed his mother.

Zach, who sat up instantly at the mention of Isaac's name and the prospect of bringing him back into this, visibly relaxed when both women agreed nothing would come of Zach's confession.

"Let me help," Zach croaked out, arms folded against his front as he leaned forward. "Please...let me help in the investigation. Before I was busted down, I had some of the best closing rates in Havenwood. Let me help. It's the least I could do...for Roxanna. For one less woman to be the victim of male violence."

Lara and Natalia turned their heads, gazes meeting. They didn't say anything. They didn't have to say anything, as they could read each other like a book. Few people in Lara's life had ever felt so connected to her as Natalia had, and apparently, still did. Even before their relationship had turned romantic, Natalia and Lara could broadcast their thoughts to each other. Especially when it came to investigative work. There was something in Natalia's eyes, the way she could reveal her emotions in any given moment, or hide them. There was something in her body language, the slightest movement. It always told a story to Lara, and in that moment, they were discussing taking on Zach for this case. Natalia thought it was a good idea, though Lara was a little more hesitant. Natalia shot a look of compassion, something that spoke of second chances. Lara sighed. After another brief pause, they shrugged, coming to a consensus.

"Sure, you can help," Lara offered. "But you've got to check your attitude, because I'm lead on this case, and I will not be railroaded. Understood?"

"Yes, of course. I'm...I'm sorry for the shit I said."

"It's okay. Water under the bridge," Lara replied, and it was. Of the things she dwelled upon, the opinion of a fellow police officer was not one of them. She had come so far to crack her glass ceiling in a primarily male workforce that there wasn't anything Lara hadn't already heard. If she alienated herself from everyone that had ever doubted her abilities, Lara would have a bowling team's worth.

The lieutenant pushed away from the table, and when Zach saw her getting to her feet, he did the same. Reaching out, he offered his hand for a shake. A peace offering. Natalia took it first, then Lara. In the brief touch of hands, an unlikely bond had been forged. It was practically palpable.

The door to the interview room flew open. On the other side was Chief Braddock, concerned.

"You don't have to say anything, Zachariah—"

"Dad, it's fine. We're good."

The chief looked relieved.

It must be difficult, having to choose between protecting your son and not showing special treatment. In a department the size of Boston's police force, Lara, despite the connection to her legendary father, could always escape it. Even being held to a higher standard because she was the offspring of Steven Nadeau. Nothing had been handed to her, she'd earned it.

"Sergeant Braddock is officially off the person of interest list. He's free to go," Natalia said.

"He's volunteered to help with the investigation," Lara tacked on.

The chief nodded, looking around the room. "Brilliant idea. More heads are better than one, right?"

"We'll get him up to speed, sir," Lara assured.

"Great. Well, I'm going to, uh...go back to my office." The chief turned on his heel and left the room. They followed suit, filing out, careful not to run into scurrying police officers.

"Lieutenant!"

Lara turned to see the towering figure of Oliver Bennett down the hallway. Of all the times Oliver could pick to show up.

"Hey, ADA Bennett," Lara greeted once he'd caught up to the trio. "Uh, Agent de Benedetto, this is Assistant District Attorney Oliver Bennett. Oliver, this is Special Agent Natalia de Benedetto of the FBI."

Oliver's eyebrows shot nearly into his hairline. "FBI? Wow...that's...hardcore."

"The chief called in the big guns," Lara shrugged. Glancing over, she saw Natalia and Zach hanging back. Natalia gave a little wave.

"Nice to meet you."

"I was passing through again, court day and all that. Thought I'd say 'hi.'" Oliver said.

Lara shot him a smile meant for show more than anything else.

"It's good to see you," Lara replied. She only half lied. She did appreciate the random visits he was thoughtful enough to make, but at the same time, she wasn't looking to encourage him into thinking anything about this could be permanent.

What followed was the awkwardest pause of awkward pauses, with Lara trying to look anywhere but right at Oliver. She could feel the judging eyes of Natalia and Zach behind her.

"Hey, Bennett, how's it going?" Zach asked, breaking through to offer his hand in greeting. Oliver clasped it, giving Zach a warm smile.

"Braddock, didn't think I'd ever see you around here," Oliver replied.

"Yeah, we were just...working some things out about a case. Seems Havenwood and Eastfall might be joining forces."

"Hey, imagine that. I think the Havenwood and Eastfall forefathers are rolling in their graves at the amount of coop-eration going on," Oliver joked.

Zach chuckled. As a new resident of Eastfall, the joke was lost on Lara, and definitely lost on Natalia. Lara knew enough that the founders of Eastfall and Havenwood loved each other about as much as the Hatfields loved the McCoys. The founders had both been outcasts from the Massachusetts Bay Colony, supposedly exiled because of their constant spats. Both groups vowed to create a better community, and thus the competitiveness among the two towns.

"So, we gotta get back to work, but it was nice seeing you, Oliver," Lara cut in, trying as tactfully as possible to move along. With a nod, and a few goodbyes, Oliver went in one direction and the trio went in the other.

"Who was that guy? He's cute," Natalia asked.

"He's just an ADA. And a friend," Lara replied as they climbed into the elevator to head up to her office.

"Mmhm," Natalia hummed. "Just a friend..."

"He's a real dreamboat," Zach piped up with an amused smile, his hands in the pockets of his jeans. They had caught him, again, on one of his days off. He looked dressed for something way more important than being interrogated. The jeans were this side of ratty, and his T-shirt had seen better days. Lara wondered if he'd been planning on heading to the women's shelter for volunteer work.

"Real dreamy," Natalia tacked on, sarcasm laced in her words.

Lara rolled her eyes, thankful for when the elevator door opened and she could escape them both.

It was odd to Lara how well she got along with Zach when they weren't bitter enemies. It was more odd when Lara found herself sitting across a booth from Zach at Bucky's, with Natalia beside her, laughing and joking and carrying on like they were all old friends. It seemed first impressions had been misjudged on both Zach and Lara's part. Beneath it all, there was a man just trying to get by on his own and not on his father's coattails. He was smart and observant, and even though he'd been broken up with Lynn Rickerson for a time, there was a deep sadness in his eyes when he viewed the crime scene photographs. Up to that point, he hadn't known what had been done to her. To see it up close and in high definition had been a shock to him, and he had to step away and take a moment to collect himself.

Now, a few hours later, they were enjoying dinner and a few after-work beers. To Lara's surprise, she was only just nursing her second beer, and dinner had been cleared away a while ago.

"...Oh for sure, you wouldn't believe it, but watching reality TV is one of my guilty pleasures," Zach said with a burst of laughter. "I don't ever admit it, but when I get home after a long patrol, I sit down and watch dudes being petty on *The Bachelorette*."

Lara and Natalia both nearly choked from laughter.

"Seriously? Does that mean you watch *The Bachelor* too?" Lara asked.

"Sometimes. Depends on the guy."

"I bet you're a Kardashian watcher," Natalia guessed.

"I used to be. The original Kardashian material was entertaining as hell. Khloe is my favorite. Can't stand the others though. I used to like Scott, until I realized I was a lot like him and decided I needed to change."

"Noooo. You? A douche? No way!" Lara mocked.

"Hey now, keywords here are 'used to.'"

After another round of beers, and even more rounds of taking the piss out of each other, the three went their separate ways.

"Tomorrow, I'll ask my captain if I can be put on retainer for the case. Worst thing he could say is 'no.' If he does, I'll just work unofficially with you guys in my off hours."

Lara stuck out her hand, feeling the gesture might be a final way to bury the hatchet. Zach took her hand, and the reaction to the touch was almost instant. Though she didn't show signs outwardly, Lara felt a jolt zip up her arm and coalesce through the rest of her body. Zach's grip was firm, warm, and strangely comforting.

"Bygones, right?" Lara asked, ignoring the sensation. If Zach felt it too, he didn't let on.

"Bygones," he nodded. "I'll see you ladies tomorrow."

Then, he was gone.

"So, uh, about last night..." Lara began, wincing at how pathetic she must sound.

"You don't have to say anything," Natalia cut in. "You got caught up in the moment, and dinner kind of felt like old times. I get it. I do."

Sure, if that's what Natalia wanted to believe, Lara could believe it too. The truth was, she missed Natalia. Missed seeing her, hearing her voice, feeling her warm body in bed next to hers. If there was one major regret from the past couple of years, it was letting Natalia walk out her door. Lara had allowed so much to drive a wedge between them. Natalia had offered so many times to help her, to help Lara work through her bullshit. But to Lara, it was simply easier to wallow, to let Natalia go, to not bring her down with her. Losing Natalia had been the feather in the cap of a stellar couple of years.

"Right, well, regardless, I'm sorry. I shouldn't have done it," Lara said.

"It's fine, Lara. You're fine. I'll see you tomorrow."

"See you tomorrow."

And with that, Natalia was gone too, and off to The Ancient Mariner.

During the drive back home, Lara felt antsy. She couldn't tell if it was because she'd only had three beers, or if it was something else. She had nothing to be anxious about at that moment, yet the closer she got to her house, the more her skin crawled and her stomach rumbled.

Parking in the driveway, she looked out her windshield at the house. It looked as it normally did, complete with the faint illuminating light of a lamp she had left on.

Still on edge, Lara hefted herself out of the unmarked and into the house. It was quiet, but then it always was quiet. That was the advantage of living set back from the busy road and being surrounded by trees. On some nights, it could be so quiet, one could hear the far-off hoot of an owl.

Nothing happened. No one came charging from the shadows where they could've been lurking, and she checked every nook and cranny of the house. So why was it she couldn't shake the feeling of anticipation?

Doing her best to ignore the sensation, Lara locked up for the night and headed to bed.

"Thanks for the dinner, Dad. This was delicious," Lara said, content and full. Retirement agreed with her father. He'd taken up various hobbies, including how to improve his culinary skills. He'd always been decent—he had to be, being a single father—but now his food was as close to culinary genius as a retired police officer could get. Even Gordon Ramsay would be proud.

It was Lara's thirty-third birthday, and on this special occasion, Steve had made a traditional Hungarian goulash with langos to sop up the meal. Langos were fried bread dough and were absolutely decadent and amazing. Lara loved her breads. Perhaps too much, as it had been necessary to pop the top button of her jeans, giving her food belly more room to breathe.

"I was just glad to cook for you," Steve replied with a smile, before taking a sip of his Sam Adams. Steven Nadeau, even at age

sixty-six, was as fit as a man could be in his later years. With salt-and-pepper hair and a lean form, he still could turn a head or two. He was a Boston boy, born and raised. His grandparents had immigrated from Quebec, and settled in the North End, competing their bakery against all the Italian bakeries. Steve had often told stories about the delicate pastries the Nadeau family had created a living on. The shop didn't exist anymore, as one of his cousins had been unable to keep it in business. Lara's own grandparents, Steve's parents, had a nice, cushy retirement, and had remained in the North End. Her mémère and pépère had been like a second set of parents to Lara growing up.

Steve's father, Lara's pépère, had been the first Nadeau to enter the police academy. Steve's mother, Lara's mémère, had been a teacher at a nearby Catholic school. They were blue-collar workers, but made an honest, comfortable living. They weren't rich, by any means, but they were happy and healthy. Steve was the oldest of three children. Lara's extended family had also been a big part of her upbringing. Unfortunately, work and time did not make it easy for her to see them often.

The house she grew up in, the house they had just enjoyed a delicious meal in, was the first place Steve's grandparents had been able to buy for themselves and their family. It was a brownstone townhome, and though it was narrow, it had its charms. Lara had many memories here, good and bad, and loved the place.

"So...you got your meal, I gifted you with the extra ammo you wanted...what more could you ask for?" Steve spoke again, lifting his beer bottle to toast against her own. She smiled slightly, clinking the bottles together before taking a sip.

"Actually...I was wanting to ask you—"

"Oh boy, this doesn't sound good," Steve interrupted with a chuckle Lara returned. The subject she wished to broach was not an easy one.

"I was hoping that...that you might finally tell me about my mother."

Perhaps it was without tact, but Lara never beat around the bush with her father. It was easier to rip off the Band-Aid, to go for the gusto, to get it over with.

The mood change on her father's face was instant. Instead of the happy, content man that had made her a delicious meal, there now sat a cool and closed off man. Lara had been able to read her father well since she was in middle school and could tell the moment he clammed up by the tension in his shoulders.

"You know I don't want to talk about her," he replied, pain and anger in his voice.

"I know, Dad, but don't you think it's time you tell me about her? I'm thirty-three years old, for Chrissake. She's been gone since I was three. No hole left by someone who abandoned us could be that huge and that painful that you'll never tell me about her."

For years, Lara tried to get information from him. What was her name? What had been her maiden name? Where had she come from? There was one picture in the house that held her image, and he, to this day, didn't know she'd seen it. It was hidden in one of his nightstand drawers. The black and white image wasn't even a full shot of her, merely a profile. Her mother was a beautiful woman, with an impish sort of smile and dark hair.

"I've told you once, Lara, and I will tell you again: I. Will not. Talk about her. Never. You don't need to know her. It's better for everyone involved if you didn't. She was a wicked woman, Lara. And you're a better person without her in your life."

Those words shocked her. She had never heard him say such harsh things. Most of the time, when she brought up her mother, the subject was met with flippant, neutral words that left no room for argument. This was different. Maybe she'd gone too far with her needling him.

"How can you say that? What on God's green earth could she have done to you to warrant that much hatred?" Lara shot back, voice rising. They had gotten into plenty of disagreements over the years, but her mother had never been this sore of a subject.

"You don't need to know. We're not talking about this ever again. So forget it."

"Dad, I'm a freakin' cop. One day, I'll figure it out. I just...I just hoped I wouldn't have to dig, because I want you to tell me about her. I want to know about the woman you fell in love with, married, and had a child with!"

As far as birth certificates go, the Commonwealth of Massachusetts didn't require much information. Lara's mother's name was there, of course, along with her maiden name. Place of birth for her mother was listed as Boston, and her occupation as housewife. Lara hadn't ever misused police resources to try and find Mave Nadeau. Maybe a part of her was too bitter and angry about being abandoned, maybe it was because she wanted to hear about Mave from her father, or maybe Lara felt she'd survived to this point, why bother trying to find the woman that clearly didn't give a shit about her?

"That woman isn't worth knowing, Lara," Steve spat, knuckles white from the grip he had on the beer bottle. "We're not talking about her."

Steve said it with such finality, but Lara wasn't done.

"You're such a bitter, lonely old man. You could've moved on after she left, but you never did. It was just the job and me. Now, you're retired, Dad, and what do you do? You cook. And you're taking carpentry classes. You're finally doing something for you. So why don't you talk about her? Talk about her, get her out of your system, and move on. It's never too late to lov—"

"I'll never love anyone else!" he exclaimed, startling Lara. Her father always had an even temperament. Steve wasn't quick to anger, and he had never raised his voice at her. In fact, the calm tone he'd always given her when he was disappointed had been more effective than shouting.

Shaking her head, Lara stood so suddenly the chair nearly fell backwards from the force. Slamming her beer bottle down onto the table, she pressed both palms down on the wooden surface, just as she would face someone in the interrogation room.

"You don't want to tell your daughter about her mother, about the *woman you love so much you could never love anyone else. You know what that is, Dad? Besides bitter and lonely? Pathetic. It's pathetic."*

Without another word, Lara turned and headed for the door. There was a hanging coat rack to the right, and she grabbed her purse where it hung on a peg. Though she heard her father calling for her, begging her to come back, Lara couldn't stop. She was so angry, so frustrated, so hurt, she just needed to be away from him. Though a girl's hero was her dad, there was no one else like a girl's mom. All Lara wanted was to know her. To know Mave would be to love her, to be as close to her as Lara could ever get. But instead, she was met with stubbornness and resentment.

The echoing sound of the door slamming woke Lara, a memory that haunted her dreams every so often. The T-shirt she wore stuck to her body from the sweat, her forehead was damp, and her heart raced.

Lara could still taste the goulash and the langos.

Fuck, she missed her dad.

CHAPTER 18

One thing he had learned since joining The Order, and being under his master's tutelage, is the ability and desire to make magic your own. There were times when one must follow a spell to a T, and there were times when magic allowed a bit of originality and creativity.

He felt he'd truly earned his right for this stroke of genius.

As the older woman led him up the stairs of a grand house, he couldn't help but already feel the pleasure welling in his gut.

"Welcome, masks are still in place?" the older woman asked after turning around to address him and the other people she had lured here. He felt 'lure' was the right word to use, as the woman had gone out with the single purpose to bring chosen people to this home for lascivious purposes. And as everyone confirmed that their masks were in place, and the front door was opened, he realized lascivious was too tame a word.

The evening was meant for debauchery and hedonism to

the fullest extent of the words. He imagined the harems of old resembled much of what would happen that night. He made sure to be the last one in the house, closing the door and locking it behind himself. He set his duffel bag underneath a side table by the door, ready for use later when everyone else had left and the owner of the house was asleep.

So what was a little bit of fun before his next kill?

The other members of this bacchanal varied in gender, size, and age. Though he was a vain man, he took carnal pleasure where he could, and tonight he would for sure take advantage of the delights that awaited.

The older woman, the one who had extended the invitation, had no idea his intentions. Luckily, she was the only one who knew his identity, and he couldn't glean the identities of the others. Knowing her, they were from neighboring towns, outside of Eastfall and Havenwood. Secrecy was of the utmost importance.

For him to be recognized would be a feat, and after tonight, the only person who knew of his presence here would cease to exist.

Not only that, but he would be one virtue closer to his goal.

Oh, but he had saved the best one for last. He got such a euphoric rush planning his final act.

And he'd chosen the perfect person.

But he couldn't think about her now. Not when he had to focus, to keep his mind clear for the task at hand.

CHAPTER 19

Tragedy struck yet again.

Lara sat in the conference room with Natalia, waiting on Zach to make an appearance, when she got the call from a dispatcher.

Despair shot through her, choking her with clawing futility. No matter how hard she banged her head against this, no matter how many leads she followed, it didn't seem to matter. The bastard doing this kept killing, and at a point when Lara felt she should be closing in, she felt farther and farther away from the solution.

As the two women scrambled to whosoever car they could reach first, Lara shot off a text to Zach, telling him to meet them at a residential home near Essex Street.

The neighborhood, informally called Manor Row, sprawled along an expanse of woods not far from Essex Street. Named appropriately, large and expensive houses interrupted the tree line, complete with long driveways and wrought iron gates. Some houses were more hulking than others, but even the smallest manor was impressive. All were brick, and some were built in the colonial style. During the

fledgling days of the settlement of Eastfall, most of the
founding families lived in this area.

When Natalia coasted around a corner, Lara instantly
spotted the house, blue and red lights strobing through the
sparse trees. They pulled down the long, gravel driveway and
parked off to the side. Zach arrived behind them, his Havenwood police cruiser blending in with the rest.

"Wow, must be nice to live in digs like these," Lara
muttered wryly to Natalia, looking through the windshield at
the house in question.

Calling it a house gave the place a disservice. The McMan-
sion had been built in colonial style, with a red brick face like
all its neighbors, and a red door. The shutters were painted
colonial blue, and the roofing looked black as tar. The land-
scaping was immaculate even though the year was winding
down and the cold would no doubt kill off much of the plant
life. A flag was attached to the right of the front door, and a
cute little Thanksgiving banner swayed in the slight breeze.

It was quaint. Lara couldn't think of a better way to
describe it. Quaint and picture-perfect. Like Ward and June
Cleaver would come out the front door and wave kindly at
you and let you know an apple pie waited for you inside.

"It's nice, sure," Natalia replied. "But we both know you
never liked the idea of a cutesy house in the suburbs."

"No. Too cookie-cutter. Too white picket fence-y," Lara
admitted, with a faint shudder.

Zach finally joined them, decked out in his patrol
uniform, hands on his hips. The Havenwood police chief had
agreed to let him work the case, citing interdepartmental
cooperation would be good for their public relations image.
Not to mention the more brains committed to this, the more
likely the case would break.

"Have you got any info yet?" he asked them.

Both women shook their heads.

"Shall we?" Lara said, stepping forward and leading the way up the walkway to the front door, where a uniformed officer let them in.

"Braddock, what the hell are you doin' here?" the police officer greeted jovially as the men clapped hands.

"Gettin' into trouble, the usual," Zach joked. "I'm also here as arm candy for these ladies."

"Why they would pick you is beyond me," the patrol officer grinned, winking at Lara and Natalia.

"Are we heading to the back, officer?" Lara cut in.

"Yes, ma'am. Head down this hallway, turn right, and you'll see the deck. The body's out back, in the woods..." Despite the fact the officer tried to hide it, Lara could tell he'd seen the body and was horrified.

The trio made their way through the house and out the sliding glass door, stepping back into the brisk late-autumn morning. Another uniformed officer stood next to a seated, middle-aged man who had a blanket wrapped around his shoulders. His face was pale, eyes unseeing.

"Lieutenant," the police officer greeted. Lara had seen the woman before. The nameplate on her uniform said she was Officer Desjardins.

"Officer," Lara replied. "Is this the gentleman that found the vic?"

"Yes, ma'am. This is his house."

"Will you keep an eye on him for a little while longer? We'll be back to hear his statement."

The police officer nodded and stood straighter, with a renewed sense of duty.

They continued, following the sound of squawking radios. It was just upon entering the tree line of the immense back-yard where they found the scene.

It was nearly identical to the other two, except the victim was a middle-aged woman, and another familiar face.

Carol Mumford, councilwoman of Havenwood's third district.

Mrs. Mumford was a conservative and had been the incumbent for the last ten years. She also practiced law part-time at the firm she owned with her husband. They had made a lucrative business out of being defense attorneys, representing the more affluent. They were good at it.

How Mumford kept her seat on the city council of Havenwood for so long, Lara wasn't sure. She could only assume it was this connection to the rich and powerful of their small town. After only living in the area for a short time, she'd heard enough about the woman to find her sleazy and out of step with the more progressive viewpoints she'd become accustomed to working in and around Boston. Mumford consistently campaigned on a platform of strict conservative, Christian family values, with a pro-life and anti-marriage equality stance.

But, no matter how horrid the woman had been in life, and how many people she may have hurt with her ideologies, she certainly didn't deserve this kind of death. No one did.

As before, Mrs. Mumford lay on her back, bruising around her neck. She was completely naked, skin pale and gaunt in the cold. Her arms were at her sides with legs splayed. Her pelvis had been sliced open, and what appeared to be an ovary lay between her legs. The same strange symbols were drawn around the organ, along with some kind of herb, and the other ovary was missing. A pink line was painted diagonally across her mouth.

The ritual had continued.

"Jesus Christ..." Zach whispered from behind her. Lara remembered he'd only seen the crime scenes in photographs, not in person. Neither had Natalia, though she'd learned over her years in the FBI to school her reactions. There was shuffling, and Lara turned back to see Zach staggering backwards and bending over to catch his breath. Lara stepped over to him, hesitantly placing a comforting hand on a firm shoulder.

"Hey, I know it's a lot to take in, but you can head back to the house if you want."

"Fuck that," Zach gasped out, the hands he'd braced on his knees squeezing tight for a moment, before standing straight. "It's okay. I'll be okay."

Lara nodded, then turned back to the scene, where one of the techs approached her.

"Dr. Rogers is on her way," the guy said. Lara nodded.

"Anything new you can tell us about this one?"

The tech shook his head. "It's exactly the same as the other two. I can't find evidence of any foreign DNA or clothing or fibers. I can say, the herb around the ovary is dill."

"Dill?"

"Yeah, I recognized the smell. My wife cooks with it sometimes."

"And the other two herbs were hazel and..."

"Yarrow," the tech supplied.

"Hazel and yarrow aren't as common for cooking as dill."

"It has to have significance to whatever this reenactment is," Natalia chimed in, having stepped closer to the body. "If this is a ritual, the herbs are symbolic of other things."

"Symbolic?" Lara asked.

"Yeah. For magic. Herbs can be used in magical spells or brews because they have a meaning to them, properties that do specific jobs. They're called correspondences."

"So, we're dealing with a wizard?" Zach asked incredulously as he finally came closer, his face an emotionless mask.

"More like someone that thinks he's a wizard," Natalia replied.

Dr. Rogers appeared, and after introductions, Lara took her crew back to the main house to speak with the owner.

The uniform had moved the man inside, a smart move as the temperature had dropped. He was seated on a couch, still wrapped in the blanket, looking shell-shocked.

"His name is Jack Davenport," the uniform said quietly, as they stood off to the side. "He's got a medical practice in Havenwood. He's married but separated. The wife and kids have packed off to her mother's in Connecticut."

"Interesting," Zach said, looking from Jack Davenport back to the uni. "Considering Carol Mumford is happily married. What was she doing here?"

"He won't say anything to me about it," Officer Desjardins replied.

"Alright, thanks, officer. We'll give it a go," Lara said with a nod. Officer Desjardins nodded in return and stepped off to go help the uniform at the front door.

"I think it's best if you talk to him," Lara said softly.

"Why me?" Natalia asked.

"You're better at empathy than I am."

Natalia snorted.

"Seems legit," Zach commented.

Lara turned to shoot him a withering look. He didn't flinch, only smiled.

"Why don't you let me talk to him? It'll be my audition for the Three Amigos," Zach continued. Though he was joking, his face said he was completely serious. He wanted to help, and to prove that he could. Lara and Natalia nodded.

Zach slipped around them and sat down in the armchair next to the couch. Jack Davenport had listed over to the side a little, using the arm of the couch as support.

"Hello, Dr. Davenport," Zach began, voice softer than Lara had ever heard it. "My name is Sergeant Braddock. I'm with the Havenwood Police Department. I'm here to help out. I was wondering if you could answer a few questions."

Jack blinked owlishly, twisting his head to look over at Zach as though just realizing there were people around.

"Y-Yes, of course," Jack replied, sitting up as best as he could.

Jack Davenport was a handsome man, the distinguished salt and pepper of his hair adding to the appeal. He was trim, body type a product of a lifetime of recreational running.

"Can you walk me through how you found Mrs. Mumford?" Zach pressed on.

"I woke up this morning, and immediately noticed she wasn't with me. So, I came downstairs to start a pot of coffee. The back door was open. I figured Carol must have taken a walk outside or something. But when I couldn't find her, I got concerned. I ventured out and...and that's when I found her."

"Dr. Davenport, you're saying Mrs. Mumford was with you last night?"

Jack looked nervous as he swallowed, but eventually nodded. At first, he didn't look like he would admit to anything, but the grief of finding her and losing her won out.

"Carol and I were having an affair. As far as I know, her husband wasn't aware."

Zach nodded. "She was with you all last night?"

Again, Jack didn't immediately answer, his gaze rooted to the beige carpeting at his feet.

"Y-Yes, me and..."

When he didn't immediately continue, Zach pushed, "Who else, Dr. Davenport?"

"We had a...a get-together last night." Davenport's face grew red, shame written in his expression and the rigidity of his body.

"What kind of get-together?"

Jack sucked in a deep breath and let it out in one long whoosh.

"It was a sex party."

A woman was dead, but for a brief moment, the thought of not wanting to touch any surface in this house crossed Lara's mind. Regardless, it was rather interesting to know the local politician who touted such conservative morality was in fact a sexual deviant. Surprise, surprise.

"How many other people were here, Dr. Davenport?"

"There were five other people here...besides Carol and me."

"What were these people's names?" Zach pressed.

"I honestly can't tell you. Everyone wore masks. Carol was the one that brought them here. She knew who they were... but I didn't."

Lara believed him.

"How often did you have parties like this, Dr. Davenport?" Zach asked.

"Once a month. Carol always brought the others."

"Do you know of anyone that would want Mrs. Mumford dead?"

"I'm sure there's a list as long as a football field," Jack replied. It was a standard question to ask, but it had to be asked, even if the interviewer already knew the answer—which Zach did. You didn't get to be a politician and lawyer like Carol Mumford and not make enemies.

"What time would you say you fell asleep last night?" Zach continued.

"Around two a.m. I was so tired...passed out cold."

"And was Mrs. Mumford with you when you fell asleep?"

"Yes, our guests left about forty-five minutes before that. We had taken some time to clean up. Her husband is away on a business trip. He makes them monthly where he spends a few days in Boston. It's when we get together."

"And the last time you saw her alive was when you both fell asleep?"

"Yes," Jack said.

"I appreciate your time and cooperation, Dr. Davenport. Here's my card," Zach produced a plain white card with his name and numbers on it. "If you think of anything else, let us know. We'll be in touch if we have any more questions."

Jack Davenport nodded and said nothing more after that. The line of questioning had exhausted him, and he fell back into a catatonic-like state. Lara saw this often with witnesses. Plus, not to mention the less-than-ideal circumstances of this arrangement. He was in shock.

Zach stood, and they convened a couple of rooms away in the dining area.

"I always knew that woman couldn't have such a stick up her ass," Zach said, breaking the silence first.

Lara snorted. "Or maybe she had the biggest stick of all," Lara said, then trailed off. Natalia shot her a look.

"Whoever killed her could have been in the house last night," Natalia said swiftly, getting back to business. "The other two scenes have been in public places. This is the first in a private residence. The backyard is fenced in, though I don't know how far back the fence goes into the woods."

"Probably the extent of his property. I've got a feeling Davenport would've locked it up tight, just to be safe. Especially with a kid," Lara supplied.

"Mumford had to have known the killer, but since she's dead, we've got no way of knowing who's on the guest list," Natalia said.

It seemed no matter what, luck just wasn't on their side.

CHAPTER 20

Upon their return to the police station, Lara began adding to the information they'd already compiled. In the conference room, the Three Amigos began mapping out connections between the three victims, as well as a list of possible suspects. Which, of course, the list was anyone and everyone at this point. The more well-connected a victim was, and certainly the more controversial a person was in the community, the more sifting through that had to be done.

"Hey, just wanted to stop by and say—Holy shit."

Lara's gaze whipped to the open door of the conference room where Oliver Bennett stood, hands in their perpetual place in his expensive suit pants pockets.

"You wanted to say, 'Holy shit'?" Zach snorted, shuffling some papers around.

"No, not what I originally wanted to say, but then I saw the think tank in here. Looks like my apartment before finals in law school," Oliver replied with a chuckle.

After more small talk, Oliver bid them farewell, and disappeared as quickly as he had appeared.

By midafternoon, they had Carol Mumford's calendar, as well as a list of known associates and contacts. The list of Carol's clients was even more extensive, as she'd been practicing for two decades.

"They don't tell you about this mind-numbing shit before you join," Zach chuckled, hours later. The trio had picked out likely candidates that might fit the profile of their killer. There were a few Carol had helped over the years, but they'd all been cases Carol won. There were also no obvious connections between these clients and Lynn Rickerson and Sierra Fitzgerald. Nevertheless, the candidates were kept on the list for questioning. They had to start somewhere.

Lara let out a groan before slumping forward and resting her head on the table. Her eyes ached from the strain of looking at so much paperwork. Red-hot pokers stabbed at the back of her eyeballs, no doubt the makings of a good migraine.

"We should pack it in for the night. Start fresh tomorrow," Natalia said, getting to her feet, as though that simple action would brook no argument. It got none from Zach.

"Agreed. I'm outta here. Evening, ladies. I'll see you tomorrow," Zach said, leaving the room with a rather jaunty tip of his head.

"Come on, Lara. That wasn't a suggestion. Let's get you home."

Summoning all the strength she had left, Lara stood and followed Natalia from the room. She took a moment to lock the door behind them, then went down the hallway to retrieve her stuff from her office.

Thinking about the still as of yet unreturned calls from Jeff McMullens, Lara held up a finger to Natalia as she dialed his familiar number on her office phone. She heaved a frustrated sigh when the phone didn't even ring but went straight to voicemail. He rejected her call outright. Too bad she was like a dog with a bone at times. Setting down the receiver in the cradle, she pulled on her coat and shouldered her bag.

As the two women headed back down the hallway toward the exits, Lara filled Natalia in on her attempts to call the Angylion employee. Lara was put off for a moment when Natalia opted for the stairs. Huffing and looking forlornly at the elevator, Lara followed.

Stepping outside into the night air was like stepping into a walk-in freezer. The temperature had dropped further, causing shock to Lara's skin and a sting that made her eyes water. Wrapping her coat tighter around her body, Lara headed for her car and was surprised when Natalia followed.

"What?" Natalia asked after Lara shot her a confused look. "I said, 'Let's get you home' and I meant it. Besides, I want to see your house. I've heard a lot about it."

"You've heard about my house?"

"Yeah. The owners of The Ancient Mariner almost bought it, but the mayor offered a better deal. They'd love to get their hands on it. I guess it's a real treasure of the city."

"I didn't realize my house was that special." To Lara, it was a place for her to set her keys and lay her head at night. She hadn't put a lot of thought into her selection when she moved here. It had all been a hasty decision.

"I'll follow you," Natalia coaxed, getting into the government SUV.

It didn't take long at this time of night to get across town and back safely nestled in her driveway. Grabbing her bag from the front seat, Lara stepped out as Natalia pulled in beside her.

"Wow," Natalia breathed. "I mean, it's pitch dark, but from what I can see, this place is gorgeous."

Lara didn't comment, merely continued on to the front door where she keyed them in. Nerves struck low in Lara's belly at having Natalia in her house. It wasn't that she was embarrassed to have her, as she did keep it clean and tidy. It was more about worrying over whether Natalia might be proud at how she'd set up her new life here in Eastfall. Landing on her feet after all that had happened. After all that had happened between them.

"Want a beer?" she asked, setting her keys down on the table by the door. The house was silent.

"Sure, I'll have one."

Lara headed toward the back of the house, where she set her things on the island in the kitchen. Reaching into the refrigerator, she pulled out two Sam Adams bottles, fingers clutched around the necks.

"This really is a nice place," Natalia commented, finally making her way into the kitchen. She'd done what Lara never did and put a light on in each room. Natalia was always cautious—occupational hazard. Or maybe Lara just didn't care enough about her safety that it never crossed her mind to clear every room of the house and make sure no boogiemen would get her. Perhaps that was an occupational hazard, too—indifference. Lara knew after years on the job that there wasn't much a person could do if someone else really wanted them dead.

"Yeah, it does the trick," Lara commented offhand as she popped the cap off and slid the bottle of beer to Natalia.

They sipped their beverages in silence for a time. Natalia's chocolate eyes wandered the kitchen, and then her body followed suit, ambling into the living room.

"You must have a pretty good-sized backyard, huh?" she asked.

"Yeah." The last time they'd been together in a living space, it ended in a knockdown, drag-out argument. That was the last time Lara had seen Natalia, actually. Lara was tired. She didn't want a repeat performance. All she wanted was for things between them to be as normal as they could. In Lara's wildest dreams, she wanted Natalia in her life again, but her heart ached at the truth. They couldn't be together. Their lives had diverged. Talking things out had never been Lara's strong suit. She had been good at actions, though.

In another couple of gulps, Lara finished off the beer. The liquid settled in her gut but had little effect other than to warm her body and instill a little bit of courage.

Natalia sipped idly at hers as she snooped around.

"It really is a nice house," she commented upon return to the kitchen.

"Care to see the upstairs?"

An innocuous question, yet Lara's tone was laced with something more, something edgier and more daring. Coupled with innocently arching an eyebrow, Lara figured Natalia would shoot her down as she had the night at Bello Italiano.

"Yes, actually. I would love to see the upstairs."

Lara tried to hide how pleased she was at Natalia's answer. She deserved a repeat of the other night. Natalia's eyes met Lara's, her brown hues darkening, bottom lip disappearing for a moment between pearly white teeth, an inviting gesture. Lara's swing had made contact, expecting an out. Instead, she'd hit it out of the park. Perhaps Natalia missed her as much as Lara missed her. Perhaps Natalia dwelled on the memories of the past—how, when it was good, it was really good.

Actually, this most likely wasn't a good idea. In fact, it was the worst idea. Lara hadn't been in the right frame of mind for intimacy for months, and Natalia was always so straitlaced and by the book.

Natalia began slowly backing down the hallway, toward the staircase, crooking a finger at Lara. They were good at sex. Damn good at sex. The meaningful communication part had always been toward the bottom of the list. But maybe Natalia, straitlaced and considered Natalia, needed a reminder of Lara as much as Lara needed a reminder of Natalia.

Like a sailor lured in by the siren song, Lara followed, leaving the empty beer bottles where they were. When she neared, Natalia held out her hand. Lara grasped it, finding the familiar feel of it to be a comfort. Natalia's hands were delicate, but at the same time, calloused from her work as a field agent, handling her weapon, and combat tactics.

Once inside Lara's bedroom, Natalia closed the door, and gently pressed Lara against the hardwood.

"We shouldn't..." Lara breathed, a last-ditch effort to give Natalia a way out of this, but it seemed the FBI agent had other plans.

Instead of words, Natalia covered Lara's mouth with her own, and the lieutenant groaned in pure ecstasy. Natalia's lips tasted and felt as she remembered—plump and soft and sweet.

Lara pressed forward into the kiss, wrapping an arm around Natalia's thin waist, bringing her flush against her own body. The slight height difference never deterred the two women. In fact, Lara often argued they fit together beautifully.

The two women took their time, reacquainting themselves with the other's mouth and the feel of their bodies against the skin of their palms. Lara skimmed hers down Natalia's hips, and then back up, snaking her fingers beneath the hem of her shirt. She moaned again at the feeling of silky soft skin beneath her fingertips, venturing just a little higher until she felt the slight swell of Natalia's breast.

Surging forward, Lara used the momentum to move Natalia back and press her down onto the mattress. Without loss of contact, Lara climbed onto the bed, straddling Natalia's hips. She took a moment to finally break their connection, just long enough to sit up and remove her button-down Fingers fumbled with the fastenings for a few seconds too long, but eventually she shed the shirt. Her skin prickled in the slight chill of the bedroom air, but it was soon abated by the scorching feel of Natalia's hands on her torso.

It was all so familiar, yet also like the first time. Lara knew exactly where to put her mouth to elicit the most beautiful sounds, and in turn, Natalia knew just how to curl her fingers to make Lara's eyes cross. They came together, slowly and with more emotion than Lara had anticipated or felt since the last time they were intimate.

Once sated, Lara curled into Natalia like a lifeline. This was what she'd been afraid of, the return of a feeling of dependency. Of need. It was a feeling she despised, because she knew herself. She knew sometimes she went too deep, felt too deeply.

In the twilight hours of the night and early morning, Lara lay awake, staring up at the ceiling, listening to Natalia's soft, steady breaths. Her mind raced, thinking about what they'd just done. Would they be able to remain professional? Or would they act as though it had never happened? There was so much that still needed to be done in the investigation. She didn't want yet another bad decision to trip her up on the job. But was this a bad decision? She wasn't sure.

When Lara couldn't get her mind to stop reeling, she gingerly slid from the bed and tiptoed around the moonlit room. Grabbing a pair of shorts and an old Boston PD T-shirt, she headed downstairs. All was silent except for the rhythmic ticktock of her Mémère Nadeau's kitchen clock. It had been hanging in her grandparents' house for years, and Lara had inherited it. She loved the sound. It was soothing, in a way, despite the metronome sound. The distant sound of owls hooting reached her, and that sound soothed her as well.

It was disorienting sometimes, living in the suburbs, even the backroads of the suburbs. She was so used to the bustle of the city that it jarred her at times to have so much quiet. Lara never realized how much the distractions of the city kept her from her head until she moved here.

Passing by her home office, she glanced over for a moment and then back forward, but what she'd caught in that split-second look made her stop abruptly.

Backing up, she peered around the doorjamb to see that the box from the attic was sitting there.

Open.

Which was not how she'd left it.

In the hubbub of everything with the investigation, Lara had pushed the strange box occurrence from earlier aside. It didn't seem as important, though it was equally startling.

Her honey-colored eyes scanned the dark interior of her office, but found no movements to belie another presence. Cautiously, Lara stepped into the room and approached the box. It was the same as she'd arranged the contents earlier. The book with its blank pages sat on the inside, as did the flower and pungent smelling herb. She sat down in her chair before reaching forward to flip on the desk lamp. The box illuminated beneath the light. The mother-of-pearl was the same, with the same initials.

Who was *AB*?

Perhaps she might need to hit up the mayor to find out a little about the history of the house after all.

Leaning closer, her eyes studied the box, looking for hidden compartments or special latches that might explain how it continued to open on its own. Fingers poked and prodded but found nothing. She hesitated for a moment, listening for sounds of stirring from Natalia. She couldn't say why, but she felt like this wasn't something she should share yet. Natalia would not believe her. She was so practical. What could Lara say about the events earlier in the day? And why she felt drawn to this space again? She picked up the book and flipped open the front cover.

Her breath caught in her throat, like it sometimes did in the bitter cold.

For a moment, Lara didn't believe what she saw. There were words etched onto the page in a fine, old-fashioned hand. She would swear the words hadn't been there before, but it's possible she had skipped over the page.

What once was thine was taken
What once was thine is within reach
Burn and steep, and thou will see
The gift that was taken from thee

Lara read the little poem several times, tracing her fingers across the letters and wondering what it could mean. Where had this message come from? Tipping the book this way and that, she confirmed there was indeed still no writing on the spine or anywhere else. She leafed through all of the pages this time, and only came up with the poem.

Was she supposed to do something with the flower and herbs?

Well, that was ludicrous, wasn't it? The book couldn't be telling her to do something, because that would mean the book was alive. Books couldn't be animated. Was she losing it again?

Slamming the cover shut with a thud, Lara replaced the book into the box once more. She shut the lid with a sharp snap. She was being ridiculous. In the morning, maybe she'd discover this had all been a dream or a hallucination. Maybe she was drunker than she thought.

Quickly, she grabbed two bottles of water from the kitchen and hurried back upstairs. Lara felt safer, and less crazy, in the warmth of her bed with Natalia beside her.

The next morning, Lara awoke in bed, alone. Her brain, still hazy from sleep, panicked, wondering if it all had been a dream. She had thought that, hadn't she? Then she heard soft humming from her bathroom, where the trickle of water sounded. Letting out a sigh of relief, Lara pulled back the covers and shed her T-shirt and shorts on her way to the bathroom.

"Mind if I join?" she asked, sliding back the shower curtain.

Natalia startled, but turned with a bright smile. "Of course. Mi casa es su casa."

Lara laughed, an honest to God laugh, and stepped into the tub.

They didn't leave the shower until their skin had pruned, their soft moans and cries having echoed off the tiled walls. The sex was a delicious distraction from her previous worries.

It was equally difficult to get dressed, considering Lara nor Natalia could keep their hands off each other. They stole kisses and gentle caresses and almost didn't make it out the door.

At the foot of the brick stairs outside, feeling refreshed and restored in that way only a night of great sex and good sleep can achieve, Lara stopped, causing Natalia to nearly collide with her.

Someone had wedged a thick manila envelope beneath

the windshield wiper of her unmarked car. Glancing back at Natalia, Lara could tell the FBI agent had noticed as well.

It was thick, yet still too thin to be a bomb or anything else nefarious. There could be a powder, certainly. Something like anthrax, maybe. Stepping cautiously closer, Lara noticed her last name printed in block lettering on the front. She glanced back at Natalia again, expecting to see her still on the stairs, but the brunette had followed her, standing at her side.

Lara reached forward and pulled the envelope free from the wiper. The little brad had been folded to seal it, with tape for good measure. She turned her wrist to see the back of the envelope. There was nothing written there.

In the interest of not freezing to death, Lara coaxed Natalia into the car and cranked up the heat. When the air turned lukewarm, Lara slid her finger beneath the slight give, and began to rip the envelope open, glancing over at Natalia every couple of inches. The agent seemed as antsy to see what was inside as Lara.

When the seal broke, Lara peeked inside and saw a stack of papers. Reaching in, she pulled them out. Splitting the pile in half, she handed some to Natalia to leaf through as she glanced over her own.

The papers consisted of financial statements and other bank records, shipping manifests, and inventory lists. No anthrax, thank God. But what was rather startling, and certainly gave Lara pause, was the logo and the name emblazoned at the top of every page: Angylion. The pharmaceutical company. There were even a couple of dossiers on some of the workers, including the few people she'd already met like Dr. Michaelson and Dr. Gibbons.

"Hey, look at this," Natalia prompted, holding up her hand, displaying a sticky note dangling from her finger. On it were four words. Latin was Lara's best guess:

Prudentia
Fortitudo
Temperantia
Iustitia

"You ever see these words before?" Lara asked.

Natalia shook her head.

"Then I think that's what we should figure out first."

As soon as she got to headquarters, Lara dropped the envelope at the forensic lab to be checked for fingerprints. She happened to have been wearing gloves for once, something Natalia had harped on before leaving the house.

When they got up to the conference room, Zach had already arrived and brought gifts of coffee and breakfast pastries.

"Bless you," Lara groaned, as she cupped the coffee cup between her hands and took a sip. It was exactly as she liked it.

"You're welcome," Zach smiled slightly. "So, tell me about this envelope you found *together*?" He emphasized that last word, eyebrows raised teasingly. Both Lara and Natalia ignored the dig.

Lara quickly brought Zach up to speed on the folder. His bright blue eyes lit up, excitement making them shine.

"So, the words! Let's find out what they mean."

Natalia pulled her iPad closer and brought up a web browser. She then typed the words into the search bar. The first result she got was a translator program, saying the words were indeed Latin. The next result was a page entitled "Cardinal Virtues." Natalia pressed her finger on the link, and it took a moment to load. On the page was a picture of four ladies dressed in Renaissance garb. All had elaborate headdresses, and all clutched various objects. According to the page, the Cardinal Virtues originated back in classical antiquity. Then, the ideas were picked up by the Christian church, and put into dogma.

The first virtue listed was *prudentia*, or prudence. In some connotations it meant wisdom or knowledge. You always know the right action for every occasion. The second virtue was *fortitudo* or courage. The third virtue was *temperantia*, or temperance. It is the ability to show self-control. The fourth and final was *iustitia*, or justice. One who has the virtue of iustitia is fair and righteous.

"Hang on," Lara breathed, recognition dawning. "I've seen the term before. '*Cardinal Virtues*.' The book Jason tried to find but couldn't remember the title. The same book with symbols that might match our crime scenes. I saw it somewhere in his shelves and shelves of rare books."

Excitement pawed at her as she turned, ready to get the hell over to *Lola's* and try and find some answers.

CHAPTER 21

Natalia sat in the front seat of Lara's unmarked, hanging on for dear life as Lara put the pedal to the metal. Zach sat in the back, calmly munching on a donut, having grabbed the whole box on their way out of the conference room.

"What? We gotta eat them now while they're fresh!" he had said.

Lara had delegated the task of calling Jason to Tom, whom she had yelled the request to as she rushed down the hallway. Tom had poked his head out of his office, confused at first, but then realized the trio must be onto something.

"I'm going to call you three the Scooby Gang," Tom had joked as he put his cell phone to his ear.

They arrived well before Jason, and to pass the time, Lara paced in front of the shop's doors. Zach and Natalia stood off to the side, polishing off one donut at a time.

Lara was thankful it didn't take Jason much longer to arrive. He seemed frazzled, having been rushed to leave the house. However, the look on his face said he knew exactly how important this was, and the moment Lara uttered the title of the book, realization dawned.

It was the book they'd been looking for.

Tight on Jason's heels, Lara followed after him to the back room. Jason knew exactly where to reach for the book. Before he removed it from the shelf, he pulled a pair of white, cloth gloves from a drawer.

The moment Jason pulled it from the shelf, Lara realized they were dealing with a very ancient tome. She'd only seen the spine with the title emblazoned in gold, but not the whole thing. It was leather bound and looked beat to hell.

"*The Cardinalem Virtutum*," Jason breathed, as he set the book carefully down on the nearby table. It was fragile, and Lara could tell he was trying his best to not destroy it.

"Jesus...looks ancient," Lara said, bending over to get a closer look.

"It's hundreds of years old," Jason replied. "How I happened on this book was absolute pure luck. I bought it from an estate sale a few years ago. I'd made a bet with Tom I couldn't win the lot. I did, of course, and he owed me—"

"What do you know about the book?" Lara pressed.

"It's an occult manuscript from the sixteenth century," Jason said. "My Latin is extremely rusty, but I had a written provenance of the book when I won it at the auction. Hang on, I'll grab it from my files."

While Jason thumbed through his filing cabinets, Lara tried her best not to bounce from foot to foot.

"What's 'occult' mean?" Zach asked, hesitating over the question as if asking it made him sound less intelligent.

"It's basically anything supernatural or paranormal," Lara replied.

"There are tons of works out there about summoning demons, conducting spells and other rituals, and how to communicate with the spirit world. The word 'occult' means knowledge of the hidden," Natalia tacked on.

"So then...Harry Potter magic?"

"Not quite Harry Potter. Think Harry Potter's edgier cousin," Natalia said.

Zach opened his mouth to say something else, no doubt another smart-ass comment, but Jason returned with a folder.

"Alright, this is what I've got, if one of you wants to start thumbing through that, and one of you can sit here and watch as I flip through the pages. Not that I'm trying to tell you how to do your police work. You're the professionals here, not me," Jason said with a chuckle.

Natalia and Zach elected to sit down with the information from the folder, while Lara pulled up a chair next to Jason as he carefully turned the pages. The paper was thin and ripped and cracking. It was a wonder it didn't disintegrate in Jason's fingers.

"Wait...wait, stop!" Lara breathed excitedly. "Go back a page."

Jason did, revealing a carefully drawn image of the exact herb and flower she'd found in the box from the attic.

"Do you know what those are?" she asked him.

"Uh, I believe the bundle is sage, used to purify the air and such. My sister burns some every so often in her apartment. She's convinced it'll ward away bad juju." The fact he laughed gave Lara the impression he didn't buy into it. "And the flower is primrose, I think."

"What's primrose used for?"

"No idea, sorry. Is it significant to the case?"

Lara's eyes stared at the page, willing her eyes to translate the text underneath the pictures.

"No, I was just curious."

Jason continued to turn page after page, until he came to

the final chapter. As the last parchment sheet flipped over, their eyes were met with a terrifying image.

It was of a man who looked like any ordinary man, except his eyes were red and blood dripped from his mouth. Gripped in his hands—no, talons—were organs. Human organs. Beneath his feet, which were clubbed as a goat's, sat a pile of skulls and bones. Beneath the pile of bones was a rudimentary image of the world.

The mere sight of it caused a shiver to race down Lara's spine and an uneasy feeling settled in her gut.

"What the fuck is that?" Lara asked.

"Not sure, but it doesn't look pleasant."

"What've you guys found out about the book?" Lara turned to Natalia and Zach.

"Um...well, it was written around the mid-1500s," Zach reported. "The story goes that this monk, who was sitting in a monastery copying texts and shit, became catatonic one day. Then, a couple of days later, he came out of his trance and began writing out this book, pictures and all. He finished it in two days and two nights. When he placed the last period, he suddenly became aware again, and had no recollection of writing the book or where the information came from."

An odd story, yet Lara knew the time period from which this book came was prone to intense superstition.

"What else?" she asked.

"Not much," Natalia shrugged. "It seems to be an important book in inner circles. Secret society sort of inner circles. It's a book of magic."

"What kind of magic?" Jason asked.

"There are some translations of parts of the Latin in this file, but the entire book hasn't been interpreted. From what experts have been able to translate, it's a book of general magic. It has both white magic and black magic."

"Anything about what the last chapter is about?" Lara queried.

Natalia and Zach rifled through the pages.

"No, there's no translation of it here, or even what it might be about," Zach replied.

"So we've got a book about the Cardinal Virtues, which the killer is using as a basis for his MO, but we don't know how to read this book so that things will make sense. Great..."

"I mean, at least we've got the book," Zach replied, trying to look on the bright side. "We can just take it to someone who reads Latin, and presto, we'll have a translation of it."

"I don't know about you, but I don't have friends that can read Latin," Lara snarked.

Zach held his hands up, palms outward as though in surrender.

"Hey, I just put a suggestion out there. Haven't been hearing a lot of those, so—"

"Okay, children," Natalia cut in. "We have the book. That's a good enough lead. Now, we just figure out some way to translate it, so we can get some insights."

Jason, who had been sifting back through the book, circled back to the last chapter. He went another page further and let out an 'ah ha!' Lara turned, eager to hear what he might have found.

"I knew I had seen the symbols from your crime scenes somewhere. Here! Look!"

On the next page after the horrifying picture of the man dominating the world, there were, indeed, the symbols found with the dead bodies. The same swirls and circles and lines. That couldn't be coincidence. Plus, there were pictures of human organs: a brain, a heart, an ovary, and an eyeball.

"It's got to be a ritual," Lara murmured, thinking out loud. "Whatever this is...it's some kind of ritual the killer believes he is fulfilling in order to gain something. Whatever it is, we need to figure it out, and figure out who the fourth victim might be."

"Where do you want to take the inscriptions to be translated? You can't believe every Joe Schmoe on the street," Zach said.

"We're going to see if Jason would be so kind as to give us scans of the chapter, along with copies of the provenance, and then—"

"I know someone," Natalia interrupted. "He's a professor at Boston College. The Bureau's used him as a resource before. He's a bit eccentric, but he'll help."

Zach clapped his hands together once, happy about the plan. Lara simply nodded.

"And I would be more than happy to get you copies. However, it will take special equipment since it is an old book, and we don't want the scanning or infrared lights to damage it. I'll get right on it, though. In the meantime, feel free to make copies of the provenance. Anything you want, just ask. I want to be as helpful and cooperative as I can be."

"We appreciate it, Jason, thank you."

It took the better part of the day to get the desired scans from Jason. The trio returned to the station to wait. Jason sent electronic copies to Lara. In turn, Lara printed the scans, and prepared a file to take to Natalia's contact.

It was odd seeing the picture of the man that wasn't quite a man. How menacing he looked, standing over top a bone heap on the world. The photocopying of the book did nothing to stem the quality of the book's pictures. Lara secretly included the information Jason had sent about the sage bundle and the primrose, hoping the professor would help.

She'd done a little bit of research about the uses of sage and primrose. Sage purified by lighting the edge just enough so it smoldered. Then, waft the smoke into every recess of a space that needed cleansing of negativity.

The primrose, on the other hand, was something different. After a cursory search on the Internet, Lara discovered that primrose could reveal and restore hidden secrets.

What did the sage and the primrose have to do with anything? What was Lara supposed to do with it? Keep it in the box and take it out every once in a while? Was she supposed to burn the sage? Was she supposed to do something with the primrose to reveal a secret?

It was all so preposterous. Lara had never been a superstitious person, never really believed in magic or ghosts or the paranormal. Lara believed in what she could see and touch. She believed people could be bad and good, but it was all due to free will and choice. Lara didn't believe in destiny or fate.

Lara definitely did not believe sage would chase away evil spirits, and primrose would reveal a secret.

While Jason finished sending all the information he could from the book, Natalia called up her professor resource at Boston College, easily penciling in a time to visit him the next day, bright and early.

"We could all make the trip," Zach suggested, sitting back in a chair with his booted feet propped up on the conference table. "Haven't been to the city in a while. Would love to go."

"We're not going for funsies," Lara snarked from her position at the table. Her pen had been scribbling away in her notebook for the past fifteen minutes. She'd wanted to refresh and organize the information they'd gathered thus far.

"No, but it's still fun to go," Zach replied, before sticking out his tongue like a toddler. Lara rolled her eyes.

"We should all go," Natalia agreed, much to Lara's dismay. "I need to check in at my field office to finalize some things on another case. You two should visit Dr. Chappelle."

Dr. Archibald Chappelle was a Classicist and Natalia's contact, who could read and translate Latin and Greek.

"We'll all go tomorrow then," Lara sighed. The thought of being so close to Boston made her squirm. While she'd parted from the Boston PD on a surprisingly good note, it still pained her to think about the city that had been her home her whole life. The places she'd explore with her father on his days off. Eastfall had welcomed her with open arms, for sure, but she wished she'd never left Boston.

CHAPTER 22

Early the next morning, they piled into Natalia's SUV and headed toward Interstate 95. Zach opted to sit in the back seat, and he sang along obnoxiously with the radio. Lara and Natalia kept shooting each other annoyed looks. At the junction of Interstate 95 and 93, Natalia turned south toward the city. They'd caught the tail end of rush hour traffic, so it was luckily smooth sailing toward Chestnut Hill.

"Alright, children," Natalia crooned, as she pulled up in front of Stokes Hall, the home of the Boston College History Department. "Behave, play nicely, and make sure you're respectful to Dr. Chappelle."

Zach snorted as he scooted across the bench seat and slid out of the car.

"Yes, mom," Lara said as she, too, climbed out of the car. "Have fun at the office. Tell all your Bureau friends to suck it."

Natalia leveled a scathing look. "I'll be back in a bit after I do some admin stuff. Don't get into trouble."

Lara and Zach stood on the sidewalk, watching the black SUV disappear down the street, heading for the FBI field office in the city. Natalia had talked about catching up on some paperwork for previous cases while they talked to Dr. Chappelle.

Lara had graduated from UMass Boston, so it was rough coming to Boston College. All Boston schools had a friendly rivalry, and all were equally worthy.

Boston College had been established by the Jesuits, an order of priests in the Catholic faith formed just before the Council of Trent in 1545, which set about the Catholic Counter-Reformation to the Protestant Reformation. In high school, Lara had wanted to attend Boston College, had even been accepted, but opted out because of tuition costs. It was a beautiful campus. Despite the fact it was early, they'd arrived in time for eight a.m. classes. Students emerged from their dorms, bleary-eyed.

"This brings back memories," Zach murmured beside her.

"Did you go here?"

"Nah, Boston University. Kind of wish I had though. I feel if I had, my life would be very different."

"How so?" she asked, watching him look off into the distance at Stokes North and Stokes South.

"If I had gone here, my old man would've pushed me in a different direction than police work. Probably business. I would've played on a hockey scholarship. I did at BU anyway."

"You played hockey?"

Zach nodded before motioning with his hand, a silent go-ahead to make their way to Stokes South.

"Yep. I was a D-Man. Set the record for highest number of goals and assists in one season for defensemen in BU history. Still play sometimes. Havenwood Fire Department likes to talk a big game with HPD. We have charity games twice a year."

"Remind me when the next one comes up. I'd love to watch."

"Oh, it's good times," Zach grinned widely and charmingly as he opened the door to Stokes Hall with a grand flourish.

Dr. Archibald Chappelle, who had been awaiting their arrival in the lobby, was the epitome of big and tall. He was at least six feet, three inches and had to be almost three hundred pounds. He wore a button-down, long-sleeved shirt and khaki slacks, which were held up by a trendy pair of suspenders. His hands were in his pockets, a pair of thin, wire-framed glasses perched on his nose, and he rocked back and forth on his heels in anticipation for their arrival. When he spotted them with his rather small, beady eyes, Dr. Chappelle's face lit up with a smile, upper lip covered by a dark mustache.

"Good morning," he greeted, voice deep, English accent thick.

"Good morning, Dr. Chappelle?" Lara half asked, half stated, as she took point and stepped up to shake his hand.

Dr. Chappelle nodded emphatically, shaking firmly.

"You have a fantastic handshake," he replied. "I am Dr. Archibald Chappelle."

"Lieutenant Lara Nadeau. This is Sergeant Zachariah Braddock. We appreciate you taking the time to see us."

"It is no problem," Dr. Chappelle said jovially, his intonation carrying the 'T' into the subsequent vowel. "Let us head up to my office, shall we? It will be quieter and more private."

"Of course," Lara said, with a small smile. "Lead the way."

Despite having just met him, Lara liked Dr. Archibald Chappelle. As they rode in the elevator to the third floor, she pondered if, in some circles, he was known as "Archie." Though he lacked the red hair necessary to make the full comparison to the comic character, as his was a dark brown.

The elevator arrived with a ding. Lara and Zach followed Dr. Chappelle to his office.

Once they stepped inside, Lara suspected the inside of Dr. Chappelle's head must look about the same as his workspace. There were papers in piles everywhere, including the floor and various other pieces of furniture. It seemed everything had its place, though, and Dr. Chappelle knew them. Scrambling forward, he hastily removed the stacks of papers from the chairs situated in front of his desk.

"Please, please, have a seat," he beckoned, rounding the desk and settling his large body in his equally large desk chair.

They did as instructed, taking their seats with ease.

"Now, what have you got for me?"

Reaching into the bag she had slung across her body, she pulled out the folder of photocopies and handed it across the desk that resembled more of a war zone than anything. Dr. Chappelle leaned forward, gently taking the manila folder between meaty fingers.

The professor didn't say anything right away as he opened the file and began to glance over the pages. He made deep humming noises and a few 'harrumphs.' Lara wasn't sure what they meant, did not feel the need to ask yet, so she took the opportunity to examine his office further.

Dr. Chappelle wasn't a fan of fluorescent lighting, as he had about four floor lamps, one in each corner of the room. Currently, he had the two nearest to his desk flipped on, creating a dim glow to the room. Lara wasn't sure how he could read in such low lighting. The room stretched to about twenty feet square. The walls were lined with built-in bookshelves, so laden with books, the wood bowed. Also on the shelves were knickknacks Dr. Chappelle had obtained in his travels—a few rocks that must have historical significance, plastic cases that held what appeared to be Roman coins, and many other odds and ends she wasn't sure of what they were.

On one section of the wall not covered with bookshelves hung a Medieval tapestry. It couldn't be a real period tapestry...or maybe it could?

Tuning back to Dr. Chappelle, Lara noticed that in her mental wanderings, he'd taken to muttering to himself.

"This is an intriguing work. As Agent De Benedetto must have told you, I am a Classicist, not a Medievalist. For the origins of this particular work, I can only make an educated guess. However, I can translate the Latin and...this is engrossing content."

The look on Dr. Chappelle's face was akin to a kid in a candy store.

"What can you tell us, Dr. Chappelle?" Zach asked politely. Natalia would be so proud of them. Being respectful, getting along, and everything.

"It is a book meant for the occult," Dr. Chappelle confirmed. "This is unlike any occult book, or any book for that matter, found in recorded human history. Where did you say you found it?"

"A local bookstore back home," Zach explained. "The owner said he bought it at an estate sale."

"An estate sale?" Dr. Chappelle asked incredulously. "This book?"

Zach and Lara nodded.

"Incredible..." Dr. Chappelle mused breathily. "This tome is priceless. If you ever decided to sell, you could make a pretty penny."

"Dr. Chappelle, what about it do you find interesting?" Zach asked.

"This section you brought me, well, it's a recipe," he replied, as though it were the most obvious thing in the world.

"A recipe for what?" Lara asked.

Dr. Chappelle didn't immediately respond, as he had

taken up translating again, eyes flying across the photocopied pages. Lara looked to Zach. From his facial expression alone, Lara was glad she wasn't the only one to find this man a bit odd. Or eccentric, as Natalia had described him.

In her pocket, her cell phone began to vibrate. She ignored it, and let it go to voicemail. Not even thirty seconds later, the phone began to vibrate again. Looking from Zach to Dr. Chappelle, who was engrossed in the text, Lara hazarded a glance at the caller ID.

She recognized the number, having dialed it multiple times over the last few days.

Jeff McMullens.

Once more, she looked at Dr. Chappelle and again at Zach who sat on the edge of his seat, waiting for the professor to give a big reveal.

Shit.

Should she step out to answer it? Or should she let it go to voicemail and call him back?

Lara warred with herself for what felt like eons, but was probably only mere seconds.

Shoving the phone back into her pocket, she opted to call Jeff back when they were finished with Dr. Chappelle.

"Incredible..." Dr. Chappelle murmured again, head shaking back and forth.

Lara figured, at this point, another gentle nudge would be ignored, so she waited, albeit impatiently. In a way, Dr. Chappelle reminded her of her father. He would come around and speak in his own time.

Sure enough, after flipping through the pictures another time, he did.

"It's a recipe for power."

Lara wasn't sure what she'd been expecting. A recipe for chocolate chip cookies? A recipe for a healing potion? A recipe for Brunswick stew?

But a recipe for power?

"What do you mean?" Lara asked.

"It is a step-by-step guide on how to obtain ultimate power and dominion over the world and all its inhabitants," Dr. Chappelle continued, reciting the last part of his sentence as though word for word from the book. "Or so it claims. Manuscripts like this could be very vague with their wording. 'World' could mean a microcosm, not necessarily the actual world. Tell me...is this from the *Cardinalem Virtutum*?"

Lara was glad to contain her surprise.

"How did you know that?" Zach asked. Natalia hadn't mentioned it over the phone.

"I've heard about it. Of course, it is a bit outside my purview as a Classicist, but I was somewhat taken with the concept when I was a young and impressionable undergraduate." The way the professor talked about it was almost fond.

"Can you tell us more about the book?" Lara pressed, getting impatient for answers.

"The *Cardinalem Virtutum* is one volume in a series of books called the *Libri Scientia Vetitum*, or the *Books of Forbidden Knowledge*. The compendium was only a legend... until one volume was found in an attic about twenty years ago. It is said there are thirteen books in total. How apropos. Each book is meant to be a collection of spells and other occult information us mere mortals are not supposed to know or comprehend."

"They're magic books?" Zach asked, unable to hide his derision.

"Oh, they are much more than that," Dr. Chappelle replied, voice soft and almost reverent. "They are said to contain the secrets of the universe. The answer to why we are here, why things happen the way they happen, where we go when we die.... To own these books and to know them...well, it would be tantamount to being a god."

Silence hung in the office, a dramatic pause after an equally dramatic revelation. It seemed preposterous, and yet Lara couldn't help but entertain the idea. With all that had happened in her life, with all the odd occurrences happening in her house, the box from the attic—it would be convenient to attribute these strange goings-on to something more concrete.

"How can we be sure these books are actually real if there's only ever been one found?" Zach asked.

"Queen Elizabeth I's chief court magician, John Dee, wrote about them in some of his journals. He claimed to have been the receptacle for the information in a volume..." Dr. Chappelle paused. "What I am trying to say is there is no proof they exist, except for the volume found in an attic twenty years ago. All the tests came back conclusive. The book was indeed hundreds of years old, written in Latin, with medical knowledge of the body that would not have been discovered for some time. Not to mention a discourse on how one could live forever, and a cure for a disease of aggressive replication of cells."

"Cancer?" Zach chirped.

"Yes, cancer."

"Has anyone tried it?" Lara asked, curious.

"No self-respecting research scientist would believe it or give it a go. Besides, some of the Latin is obscure. An ancient dialect, perhaps. No one has been able to translate the entire thing. In fact, legend says these books were written in a variety of ancient languages."

"Where does the information come from?" Lara asked.

"Well, they say certain people were chosen to be a vessel for the information but were completely unaware of what they were writing."

Lara remembered the story about the monk in a

monastery that went catatonic but somehow crafted a whole novel in mere days.

"But where is the information coming from?" Lara asked, leaning forward in her chair.

Dr. Chappelle shrugged. "Who knows? God, a pagan god or goddess, the universe, some other divine being, someone from another dimension..."

"Wild," Zach breathed.

"Indeed. But fascinating if you love learning about the occult," Dr. Chappelle said with a small smile.

"So, the recipe in this one..." Lara said, trying to bring the professor back around to the topic at hand.

"Ah, yes, the recipe. It is a handbook for using the Cardinal Virtues in order to gain mystical power. If you target certain people that represent each Virtue, ideally women according to the list, and take something from them, you will gain ultimate power."

"And by taking something from them you mean their internal organs?" Lara asked.

"Yes, see the pictures...they are so you know what you're cutting out is the right thing."

Bile rose in Lara's throat.

"What happens when you've got the organ parts?"

"Well, you also have to place the bodies in the correct manner, with the proper herbal offerings and colored paints. The paint is to go over the part of the body that best represents each Cardinal Virtue. So, the forehead for intelligence, chest for bravery, so on and so forth."

Lara slid a side glance to Zach, who sat rigid in his chair. Natalia had not told Dr. Chappelle any details of the case.

Tiny pieces of the puzzle began to click into place.

Someone had come across information about the *Cardinalem Virtutum*, and—believing that it would actually work—began a crusade to kill innocent women in a bid for ultimate power. Despite its occult roots, the ritual sounded like the profile of a crime committed by the quintessential serial killer—most likely a white male, lifelong misogynist, who did anything and everything he could to oppress and punish women. And whoever the killer, they truly believed they could gain ultimate power.

"Why the Cardinal Virtues?" Zach asked. "That's something we learned in Sunday School at St. Mike's."

"Now we're getting solidly into my area of expertise," Dr. Chappelle grinned. "The idea of the virtues goes back to classical antiquity, to Plato's *The Republic*. Each of the virtues, according to Plato, are meant to be archetypes of what makes a good city. Each social stratum in a city had their corresponding virtue. Courage for the warriors, prudence for the rulers, et cetera. The virtues are then mentioned in Aristotle's works, Cicero's, and those of Marcus Aurelius. Because the virtues were also meant to be traits the best kind of person possessed, it is possible the ritual derives from the want for power over oneself or reaching the height of the human condition. Whatever that may mean."

Lara remembered the philosophy class back in college every student was required to take. What makes a good person? What makes a bad person? Lara had hated philosophy, but that class discussion had almost redeemed the subject.

"Okay, so, just to recap..." Because Lara's head reeled with all this information. "Allegedly, there's a series of books containing the knowledge of the ages, and a local businessman owns one of the thirteen, which contains a how-to guide on obtaining supreme mystical power. Another one was found in an attic twenty years ago."

Dr. Chappelle nodded his head. "Yes, that is all correct."

"Do you know the titles of the rest of the books?"

"Only a few," the professor replied. "The volume found in

the attic is called *Mysteria Corporis*, or *Mysteries of the Body*. Historians have reported other potential titles as *Liberi Veneficarum*, or *The Witch's Book*. Another one is *Amor et Passio*, or *Love and Passion*."

"So, we know a few of their titles, but other than that the books are a legend. A legend involving random people chosen to be vessels for these revelations, and they write them down without realizing."

"Yes, that is correct."

"Hmm..." Lara hummed, too stunned to process any of it. A nagging in her gut made her think that maybe it wasn't as outlandish as it seemed. The books could exist, but certainly they didn't offer *all* this knowledge?

"So, what, this guy kills his last victim, and he believes he's imbued the supreme power of the universe?" Zach asked.

"Yes, it takes four victims and careful planning of the ritual. It has never been attempted in known history of the books."

Zack jumped in again. "So, the four Virtues are Temperance, Courage, Prudence, and...?"

"*Iustitia*. Justice."

Which could describe anyone in Eastfall and Havenwood's Police Departments, as well as the other occupations associated with the justice system.

"Well, we thank you very much for your time, Dr. Chappelle," Lara said, attempting to wrap this up. "I think we've covered everything we needed to. Would you be able to email us a translation, professor? If it isn't too much to ask?"

"It is not a problem at all," Dr. Chappelle replied. "I translate old manuscripts such as this for fun. Should have it completed in a jiffy."

"Great, we really appreciate it," Lara said, eyeing the pages in question. Buried amongst the papers were the pictures of the primrose and sage.

"Really, it is not a problem," Dr. Chappelle said with a cheery smile.

Lara and Zach stood, as did Dr. Chappelle, and shook the man's hand. They declined his offer for him to personally guide them back to the lobby, and instead elected to make their own way.

"What the fuck..." Zach muttered under his breath as they took the stairs to the ground floor.

"My thoughts exactly," Lara agreed.

"That was...a lot of craziness in so short a time," Zach couldn't help but chuckle.

"You're fuckin' tellin' me," Lara replied.

"We're going to need to unpack that...a lot," Zach pointed out when they reached the curb where Natalia had stopped earlier. According to a text, Natalia would be there to collect them soon. Sure enough, it wasn't long before Natalia pulled up to the curb, looking expectantly at them through the window.

CHAPTER 23

L ara and Zach spent the first leg of the trip back to Eastfall explaining to Natalia what they had learned from Dr. Chappelle. The FBI agent's face was a mask of resolve, taking in the information. Though they were no closer to naming another suspect, they at least had an idea of the killer's motive. Not to mention his belief in this supernatural text made him delusional and psychotic, as well as a sadistic butcher. A dangerous combination.

The rest of the ride was spent in silence. Lara's thoughts whirled. Magic, books, power... She couldn't help but wonder about the book she'd found in the attic. Could that have any connection to the case? To what Dr. Chappelle had said. It seemed absolutely fantastical, too difficult to believe. Yet, could there be a chance...?

Zach had nodded off in the back seat, and judging from the heavy breathing, he was in deep. Lara took this opportunity to pull out her cell phone.

Jeff had not left a voicemail. Not a surprise.

Lara hit the recall button, and the call went to voicemail directly.

"Dammit," Lara hissed, pulling the phone furiously from her ear. She crammed it back in her pocket, pissed off at this whole game of phone tag.

"What is it?" Natalia asked softly.

Lara told her about the phone call from Jeff in the middle of Chappelle's analysis of the book.

"He'll call when he's ready. If you've got a feeling he could be a valuable ally, then he's got to come to you on his own terms."

Lara glanced over at Natalia, eyes scanning her profile from the soft line of Natalia's jaw to the aquiline nose and dark eyes. Something bothered her.

"Everything okay?" Lara asked quietly, changing the subject. She took a quick glance back to make sure Zach slept on. His body bobbed and shook with the motion of the car but remained asleep.

"Yeah," Natalia replied.

"Oh really? Because you've got that look on your face you get when you're halfway to frustrated and anxious."

"I just...I shouldn't have gone to the office."

"What happened?" Lara asked.

Natalia shook her head, adjusting her grip on the steering wheel. Her knuckles went white for a moment. "Just... hypocrisy and bullshit."

"Okay," Lara said, tone inviting, pulling at Natalia to tell more of the story.

"I just...I don't know anymore. I thought joining the FBI would be the right thing. Maybe I should've done local policing."

This was the first time in a long while Lara saw Natalia in a vulnerable moment. As an FBI agent, she always had everything in order, every decision carefully thought out, every life step planned to the minute. She had to in order to achieve such distinction at such a young age. That was something they had disagreed—Natalia couldn't understand why Lara wasn't more ambitious, why she hadn't considered climbing up the ranks in Boston or even joined the Bureau. Lara had been content in her position as a detective in Boston. Now, she'd even say she's warming up to being a lieutenant in East-fall. At times, there was so much extra crap that came with being a lieutenant—more paperwork, politicking, press conferences....

"It isn't all rainbows and unicorns on the local level either," Lara pointed out. It was something her father had always harped on—the grass wasn't always greener on the other side.

"Yeah, but in government you get more backstabbing and power moves," Natalia huffed.

"Okay, true. Someone trying to sidestep around you for a promotion?"

"No, actually, it's kind of the opposite," Natalia said, before flipping the lane change indicator to shift right. "I've had three separate bigwigs tell me I need to apply to a higher leadership position, Supervisory Special Agent."

"That's fantastic, Nat," Lara replied with quiet enthusiasm.

"Yeah, except it feels...wrong. I'm convinced they've been trying to push out my current Supervisory Special Agent from his job, and they want to put someone else in that position. Someone easily manipulated."

"Jesus."

"Yeah. Also, did I mention—two of the Assistant Special Agents in Charge are banging."

"What?"

"Yeah. Everyone knows. Even fuckin' HR knows. But they won't do anything to stop it. They're both married, they both have children, and, oh yeah, it's highly unprofessional."

"Wow, what the hell?"

"Yeah," Natalia sighed. "The Special Agent In Charge knows all about it but won't do a damn thing to stop it. I'm pretty sure the SAC is being led around by the balls by one of the ASACs. It's a shit show, Lara. I've never seen anything like it. Just...the level of unprofessionalism...it's astounding."

"So, what's with them trying to shoehorn you into supervisory? Hadn't you applied twice and been turned down both times?" Lara asked.

Natalia nodded. "Yes, ma'am. Applied for supervisory special agent twice, denied twice. And now all of a sudden, they want me in the position, even though it's still technically filled."

"Something's going on there...something shitty."

"I don't think it's a coincidence they put me on your case," Natalia said, probably a suspicion she'd fostered since the beginning.

"Why?"

"Your guess is as good as mine," Natalia shrugged, taking the exit for Route 1 that would bring them into Eastfall. "Whatever it is, I don't like it. I don't like being a pawn in anyone's game."

Preach, Lara thought.

"Whatever it is...you'll figure it out," Lara said confidently. "And if it's something illegal, you'll figure that out too. And be the best SAC that office has ever seen."

Natalia smiled softly, eyes sliding toward Lara for a moment, before refocusing on the road.

"That's always been the plan...as you well know."

Lara chuckled. "Yes, I do know."

The remainder of the drive back to the police station passed quickly in silence. After Natalia pulled into a parking space, Lara hopped out and opened the back door. Reaching in, she poked a fingertip against Zach's ridiculously strong jaw. When he didn't budge, she poked harder. That caused him to stir, but he didn't wake. This time, Lara went for the nose, pinching the nostrils closed. Zach startled, jerking upright, blue eyes open and bleary from sleep.

"Wha...Wha' the fuck?"

"Wakey, wakey," Lara teased, laughing. Natalia, who had watched the exchange, laughed along.

"Damn," Zach grumbled, rubbing his eyes. His hair was messier than normal from his napping. The longer bits of his hair fell onto his forehead, giving him that artfully tousled look. It was entirely unfair.

Once back inside, the three took the elevator up to Lara's office and were surprised to see Chief Braddock waiting for them.

"Welcome back," the chief greeted as they piled in the doorway. He leaned back in Lara's office chair with an air of calm, but sternness. "I hope your jaunt to the big city was worth it."

While giving the chief a rundown of Dr. Chappelle's information, Lara watched the older man's face carefully. She didn't envy him his position as chief of police. It couldn't be an easy job, not even in a place like Eastfall, and especially when a psychotic serial killer was on the loose.

"So, we're looking for an occult-obsessed nut job? Should be easy to root out," Chief Braddock said, words dripping with sarcasm. He stood, relinquishing Lara's chair and sidling past them and into the hallway. "Look, I know this is all delicate business, but you've got to find the guy. And you've got to find him fast. My balls are in a tight vise right now thanks to the mayor and the rest of the city council. Not to mention Havenwood's mayor and city council. I need someone down in holding by the end of the week."

The threat hung invisible in the air. If Lara couldn't find

the guy responsible, then her future in Eastfall sat on a thin, fragile line. It was hardly fair, but there was no use arguing this with the chief. The job wasn't always about good police work. It was also politics, re-election campaigns, image....

"Yes, sir," Lara replied, voice firm. The chief's blue eyes, the exact same as Zach's, looked from Lara to Natalia to Zach, and then back to Lara. With a quick nod of his head, he made his leave.

"You know...you could stay with me. Save the Bureau some money."

"Is that really a good idea?"

"Why wouldn't it be? I've got a spare room with a comfortable bed. We could commute to the station. Save the planet and all that."

After a few more hours put in at the station, the three had gone to eat at a local Mexican restaurant. Zach had eventually bowed out, seemingly to seal the deal with some woman at the bar he'd been flirting with. Natalia and Lara stood out in the frigid parking lot. They didn't move, as if they both wanted to go home together instead of separately, but neither wanted to take the initiative.

Natalia sucked in a breath and let out a deep sigh.

"Why do you always make it so hard to say no to you?"

Lara shrugged. "Dunno, must be a gift. But, seriously, I'll behave. You could stay in the guest room. I could make crepes in the morning?"

She knew she'd hooked Natalia with that final offer. Crepes were a staple of the Nadeau family. They were a paper thin, pancake-like breakfast food filled and folded with just about anything imaginable. Lara had learned how to make them from her mémère when she was a teenager. She didn't make them as much anymore, not since her father's passing.

"Alright. I'll come over, but not to stay. I'll be back at the B&B tomorrow," Natalia relinquished.

Lara grinned widely. "I'll pull down the sheets for you. Maybe even put a little mint on your pillow."

Natalia rolled her eyes and climbed into the SUV.

Another hour later, Lara rolled away from Natalia's naked body, sweat glistening on their skin, gleaming in the dim light of her bedroom. Lara had had every intention of pulling down the sheets in the guest room for Natalia, but it seemed the dark-eyed beauty had other ideas.

Natalia turned, curling into Lara's side and draping a leg over Lara's body.

"We were always good at this," Natalia whispered.

"Yeah. We always let our bodies do more of the talking," Lara agreed.

Natalia was silent, tracing lines between some of the beauty marks on Lara's body.

"I'm renowned in my office for my negotiation tactics, but when it comes to trying to have a meaningful, and logical, discussion about a disagreement between us...I can't seem to get out the right words. And Christ knows you're not good at smoothing over an argument."

Lara couldn't argue with that statement.

"We always smoothed over an argument with sex and... that's never good," Lara sighed softly.

"No. No, it's not," she agreed. Sex was better than facing feelings. Lara had always been convinced of that, though she'd been better about it before everything went to shit.

Sometime later, after Natalia had fallen asleep, Lara

remained awake. Tipping her head, Lara took in Natalia. The other woman had turned away in her sleep. The soft moonlight played along the olive hue of her skin and gleamed against the dark color of her hair, making it appear blue. Natalia was achingly beautiful, and intelligent and strong. Lara wished she was worthy. Natalia deserved better.

Her mind turned to the box from the attic. How peculiar the circumstances in which she found it. The ghostly footsteps leading her to the box. The strange woman she'd seen at the Harvest Festival. Could this case be connected to any of this otherworldliness?

Restless, Lara rolled from the bed, dressed, and tiptoed downstairs, wincing at every creak and groan of the stairs and floorboards. Just as it was every evening, the house was quiet except for the sound of her mémère's clock. Making her way to the kitchen, Lara scavenged for a snack, settling on a bag of Doritos. Leaning up against the counter, Lara munched on the cheesy triangles.

Thoughts of the visit to Boston whirled through her head, trying to hash through the craziness for some nugget of reality. Taking her bag of chips, she headed for the office and settled down at the desk. Glancing around, Lara didn't immediately spot a napkin or paper towel, so she brushed the cheese dust off of her fingers and onto her shorts.

Powering up the laptop, Lara checked her email first. When she saw she'd received a message from Dr. Chappelle, she sat straighter, alert. Her heart hammered in her chest, as she clicked on the message.

Greetings, Lieutenant Nadeau,

    I have not had the opportunity to work through all of the photos you left with me; however, I have deciphered a rather interesting section. It has nothing to do with the Power spell, but I thought I should report my findings, as I feel you included this for a reason.

I am unsure of the type of spell, because the title is warped by age or by water damage. However, I can tell you that it is a spell. It calls for the burning of sage, as a way to purify the air in your immediate space. Once this step is complete, the caster is to drink a tea steeped from the primrose flower.

Again, as to the purpose of this simple ritual, I cannot say, but I thought you might wish to know.

I will come back soon with the rest of the translations,

Dr. Archibald Chappelle

Swallowing thickly, Lara's honey eyes slid to the box.

Should she try it?

Dr. Chappelle's email jogged something in her memory, something she'd read before. Reaching for the box, she flipped open the lid and took out the book. The words were still there.

Burn and steep, and thou will see.

Setting the book aside, Lara pulled out the bundle of sage and the primrose.

With resolve set in her shoulders, she returned to the kitchen, setting the plants on the counter carefully. Searching through the cabinets, Lara found a teakettle. She used to be a tea drinker before she realized alcohol was better at helping her feel numb. Quickly, she filled up the kettle and put it on the stove.

While she waited for the water to heat and boil, Lara pulled out her phone and searched for 'primrose.'

Primula vulgaris, also known as primrose, came in a variety of colors, but hers was a pretty yet subtle shade of yellow. It was native to many places, among them Western Europe. The leaves and flowers were both edible and often used in teas, a relief to Lara, as she'd not been sure the thing wasn't poisonous. After more searching, Lara was interested to find that in the tradition of Wicca and other practices of witchcraft and herbology, the primrose flower was used as a way of revealing truths and divulging long held secrets.

What secret will you reveal today, primrose?

The kettle began to whistle, causing Lara to startle. Letting out a deep breath, she pulled a mug from another cabinet and began to pluck the green leaves from the flower, dropping them in the bottom of the cup. Once finished, she set the rest of the primrose aside and poured the steaming water over top until fully submerged.

Returning the kettle to the stove, Lara stood back, picking up her phone once more while she waited for the leaves to steep. The email had said she would need to burn the sage to purify the air around her. Thumbs worked quickly over the phone screen as to how to safely burn sage.

Tossing the phone back down on the counter, Lara rummaged around in drawers before she found a box of matches. Wedging the box beneath her chin, she took the sage and the cup of primrose tea and slipped through the back door and onto the patio.

It was dark in the backyard, except for the glow of the porch light. The ring of light reached out just enough to cover the wooden deck, then ended in darkness, stretching to the trees beyond. The night was veritably silent, except for the rustling of underbrush from some anonymous animal. It was as if someone had cranked down the temperature further. Lara could see her breath and the wisp of steam from the hot tea. She had to make this quick, or else get frostbite.

Fingers shook, whether by the temperature or nervousness she wasn't sure, but she ignited the match regardless. Holding the flame in one hand and picking up the sage in the other, Lara lit the edges of the herb. With a quick puff, she blew out the match, then the edges of the sage after she'd let them burn. The herb continued to smolder, emitting a sweet scent. Smoke wafted from the sage, and Lara waved it around, even spun in a circle. The scent filled her nostrils, cloying at her senses for a moment as it suspended above, then settled around her.

"Please," Lara muttered. "Don't make me feel like more of an idiot." To whom she was speaking, she had no idea, but maybe they'd be listening.

Satisfied she had done enough, Lara set the sage down on the patio table, suspending the burning end over the edge.

The moment of truth. Time to drink the tea.

Her dark eyes glanced almost accusatory at it before picking it up. She swallowed a couple of large gulps hurriedly before she could lose her nerve, careful to not swallow the leaves. It didn't have much of a taste, though the warm water soothed and settled in her belly, heating her body.

Lara waited.

She didn't know what to expect. Fireworks, an angelic choir, a beam of light coming from the sky?

Nothing. She felt nothing.

Sighing, Lara drank the rest of the tea, then shook the primrose leaves into the grass. The sage had burned down more, creating a cocoon of the sweet smell around her. It was soothing, and Lara was disappointed to have to stanch the smolder.

It was a relief to step inside, warmth returning to her toes and fingers.

A failed experiment. Lara intended to throw the rest of the primrose and sage back into the box with the book and put it back under the floorboards.

Walking back down the hallway toward her office, she sat

at her desk and picked up the book, every irked nerve urging her to put it in the trash can and be done with it.

When she touched the book, Lara paused. It warmed at her touch, warmer than leather should be. Lara peeled back the front cover and gasped, nearly dropping the heavy tome when she noticed the pages were no longer blank.

CHAPTER 24

L ara clapped her hand over her mouth to hold back the startled scream threatening to let itself be known. All she needed was to wake Natalia and have to explain how she was losing her Goddamn mind.

The words that had once been there were gone, now replaced with new words. Lara slammed the book shut and threw it across the desk as she stumbled up from her chair, causing the thing to topple over.

So much for not alerting Natalia.

Relief rushed over her when the FBI agent didn't come storming down the stairs, gun drawn.

"Okay, it's okay. Calm down, Lara. It's okay," she whispered to herself over and over, attempting a few deep breaths that didn't calm her frazzled nerves.

The pages were blank. Now, the pages overflowed with words and carefully drawn images. Had she finally lost it this time? She was scared to look again, afraid to confirm what she feared the most—that'd she finally lost it.

Lara's curiosity got the better of her. Kneeling down, she retrieved the book. It was still unnaturally warm, like a late spring day. She could feel it in her fingertips, and if she felt it, it had to be real, right?

Carefully, as though the book would bite, she wedged her thumb beneath the lip of the cover and flipped it open again.

A Grimoire for the Novice and Advanced Practitioner
Compiled Over the Ages by Ancestors Long Passed

A grimoire? Ancestors long passed? What the fuck was this thing?

Emboldened and slightly more confident that the book wasn't about to take her hand off, she flipped through a few more pages. Some were written in what appeared to be Latin, some looked French—probably an old dialect—and some, toward the back of the book, were in English.

The pages written in English advertised salves for burns, a draught for healing a headache, a quick fix for gout, and a whole slew of other things, including how to grow a money tree.

A fucking money tree.

Lara pored over the contents, losing track of time, until the first rays of the sun began to illuminate the sky. Even then, she continued to flip through the book, swearing that every time she checked back, the pages written in Latin or French had translated themselves into English.

Her eyelids grew heavy from lack of sleep, and she couldn't help but wonder just how much she'd lost her mind.

Upstairs, Natalia stirred, her footfalls tracking to the adjacent bathroom. Lara slammed the book shut and put it in the box. Heading for the kitchen, she began a pot of coffee, acting as though she'd not been out of bed for the majority of the late night and early morning.

The FBI agent appeared, wearing one of Lara's shirts.

"Morning," she said with a soft smile, blinking sleepily at Lara. No one should look this good in the morning. "You okay? You weren't in bed."

"Yeah, I'm fine," Lara said, forcing a smile. She wasn't. Of course she wasn't! She wanted badly to say something to Natalia, but she didn't know how. Maybe now wasn't the time. "Just wanted to get up, start some coffee, and prepare the batter for crepes."

"How sweet," Natalia grinned, leaning forward, bracing her elbows on the island counter. "Did you sleep okay?"

"Yep," Lara replied, strained. "You?"

"Slept pretty damn well, actually," Natalia replied with a grin.

"Good." Lara, without thinking, reached for the mug she'd used for the primrose tea. Realizing this, she changed course and grabbed two fresh cups from the cabinet. She wasn't going to take any chances. Who knew how long it took for the effects of the sage to wear off.

Natalia, none the wiser, sat happily and waited for her plate.

The two women leisurely enjoyed their coffee and crepes until Zach texted Lara, inquiring their whereabouts and when they would get to the station.

An hour later, they stepped into the conference room, finding Zach standing in front of the whiteboard where they had tacked up pertinent details to the case.

"About damn time," Zach grumbled, though with a twinkle in his blue eyes.

"What are you thinking?" Lara asked, draping her jacket over the back of one of the conference room chairs. "You were looking at that board pretty hard."

"I dunno," Zach shrugged, taking a sip of his extra-large Dunkin coffee. "Just trying to wrap my head around the fact that there's an actual psycho out there, thinking he'll gain mystical powers if he completes this crazy-ass ritual. I mean, come on, how in the hell do you really believe you've got magic powers, and you're going to take over the world with them?"

Lara stood, silent, looking at the board, and trying very hard not to think about the book—*grimoire*—that had revealed itself to her. She'd been tempted to check the book again, make sure it hadn't all been a dream. She couldn't bring up the magic book to her colleagues, once blank and now miraculously not. Yeah, that'd go over well.

"It's amazing what people will believe," Lara mused, looking at each victim's picture in turn. "I want to know what connects them..."

"A teacher, a cop, and a politician. Connections could be made easily, in theory, but it's got to be different here. They didn't know each other, or so it seems," Natalia said.

"Hang on. We haven't added the Cardinal Virtues angle yet," Lara said, reaching to the tray for a dry erase marker. On the whiteboard, she wrote the four virtues in English, rather than Latin. "So, Lynn is obviously Prudence, which represents wisdom, according to the Internet anyway. Makes sense, because she's a teacher."

Lara wrote the name of the virtue under Lynn's picture.

"Sierra would be Courage," Zach jumped in. "Saving a family from a fire is pretty damn brave."

"My thinking as well," Lara replied. "Justice didn't seem to fit her in this case, despite the fact she's a cop."

"So, Mumford would be Temperance, which doesn't make sense, considering she doesn't exactly embody self-control or abstention. At least, not after finding out what kind of person she really was," Natalia said.

"She doesn't quite fit the MO. Maybe it wasn't personal before. Lynn and Sierra were a necessary means to an end. Maybe he saw Carol for what she was, got angry, and decided to use her as the ultimate irony?" Lara mused.

"It's possible." Zach nodded. "Which would support our theory that he was at the sex party. Figures that the one person that could tell us the identities of the people at these parties is dead."

Lara sighed, shaking her head. "I'll be right back. I'm gonna hit the head."

On her way to the restroom, Lara paused when she saw Oliver Bennett sitting with another lieutenant in their office, deep in discussion. They laughed and chatted, no doubt talking about a case coming up. The dark-haired man glanced over his shoulder and spotted Lara. She smiled slightly, as did he. He nodded back, and Lara held up a finger for him to wait a minute.

When she'd finished, Lara stepped into the hallway to find the lieutenant had gone and Oliver waiting for her.

"Morning," he greeted, hands in the pockets of his well-tailored suit slacks.

"Hey," she replied, sheepish. "Sorry, I haven't really been around much lately...to talk and whatnot."

Oliver pulled a hand from his pocket to wave the comment off. "Please, Lieutenant, you have a million other things you need to worry about. I know this case can't be easy for you."

"Yeah. It seems like every time we take a couple of steps forward, there's something new blocking us, and we have to step back to get around it."

"Yikes. Run of bad luck?"

"Seems to be a constant in my life," Lara chuckled ruefully.

"I can't imagine. With the death of your father and then what happened after at the bank..."

Lara tensed, eyes lifted to meet his dark stare.

"What the fuck did you say?" she blurted.

Oliver, realizing he'd made a horrible slipup revealing something he shouldn't have known, tried to backpedal.

"Uh, well, shit...I'm sorry, I didn't mean to pry."

"How the fuck do you know about that?" Lara's honey eyes were like molten gold, lit with fury and betrayal. No one in Eastfall except for Tom and the chief knew the whys of her transfer. Most knew she'd fucked up somehow. Lara tried to remember if he had slipped up in their conversations before. What else did he know?

"I'm sorry, I just...I did some digging, strictly to understand you better...I consider you to be a good friend, and you don't exactly open up—"

"Yeah, for good fucking reason," Lara seethed, stepping right in to interrupt. "I can't fucking believe you. The fact you went behind my back, and used your pull as an attorney to dig up shit on me?"

Lara shook her head, the anger so encompassing and consuming she could barely form the words to chew him out.

"I'm so sorry. It was a total invasion of privacy, I completely understand. I'm the biggest ass, but I—" Oliver pulled his hands from his pockets, advancing toward her as though he meant to touch her. Panic squeezed at her throat as Lara backed up, feeling trapped, with only the bathroom behind her. Seeing an opening, she ducked around him.

"Don't. Don't fuckin' talk to me again, Bennett. From now on, this relationship is strictly professional. God, I can't...I can't fucking believe you'd be that nosy."

Lara turned and rushed back up the hallway, ignoring his attempts to stop her.

Her chest felt like fire, eyes burning from unshed tears.

There was a reason she'd come to Eastfall—to escape her own fuck-ups that had happened in Boston. She was naive to think it would've stayed hidden forever, but Lara had hoped it would stay hidden a little longer. Just long enough to prepare herself for the disappointment and the potential vitriol that would come with it.

Not bothering to stop and grab her jacket, Lara took the keys to the unmarked out of her pocket and hurried to the parking lot. She got in the car, turned over the engine, and started driving.

The T had been on time and easy to catch the night she stormed from her father's. An argument over her mother...on her birthday, no less. She should've known. It was typical of the man. Steven Nadeau had been a loving father and did the best he could as a single parent, but damned if he would ever talk about Mave. He wouldn't even mention her by name, for Chrissake.

Inside her pocket, Lara's cell phone began to vibrate. Pulling the device out, she saw it was her father. Rolling her eyes, she hit the ignore button and shoved the thing back into her pocket. A beat or two later, the phone vibrated again. This time, she turned it off.

Lara didn't sleep much that night. As she lay in bed, she tossed and turned, trying to quiet her mind enough to doze. She thought of the hidden picture of her mother. She thought back to all the moments in her life when she'd wished she'd known who her mother was. She thought back to all the hushed conversations her father would have with her grandparents and now wondered if they'd been about Mave.

She'd just begun to nod off when a repetitive pounding began. It took her a moment to realize it wasn't a headache forming, but the incessant knocking of someone at her door. At first, she ignored it, thinking it was her father trying to get her to see reason. But when the knocking didn't stop, Lara groaned and flung herself from the bed.

Sleep deprived, Lara didn't bother looking through the peephole before pulling open the door, security chain catching. On the other side stood a uniformed police officer and Charlie Renetti, her mentor and partner. Blinking blearily, it took her a second to process that he was there and it wasn't a dream. She closed the door enough to remove the chain, then flung the door wide.

When she saw the expression on Charlie's face, she knew it wasn't good news. And because it was Charlie, she knew it had to be her father. Who else could it be?

Pressing a palm to her mouth, sobs punched from Lara's chest as she listed backwards, stumbling and losing her footing. Charlie rushed forward, his mouth moving but no words made it through the silent haze. She felt his touch as he guided her backward to the couch.

Lara wouldn't remember much else from that early morning house call. The word 'aneurysm' would come to mind and the fact he'd tried to call her before dialing 911. Her father had known something wasn't right, so he tried to reach out to her.

And she had ignored him.

The last conversation she ever had with her father had been filled with malice, words she wished she could take back more than anything. Filled with words said in anger, filled with words she could never truly mean, not in a thousand years. And he had died that night, alone, believing his daughter thought him pathetic.

Lara wasn't entirely sure where she ended up, but her surroundings looked like the wooded expanse near her house. She'd been driving and driving, no clear destination in mind, just the need to get as far from the police station as possible.

When she spotted a good pull off, Lara maneuvered the car from the main road and threw it in park. The heater did nothing to break the chill from her bones, and it didn't help she had left her jacket behind.

Fuck.

Fuck!

Lara slammed her palm repeatedly on the steering wheel, emphasizing each hit with a different expletive. She felt out of control, like her consciousness spun dangerously close to the abyss. It was like something had been taken from her, like she'd been violated. It was ridiculous to think so. It wasn't like someone couldn't find the information if they knew where to dig.

It was the principle of the thing. Her lowest points should be hers to share when she wanted and with whom she chose. What was worse, she'd let the guy into her bed. Not that the sex meant anything, but she'd trusted him enough with that intimacy. In time, she might have trusted him with what had happened to her dad, and what had happened after. But now?

Fuck that guy.

Resting her head back on the headrest, Lara thought she might actually fall into blessed sleep, something she'd been lacking the past few nights, when a knock came at the window. Lara jumped, reaching for her hip where her gun sat, holstered.

It was Zach.

He twirled his finger, motioning for Lara to roll down the window.

"Hey," he said softly, ice-blue eyes kinder than she'd ever seen them. "You okay? You went to the bathroom and never came back. Nat and I were worried."

Nat.

How things have changed. Days ago, the man was a murder suspect, now he used nicknames.

It was on the tip of her tongue to say she was fine. That she had just needed some air.

But the dam burst, and she began to sob.

CHAPTER 25

*Z*ach looked about as uncomfortable as Lara felt. She didn't consider herself an overly emotional person. In fact, it had been a very long time since she had had herself a good cry, and Zach looked like he didn't know how to handle a near hysterical woman, but he took it in stride.

Quick as a fox, he rounded the hood of the car, and sat himself in the passenger seat. Zach made no move to touch her. At least he knew that much.

"Hey...hey, it's okay, deep breaths..." he coaxed, trying to use tactics that would normally be saved for negotiations and jumpers.

"H-How did you even find me?" Lara blubbered.

Zach blanched, as though that was the last question he'd expected from her.

"Uh, well, all city police vehicles have tracking transponders on them..."

Of course. She'd been so preoccupied, she hadn't considered that.

A fresh wave of emotion swept over Lara, tears streaking

220

down her cheeks. Part of the problem was she didn't deal with and process her emotions. She knew that, but it didn't make any difference that she knew. She had no idea how to deal with the emotions, where to put them, how to let them go. That was her whole problem. That was what had led her here, now.

Pressing a palm to her sternum, Lara tried to catch her breath. It felt like utter despair clutched at her heart, like the panic attack she'd had not long ago.

God, she missed her dad. Without him, Lara felt adrift, lost in a sea bereft of sage advice and corny jokes. Everything had gotten so much worse since his death. Steve Nadeau had been the only parent Lara had ever known, and as quick as her mother had left, so had her father.

Before she could apologize for the shitty things she'd said.

"What happened, hm?" Zach hummed. His voice was enough, better than a comforting hand on a shoulder. It had a calming effect, much like Natalia's voice. It had always struck Lara as strange how a few words from that woman always brought her back to earth.

"N-Nothin'," Lara breathed.

"This sure doesn't look like 'nothin,'" Zach pointed out. Lara could feel his crystalline gaze on her, though she couldn't bear to turn and look him in the eye.

"Just...things I don't want to deal with," Lara replied vaguely.

"Ah, yes. Sounds kind of familiar," Zach said. She felt, rather than saw, him nod.

When Lara didn't volunteer anything else, he allowed the silence to stretch further.

"You know," he began again, "it does help a little when you talk about it. I know this from experience now."

"Losing my dad was the hardest fucking thing," Lara said,

voice watery and thick from crying. "I thought I'd be able to recover from that, but it's what happened after that fucked me up royally."

"What happened after?"

Boston Massachusetts: Eighteen Months Ago

First Boston Bank and Trust had been Lara's bank since her sixteenth birthday. According to her father, it was the best birthday present a young person could receive, as it taught fiscal responsibility. Lara had soon learned to read between the lines—it was time to get a job, and this was where you put the money from that job.

It had been a month and some change since he passed unexpectedly, and a couple of weeks since Lara returned to duty. She had gone to the bank that day to settle the last of her father's affairs. It was painful, more painful than any trip to a bank should be. It was so final, like she was being forced to accept the fact that her father was dead and never coming back. Standing in line, Lara tapped her foot as she waited impatiently for the next available teller. Her attention naturally wandered, taking in the turn-of-the-century decor. The bank had been standing for a least a hundred years with all the ambiance of a 1920s James Cagney gangster movie. Lara had never really been a big fan of the art deco style, but there was something about the bank—one could not deny its beauty.

Ahead of her, the line progressed, bringing Lara to second in line.

That was when the masked men stormed in.

There were three, armed with semi-automatic rifles and carrying duffel bags. Shots rang out as the first one through the door lifted his rifle toward the ceiling. The spray of bullets struck—poor ceiling probably hadn't seen an upgrade since the opening of the building—causing plaster to rain down. Screams echoed around her, and for a moment the atmosphere was chaos. On instinct, Lara had dropped to the ground, police training kicking in as she dragged the woman in front of her to the floor as well.

"No one move!" one of the men shouted with a generic voice, generic accent, and generic line. His height was just as average, and the ski mask covered any identifying features. The guy, presumably the leader, stepped up to the counter and vaulted over. As he threatened the tellers to stuff all the cash they had into a duffel bag, the other two gunmen, also average in every way, herded all the remaining bank patrons into a corner.

They were now hostages.

Lara ran through every scenario she could think of. She could hear one of the instructors from the academy yelling in her ear to not play the hero without backup. She didn't have her badge or sidearm. Luck, however, was actually on her side, as she did have her Sig Sauer P238 tucked into her ankle holster, hidden beneath her slacks. Lara had to tread carefully, as these guys looked damn nervous and one of them was bound to have an itchy trigger finger. One never could anticipate how far hostage takers were willing to go.

When the leader was satisfied he'd been given all of the on-hand cash, he turned to a bank employee who appeared to be one of the managers—a balding man, probably in his fifties, dressed in an ill-fitting suit.

"You! Open the vault!"

They meant to go for the safety deposit boxes next.

Once the manager had disappeared around the corner to the vault, the leader followed, ordering one of the others to come with him and the remaining robber to stay and watch the hostages.

One gunman. Lara would say her odds had vastly improved.

At the time, Lara wasn't sure how long they sat there, but it seemed too long for men in a hurry. In hindsight, Lara would guess they were looking for something specific and were frustrated when they didn't find it. It had been at least fifteen minutes, however, longer than a run-of-the-mill bank robbery. The place had to be surrounded by now—police cruisers and officers, uniformed and otherwise, and not to mention the SWAT Team.

Someone had to have had the wherewithal to hit the silent alarm.

Lara had always been good at reading people—their body language, their facial expressions, everything they said and didn't say. The man left to watch them was definitely not the most strong-willed of the three. Anxiousness poured from him with shaking hands and a fidgety stance. Side to side he swayed, head swiveling this way and that at every little noise. If there was anyone she could successfully take down, it'd be this guy.

When the bank robber turned his back, Lara saw her chance. Surging to her feet, she tackled the man from behind, a move that would have made any rugby player proud. They fell to the ground in a tangle of limbs, scrapping. On her best day, Lara would've had the man on his stomach, arms cuffed behind his back in seconds, but she was still raw from her father's death, mentally and physically. It didn't take long for the man to overpower her, socking her in the gut with an elbow, effectively knocking the wind out of Lara.

With an oof! *she slid across the marble floor. Heart racing in her chest, Lara knew she'd made a huge mistake thinking she could do this on her own. In a flash, she reached for her ankle holster, pulling out the Sig just as the robber lifted the rifle.*

"Put the gun down, asshole," she huffed, breathless. "I've got your forehead right in my sights, and I'm a damn good shot."

The man, panic clear even behind the ski mask, lunged forward, grabbing the woman that had been standing in line in front of her. Fear hit Lara harder than any punch to the stomach could have.

"Don't move, or I'll blow her fucking head off," he shouted back, pressing the muzzle of the rifle against the woman's cheek.

"Let her go. No one needs to get hurt. You guys are getting your money, just let these people go."

"It's not about the money..." the man murmured, a glassy film covering those dark eyes.

What else could it be about if not the money?

"P-Please," the woman whimpered, her fear causing her knees to buckle.

"You're going to be alright, ma'am," Lara reassured her. "What's your name?"

"Amanda."

"It's going to be just fine, Amanda."

Amanda couldn't have been much older than Lara. Married, judging by the gold band on her left ring finger. No doubt had a kid or two.

"Shut the fuck up!" the robber exclaimed, pressing the muzzle harder into Amanda's cheek. "Gimme the gun!"

"I'll give you the gun once you let her go."

"Fat fucking chance, bitch. Put the gun down, then I'll let her go."

"I have no guarantees you won't hurt her if I do put the gun down," Lara replied. "You've gotta work with me here."

"Fine. I'll let her go, then you drop the gun."

Lara held up both of her hands, twisting so the palms faced toward the gunman, the Sig dangling from her index finger.

The guy threw Amanda to the floor. The screech of her body as she slid caused Lara to wince, but she was safe. True to her word, Lara slowly lowered the gun to the floor, letting it gingerly skate from her hand.

To the day she died, Lara would never forget the look of unabashed, crazed violence that slid over the robber's eyes. She'll never forget when he raised the gun, and how she thought that that was it —she was going to die. Instead, he popped off two shots. Both hit Amanda, still lying helpless and innocent on the floor.

Lara screamed out, diving for the woman to shield her. Another round ripped through the fleshy part of Lara's shoulder, but she could barely feel the pain with adrenaline racing through her veins. Her Sig near, she dove for it, immediately rolling, arms up, and squeezed off the whole clip. Every round hit him squarely in the torso, his body jerking with each impact. He finally fell to the floor, rifle clattering next to him. The rest of the hostages sprang into action, reaching for the gun, just as the air vents above them shot out of their frames, and armed SWAT members dropped down from the ceiling.

The team quickly and efficiently advanced, securing the room before going after the men in the vault, a fact conveyed to them by one of the hostages.

"Medic! We need EMTs in here!" Lara shouted, palms pressed to the gunshot wounds in Amanda's torso. The young woman's life blood spilled to the floor, a crimson puddle quickly forming and spreading, advancing to soak into Lara's slacks as she knelt. "Hold on, Amanda, okay? You hear me? Hold on!"

Amanda gulped, blood sputtering past her lips as she tried her hardest to breathe, but a bullet had lodged itself into a lung, causing its collapse.

A SWAT member had to forcibly remove her from the scene, as EMTs came zooming in, stretcher in tow.

"It was too late," Lara hiccupped, back in the unmarked police car in the God Knows Where part of Eastfall. "She was dead. Her blood all over the floor of that damn bank, just there to make a simple deposit. She's dead because I tried to play the big damn hero."

"You did what any of us carrying a badge would," Zach said. He had listened the entire time, not interjecting to ask questions, just simply listening. That meant more to Lara than she realized. "As much as I hate to admit, we lose people in this job. Look at me...look at what happened."

Lara nodded. They had had similar situations, hadn't they? She wasn't sure why she hadn't made that connection before. Her own grief, perhaps. It had been clouding everything.

"I'll sit here and tell you that you can't blame yourself until I'm blue in the face but at the end of the day, you're gonna do it anyway. The only way that can be fixed is, well, professional help. Have you talked to anyone?"

"I went to sessions, sure," Lara replied. "To as many as I needed to get back on active duty. Said the right things. I wasn't back too long before..."

"Before what? The thing that sent you here?" Zach asked.

Lara nodded.

"It was a series of things, really. Careless things. But they eventually added up. One day, my partner and I were chasing after an armed robbery suspect. This was a guy I'd arrested before. A poor sap that just would never be able to stay out of the system. I tackled him, and he went for me with his fists, so I fought back. But I fought back a little too much. I started waling into him...I still don't know why he didn't press charges."

She reached up, pressing a palm to her forehead.

"Fuck," she continued, "I was so damn lucky. My captain —pretty sure he pulled in any and every favor he had with people he knew. And he got me here. Thought it would be better for me—less stress with smaller city policing."

"Has it worked?"

"I mean...haven't beaten anyone up yet," Lara chuckled.

"Haven't you?"

A few simple words that held a whole hell of a lot of meaning. Lara knew exactly what Zach implied. He probably didn't know her poison of choice, but he suspected she did something to cope. And it wasn't anything healthy.

"Nope. I haven't. Been pretty good," she replied.

He didn't try to argue that Lara was delusional, which gave her some relief.

"We should get back," Zach said, after a long length of silence. "Nat's worried about you."

"Yeah, I guess we should, before she sends out search and rescue for the both of us."

"Does she know?" he asked.

Lara nodded, swallowing thickly as another wave of emotion crashed against her insides. By God had Natalia tried and tried to help her after the bank, but it had been the major point of contention in their relationship.

"She knows. We broke up not long after. I don't blame her. I wasn't the same person."

"No one ever is," Zach sighed. "Alright, come on. I'll follow behind you."

CHAPTER 26

On the way back to the station, Lara and Zach ran into a roadblock. Fire trucks, patrol cars, and an ambulance had veered off the road or parked at an angle to keep cars from passing. Lara came to a stop and stepped out of the car. Zach did the same, parking behind her and coming to stand next to her.

"Car wreck?"

"Must be," Lara agreed.

They walked closer to check out the action. The EMTs rolled a stretcher from the back of the ambulance toward a sedan. The car was unrecognizable, a mangled mass of metal wrapped around a tree.

"Zach Braddock, the hell you doin' on this side of the town line, stud?" a uniformed officer greeted as he came over, a notebook in hand.

"Hey, Ramirez, how the hell are ya?" Zach greeted. They slapped hands, then did a complicated looking handshake.

"Been okay, been okay. Married life...most people complain about it, but I'm friggin' loving it." Officer Ramirez laughed.

"It's not an easy job, but someone's gotta do it," Zach joked. "What happened here?"

"Poor guy. We're thinking he lost control. DOA."

Dead on arrival. Poor guy indeed.

The EMTs rolled the stretcher back to the ambulance, the still body of the driver laid out across the board. The face was a bloodied mess, arms and legs limp and lying at odd angles, clothing shredded by broken glass and jagged metal.

Lara had to do a double take, realizing she knew the driver.

"Holy shit," she breathed, rushing over to look closer at the body. She motioned for the paramedics to stop and leaned in to see the victim's face.

It was him.

Jeff McMullens.

The man she'd met just days before. The one she tried and tried to get in contact with. The one that attempted to call her back, but she didn't answer.

Bile rose in her throat and her stomach churned at the sight of him. She swallowed, trying to convince her body not to empty the contents of her stomach.

Guilt.

She felt guilty.

Maybe if she'd just picked up the phone...

What would he have said?

Would he have given her information about the murders? Or perhaps something else?

"You know this guy?" Zach asked, appearing at her side.

"He works in R&D for Angylion. He gave me Mayfield's name. I've been trying to get in touch with him."

"Shit luck," Zach murmured.

Lara wasn't convinced luck had anything to do with the accident.

It was a hunch. One of those gut feelings that felt like a

bit of a premonition. There was more to the story than Jeff McMullens simply losing control of his car.

———

Upon their return to the station, Natalia accosted her, doting and pecking at her like a mother hen. She had worried over Lara's hasty exit. After more reassurances, Natalia seemed to calm, and they returned to work.

Sitting down at the conference table and overlooking the organized chaos, Lara sighed, anxiety overwhelming her thoughts. The envelope she'd found lodged under her windshield wiper caught Lara's eye. She reached for it. For the next few minutes, she looked over the papers. The information the pages contained seemed so innocuous, like going over someone's personal financial files with tax returns and bills and insurance claims.

She leafed to an invoice list of supplies for God knew what. The list seemed filled with the names of natural, herbal ingredients for medications, as well as other medical and laboratory supplies for the R&D department.

In the footnote at the bottom of the page, Lara noticed a series of numbers accompanied by a last name she hadn't noticed before. She quickly thumbed back through some of the other papers and saw the same numbers, which appeared to be a date, time stamp, and a numeral identifier of the person that had logged in to generate the information.

And a last name.

These specific pieces of information had been gathered by the owner of the numeral identifier and the last name with specific purpose to give the information to her.

The last name was McMullens.

Her mystery informant had been Jeff McMullens.

The researcher from Angylion had slipped her insider information in the hopes of aiding her in this case.

He'd tried to call her, and Lara had ignored it.

Now he was dead.

Between this ugly truth and the fact he'd given her classified information had Lara's suspicions raised that his accident hadn't been an accident.

Could she have prevented this?

If she'd just answered her Goddamn phone...

Lara crumpled some of the papers in her haste to flip through them again, looking for anything she might've missed in her cursory glances. Nothing out of the ordinary popped out, except for a hastily scribbled word she'd overlooked. It was the same handwriting as the sticky note with the names of the Cardinal Virtues.

Wardrobe was all it said.

Wardrobe?

Did he mean clothing? Or did he mean a piece of furniture?

Looking over the paper, Lara saw it was a copy of a packaging label. The image was so small, she'd skimmed right over the name at previous glances. It was Jeff McMullens's name and his mailing address.

Lara jumped to her feet, scrambling to explain what she'd discovered to her two partners. When she was done, she didn't wait for their response and ran from the conference room and down the hall to the stairs. She went up, taking them two at a time, chest burning from exertion.

The door was open and the light was on in Chief Braddock's office. Lara completely ignored the chief's secretary and barreled into the room. She must have looked like a crazed person, eyes alight as she held the packaging label.

"Permission to search a dead man's house, sir," she puffed out through short breaths.

"What?" the chief asked, not accustomed to his subordinates making themselves at home by coming into his office unannounced.

"There was a wreck...on Wessex...not an hour or so ago..."

"Yeah, I heard it on the radio. DOA," the chief said.

"I think there's a connection between the DOA and my murder case. Permission to obtain a warrant to search his house?"

"Do it. I'll see if I can get it into a fast lane for a judge," the chief said.

Lara drummed up the paperwork for a warrant in record time, shooting an electronic copy to the chief to work his magic. Luckily, the chief was a man of his word, and the warrant returned with approval.

The anticipation roiled and expanded in her gut when Lara pulled up to Jeff McMullens's apartment building, Zach in the passenger seat. Natalia had opted to stay behind and root through the contents of the folder again.

Zach called on the drive over to talk to the superintendent of the apartment, and luckily the man met them out front.

He introduced himself as Neil Mooney. He described Jeff McMullens as a good tenant, keeping to himself mostly, no noise complaints, and always paid his rent and utilities on time.

Neil led them through the breezeway to the back of the building where Jeff's apartment was after taking a cursory glance at the warrant, quickly satisfied that it was legitimate.

"That's odd..." Lara heard Neil say.

Peering around him, Lara reached out and clasped her

palm onto the superintendent's shoulder, stopping him from moving forward.

"Zach..." she warned.

The police sergeant took notice immediately, pulling his sidearm from its holster.

"Mr. Mooney, do us a favor and wait right here," Lara said, reaching for her own side piece.

The door to Jeff McMullens's apartment stood ajar, the doorjamb splintered at the lock.

"I'll go first," Lara said, and pushed forward before Zach could argue.

Leading the way, Lara moved quickly from room to room, until they were both assured the intruder wasn't still lurking.

The place had been emptied.

The only things left behind were a few pieces of furniture, but everything else was gone. Indentations in the carpet were the only indicator anyone had even lived in the apartment.

Neil, apparently tired of waiting outside, came through the front door, looking as confused as the two police officers.

Someone had scrubbed Jeff McMullens's apartment, and Lara had a feeling they sought what she wanted.

It had to be Angylion trying to prevent McMullens from blowing the whistle.

This was an entirely new development Lara hadn't anticipated.

Could there be a connection between her murderer and Angylion?

"There's nothing left in his apartment?" Natalia asked, confusion etched across her face.

"Nothing but a couple of tables and a chair."

They had added Jeff McMullens's name to the board, with

his connection to Angylion and Lynn's connection to their clinical trial. Lara had a hunch both were linked. How, though, was not apparent at present.

"Anything and everything that could've been hiding classified documents is gone," Zach pointed out.

Lara's honey eyes glanced at the manila envelope. She needed to keep its contents safe.

"Um, pardon me for interrupting..."

Three sets of eyes shot to the door to the conference room. Oliver's tall, lean frame filled the doorway. He shuffled from foot to foot, looking sheepish, a folder clutched in his hand.

"Something we can help you with, ADA?" Zach asked.

"I was wondering if I could speak to the lieutenant for a moment...in the hallway?"

Lara stiffened. She had hoped to delay this confrontation, but it seemed fate had other plans. Nodding, she stood from the rolling chair and stepped into the hallway, closing the door behind her.

"Look, Lara, I—"

"I'm pretty fucking pissed at you," Lara steamrolled him, shutting him up.

"I know, and I'm so—"

"Like, really fucking pissed. You invaded my privacy, Oliver. Instead of just talking to me, you investigated me. Like I'm a case you're trying."

Oliver knew to stop there, to not attempt to interject again.

"I'm sorry I can't be what you want me to be for you," Lara replied, her voice growing softer. "I'm not...I'm not the 'take home to the parents' kind of girl."

Oliver nodded, his eyes grave. "It's okay," he began. "I kind of figured it was just strictly a physical thing. I'm sorry for trying to make it more. I'm sorry for going behind your back and doing what I did. Besides, I don't have parents to bring you home to." The last sentence was lighter, as if he tried to make a joke of it. Before explaining further, he thrust out his hand, all but shoving the manila folder into her hands. Lara accepted it, looking from it to Oliver's dark eyes.

"What is this?"

"Open it."

Lara did. It was a case file from Chicago, Illinois. The second thing she noticed was the mug shot of teenage Oliver. Eyebrows furrowed, she looked back to him.

"They're my juvenile records. Before I turned eighteen. I wanted to show you these so you'd...I dunno...so we could be even. That is my dirty past I wouldn't want people knowing about. It seemed only fair to show you."

Lara didn't respond and instead let the file do the talking.

They were copies of Bennett, Oliver's juvenile record from his hometown of Chicago. Oliver had only ever briefly mentioned this fact but had never gone into detail. A police report detailed the discovery of Alana Bennett's body, a heroin needle lodged in the crook of her elbow. The officer that first responded believed it was a cut-and-dried overdose. The report went into a little bit of detail of how he was a frequent visitor, having been called to the residence over the years for domestics and drugs. Something about the father being absent, always had. Living in squalor. Barely any food. Prostitution.

"Jesus Christ," Lara breathed, looking to Oliver again.

"I just wanted you to know you weren't alone in the dead parent department," Oliver replied, his hands in the pockets of his Hugo Boss suit. "My father walked out on us when I was five. My mother—well, she had lost her way even before my father left. Our abandonment was the catalyst. She was inconsolable. She hadn't had a solid job to begin with. Eventually, she lost that. Bills started piling up, and she couldn't afford the drugs. So, she resorted to the oldest profession. I'm sure my mother loved me in her own way, but she had a helluva way of showing it."

"Fuck, Oliver..." Lara breathed.

He shrugged, his eyes firmly glued to the tips of her shoes. "She OD'd. I found her when I got home from school. I was fifteen. That officer who wrote the report, he'd been helping me over the years as much as he could. Mentoring me. He saw the potential in me and gave me the ambition to remake myself. I was damn near top of my class in school. Got a full ride to Harvard. Moving here was...the new beginning I needed. Before then, since I was still a minor, I hopped around from foster to foster. The detectives called in to work the case even dragged me to court, damn near fully charging me with murder, because they thought I'd made it look like an OD. That experience made me want to be a lawyer. Because I was a minor and cleared of the charges, they sealed my records. And it was as if I started over. And here I am."

Lara closed the folder with a dull snap. "So you've got a past. Seeing this doesn't mean I've fully forgiven you. But...I get what you're trying to do."

"I don't want this to excuse what I did," Oliver said. "I just wanted to make us even. Now we both know our darkest secret."

Lara considered Oliver carefully. Clutching the file, the heaviness of it gave her pause. Like something inside of her urged her to read the contents closer. She tucked the folder under her arm, gave Oliver the best smile she could that conveyed she wasn't entirely pissed anymore but not all was forgiven, then ducked back into the conference room. There was a case to solve, and personal shit couldn't get in the way now.

CHAPTER 27

A few hours later, a knock at the conference room door interrupted the trio's brainstorming. In walked the chief, Tom, and Mayor Lothrop.

"Sir," Lara greeted, standing at attention. Zach and Natalia did the same.

"Lieutenant. Sergeant," the chief greeted. "Mayor Lothrop, this is Special Agent Natalia de Benedetto. She is a liaison from the Boston Bureau office, helping out the team. My son, Zach Braddock, I think you know. He is also assisting in the investigation. And, you know Lieutenant Nadeau."

"Pleasure," the mayor replied. He didn't seem his usual cheery self. Instead, he was all business, even a little annoyed, like he didn't want to have to be here.

"The mayor stopped in to check up, see the progress of the case," the chief continued, his eyes taking in the white-board and the few connections they'd drawn. "Could we get a progress report, Lieutenant Nadeau?"

Lara was confused, until she realized the chief wanted her to come alone to give the report. Nodding, she looked to

Tom who seemed as clueless as she felt, then glanced over her shoulder at Zach and Natalia, who both shrugged.

Lara followed the three men to Tom's office. Tom offered his chair to the mayor, who accepted graciously. The chief took a spot behind the mayor, leaning his backside against the windowsill, and Tom stood off by a filing cabinet, resting his elbow on top. The vibe in the room screamed intervention, so Lara stood in front of Tom's desk, shoulders tense.

"So, uh, the progress report—" Lara began, but the mayor interrupted.

"Actually, I don't need one," he said, resting his elbows on the arms of the chair. "There have been three murders: a teacher, a police officer, and a Havenwood city council member. There are no suspects, no arrests made...have I left anything out?"

Well, he'd left out a whole hell of a lot of details, but Lara didn't feel she could or should correct him.

"No, sir, you did not," she replied.

The mayor sighed, massaging fingers at his left temple, before pinching the bridge of his nose.

"I've been speaking closely with Havenwood's mayor and city council," Lothrop said. "They are deeply concerned of the events unfolding in Eastfall. They have asked me to come personally to see what progress has been made."

Lara didn't like where this was going.

"You can imagine what sort of position this puts me in," Lothrop continued. "I have another mayor and two sets of city councils worried sick. They're terrified they might be next, like poor Carol Mumford."

Lothrop shook his head, as if to show a semblance of remorse or sadness. Honestly, to Lara it didn't look much like he cared for the loss of human life. More like what this would do to his public image if the murders remained unsolved.

"What can I do to alleviate your fears, sir?" Lara asked, hands clasped into fists at her sides.

The long pause seemed answer enough. She had a hunch of what was coming, had seen the same look in the eyes of her captain back in Boston when the transfer to Eastfall had been initiated.

"I am sorry to have to do this to you, Lieutenant, but I think it's best if we put another lead on the case," the mayor sighed.

"Mayor Lothrop, this isn't—" the chief started, standing alert and stepping closer. He looked startled, like he hadn't known *this* was the true purpose of the mayor's visit. Tom was in much the same state, having moved his arm from the filing cabinet immediately after the mayor's declaration.

"I know it's highly uncouth and uncharacteristic of me to step on your toes like this, Chief Braddock, but my hands are tied. As mayor, it's my duty to heed other's concerns," the mayor tried to assuage, turning the chair to speak directly to the chief. He then turned back to Lara.

"You will not be transferred away, of course, or put on leave," Lothrop began again. "You may continue with other cases. I think it best, and I bet the chief would agree with me, to put Captain Sharpe here as primary. Of course, you may still offer some support. Sergeant Braddock and Special Agent de Benedetto can remain to help Captain Sharpe. We in Eastfall will always welcome federal help, if it means these murders will stop and the killer brought to justice.

"You see, tourism numbers are down enough already, and we can't lose more time on this. We've got to think of our holiday parades and festivities coming up. No one will want to visit if there's a murderer running around. I'm sure you understand, Lieutenant."

Lara's jaw clenched, biting back a few choice words.

Words nowhere near professional nor appropriate to say to a superior.

"Sir, with all due respect, I do not understand. I believe I am, and will always be, the best person for this case," Lara said as tactful with her annoyance and anger as possible.

"I understand your frustration, and I would be mad at me too. Unfortunately, like I said, I and other council members think it best you step down from this investigation and let Captain Sharp handle it. He is your supervisor, after all, and a very capable investigator. He will no doubt benefit greatly from the information you've already gathered."

Fuck, no.

Her breaths came quickly, that familiar panic rising within. The chief couldn't meet her eyes, no matter how much she tried to catch his gaze. It wasn't his decision, but he had to listen to the few people higher than him on the ladder.

"Mayor Lothrop, I would like for it to be noted that I do not agree with this decision at all and believe Lieutenant Nadeau *is* the perfect person to crack this case," Tom interjected. Lara appreciated the defense. Like her, Tom had no choice in this matter. He followed orders to the letter, just as she did.

"Noted, Captain," the mayor replied, his eyes never leaving Lara. "You know you're not being put on leave, right, Lieutenant? You'll still be able to work cases. But, again, given your history and record from Boston and the fact nothing has come of the investigation so far, we all felt this move to be in the best interest of this case and this city."

For a time, Lara couldn't bring herself to respond. She felt utterly betrayed, but not by the chief nor Tom. Lara believed she'd been handling this case to the best of her abilities and felt close to a solution. But once more her past decisions and actions came back to bite her in the ass. It stung. It really did.

"Yes, sir, I understand now," Lara replied, dejected. "I'll surrender the case to Captain Sharpe." Lara turned on her heel and escaped down the hallway before the mayor could take away her badge next.

"Captain Sharpe will be taking over the case," Lara announced, lingering in the doorway of the conference room. Natalia and Zach's heads jerked in her direction, faces turning to masks of confusion.

"Wait...what?" Zach asked.

"Tom's taking over. The mayor has taken me off the case. He's getting pressure from outside, and therefore is pressuring the chief to make this official. I'm...I'm gonna go home for the rest of the day."

"Lara, this is bullshit—"

"Yes, Nat, it is, but I don't have a choice. I'm going home. I'll talk to you guys later."

Lara felt herself spiraling.

This whole clusterfuck felt like Boston all over again. She could see the disappointed look of her Boston captain, clear as day. She could hear the disappointment in his voice, listing off the carelessness she'd exhibited in her paperwork, almost preventing a criminal charge from sticking, and how she'd need to be psychologically evaluated for the excessive force she'd used in a takedown.

Those worthless feelings that had become her best friends came roaring back. She was such a fuckup. It didn't matter all the hard work she put toward this new place, this new chapter of her life. It still wasn't good enough.

Why had this happened? Lara believed wholeheartedly

she'd been making strides in this case. Clearly not fast enough for Mr. Politician.

Mayor Lothrop had glossed over the nitty-gritty details of the case. It made Lara wonder if maybe the omission had something to do with Angylion. The pharmaceutical company was a thread she had yet to pull on, though proof of any connection to the murders was a reach at this point. Of course, she included mention of Angylion in her notes, which the chief was privy to. Had the chief told the mayor? Was the mayor protecting Angylion? It certainly was the largest business in the city, giving a huge boost to jobs and tax revenue. Did her removal have something to do with Jeff McMullens's death? Had she gotten too close to something?

As Lara drove home, she contemplated next steps, because like hell she'd let this case go.

But, could she do this right? Could she do *anything* right? It was as if Steven Nadeau's presence had been the only thing keeping her on the straight and narrow. Now he was gone, Lara fucked up everything, having rolled downhill pretty damn steadily over the past year and a half, hitting every fucking rock on her descent.

Her mom had taken off when she was a kid, not giving a fuck about her and who she could become. She'd never really had a large group of friends, only a few close ones that she didn't even talk to anymore. She'd gotten a woman killed. She didn't have a damn thing to show that she had made something of her life other than her job.

And apparently, she couldn't do that right either.

Once home, Lara grabbed a beer from the refrigerator. The first disappeared before she even noticed. The day turned to afternoon, casting an annoyingly bright pall over the house and backyard.

After three beers, she forced herself to stop, to not go for a fourth. Lara couldn't feel the cold chill as she sat at the table on the back patio. It felt better to be outdoors, to have the scent of fresh air filling her senses. Being inside felt stifling, like the walls would close in.

Zach and Natalia had been blowing up her phone with text message after text message since she'd left the station. Lara considered ignoring them, but if she did, they'd be over in a heartbeat, busting down the door. She shot back a text asking for some space.

Lara wanted to be alone. It felt better that way. Less people in her orbit she could ruin.

Time passed, and Lara watched the shadows stretch and move across the backyard, until it disappeared altogether, and night set in. Her hands were numb from the cold, as were her legs and feet.

Beer had only done so much to warm her, so she decided to drag herself inside to try something else. There wasn't much in her refrigerator or pantry, but she made do, eating an entire box of Kraft Macaroni & Cheese.

A hockey game was on, Bruins versus Capitals, and Lara settled herself on the couch to watch. Her belly felt warm, and the food had relieved some discomfort from the cold. But it didn't brighten her spirits much. Neither had the beer, for that matter. What good was the shit if it didn't work anymore?

Her vision became blurry as exhaustion took hold, making the events of the second period of the game fuzzy. Eyelids closed fully, and Lara slept.

"Lara...Lara..."

Eyelids cracked open to find a woman knelt beside the couch. She seemed familiar to Lara, but she couldn't immediately identify her. The flickering of the television and dim light from the lamp illumi-

nated the woman's features with an ethereal glow. She was petite, her face pixie-like. She had beautiful blue eyes, a smattering of freckles, and a carefully coiffed mop of dark tresses.

The woman wore clothing that didn't belong in this century.

Lara sat up on the couch, head clearer than it had been in hours.

"Wh-Who are you?" she asked, voice cracking.

The woman didn't reply, only smiled before placing a finger to her lips.

Lara's eyebrows furrowed.

The dark-haired woman stood and crooked the same finger at Lara, bidding she follow.

What else could Lara do but comply?

Straightening out her skirts, the woman moved around the couch and headed toward the front door, as though she knew exactly where to go. She disappeared into Lara's office, and Lara rushed to keep up.

The woman had opened the box from the attic and lifted the book from its confines. She set it down on the desk and opened the cover. Rifling through the pages, the woman finally stopped, finding what she sought. She lifted her blue gaze to Lara and pointed her finger at a page. Lara moved to take a step closer, to see what it was she needed to see, but her vision wavered, and the woman disappeared.

Lara tried to step forward again, but found her feet weighed down. Glancing at them, she saw nothing physical keeping her there, as though invisible weights kept her rooted to the spot. The more she tried to move forward, the more she sunk into the floor.

Like quicksand, the floor sucked her down and down inch by inch until she was up to her neck in hardwood flooring. It didn't matter if she screamed, cried out for help. No one came. The more she struggled, the more she sank, until she disappeared.

Lara shot up, a gasp caught in her throat.

It was pitch dark outside. The television programming

had turned to infomercials. The lamp still shone its dull light across the floor. Her heart hammered in her chest.

Slowly, Lara stood, digging her fingertips into her eyes and rubbing as though that would clear the haze. She shuffled into the kitchen to get some water. Pulling down a glass from the cabinet, Lara filled it with water from the faucet and stood at the island, taking large gulps.

Once the water was gone, Lara replaced it with vodka, taking equally big gulps. The liquid burned as it slid down her throat, waking her just a little bit more. When the clear fluid had disappeared, Lara poured herself another couple of fingers, and headed to the staircase. Better to sleep in her bed and not risk a tweaked back.

As she stood at the bottom of the steps, Lara paused, glancing over at the darkened interior of her office. The bizarre dream had jogged a thought from the previous evening. She would want to gather her notes to make copies for Tom. Stepping into the office, she froze when she saw the book out of its box and lying open.

Just like her dream.

CHAPTER 28

Lara stayed as far from the book as she could. She backed away, took herself right up the steps, and collapsed onto her bed.

She didn't remember anything else until the sun shone on her face, having forgotten to close the black-out curtains. Groaning, head pounding, Lara sat up.

At first, when her eyes snapped open, she thought she'd been hearing things again. Perhaps the ringing had merely been in her dreams.

Was it the book again? Oh God, the book. Lara tried to stand up and the sound...

It took a bleary moment to realize the ringing hadn't been in her head but was in fact the shriek of her cell phone. The number blinking on the display was not one she recognized.

She curled her fingers around the device and hit the green phone icon.

"'Ello?"

"Hi, is this a number where I can reach Mr. Steven Nadeau?"

The voice on the other end of the line was a woman. She

sounded haggard, exhausted, run through the wringer. She sounded in desperate need of a vacation.

"Um...Mr. Nadeau passed away about a year and a half ago. I'm his daughter. Is there something I can help you with?"

A beat of silence.

"Oh dear. I am sorry to hear of his passing. Mr. Nadeau was so kind to all of us. My deepest condolences to you. I had no idea of the loss," the woman replied, her tone genuine.

"Thank you, I appreciate that. Now, how can I help you?" Lara was no longer sleepy.

"Right, well, news of his passing explains a lot. He had left this number as an emergency contact if anything should happen. You are listed as his daughter."

Frustration creeped into Lara's chest, hating the fact she still didn't have an answer as to who this woman was and what she wanted.

"I am...I'm sorry, but—who are you?" Lara interrupted.

"Right, sorry. My name is Janice Adkins, I'm the head nurse at Briargreen Institution. Your father has been paying visits and part of the bill for a patient's stay here at our facility."

Lara blinked, the fog of her brain slowing the processing speed. Her father had done what now, and with whom?

"What's the patient's name?"

"Hang on, let me check if you are also on the medical release. Verify your first and last name for me."

"Lara Nadeau."

"Yes, Ms. Nadeau. You're on the release form. The female patient's name is Mave Morgan Nadeau."

"Wait," Lara cut in, feeling her heart stutter and her stomach drop. "*Mave?*"

If Nurse Janice said more after that, Lara's hearing tuned out. The entire fabric of her reality ripped open right then, letting some sort of cosmic energy slash through and lash her to pieces.

Her mother was alive?

Her mother was alive, and her father had known.

Her mother had lived in a fucking insane asylum for who knew how long, and *her father had always known*.

It was like the ultimate kind of betrayal. To believe one thing for the majority of your life, and in an instant have that turned completely on its head.

"Ms. Nadeau? Ms. Nadeau?" Nurse Janice's voice brought Lara back. "Did you hear me?"

"N-No, I'm sorry, Nurse Adkins, I...I didn't."

The pause over the line was more tangible than any Lara ever felt before. She could practically feel the pity leaking through the phone.

"It's okay. You're totally clueless about all of this, which is highly unusual for me, and I work in a mental institution," the woman continued, trying to insert a bit of humor. "Mave Morgan Nadeau—your mother, if the file is up to date—has been here for going on twenty-five years. Your father comes— sorry, he came—at least once a month to see her. Sometimes, he would come more, depending on whether it was a holiday or her birthday."

Lara couldn't breathe, couldn't swallow, nothing would make the nosedive sensation cease. Maybe she shouldn't have had those beers last night, but then again being ripped away from a case and chased by a book wasn't normal.

"We didn't know what had happened to him. He had paid in advance for a good while, and of course, we took notice when the payments ran their course and now we're making contact. We don't want to put her out. The last time we tried that it—it didn't go well. Besides, Mrs. Nadeau is—well, she's asking to see you."

"She's asking to see me?" Lara asked, breathless.

Her entire life, she never knew her mother. Her entire life, her father would not even mention her mother. And it was a cruel irony that the last conversation she had with her father was over the woman that apparently *had* been around all along, but the mere mention of her drove her father into a defensive tizzy.

"Yes. She keeps mentioning your name," the nurse said, then got quiet. Lara had the feeling she wanted to say something but didn't feel it was her place to do so.

"You're wondering why he never brought me," Lara guessed.

"Yes," Nurse Janice sighed. "They always talked about a daughter, but at first, we all just assumed it was because you were young and they didn't want you to see her like this. But then the years rolled by and we never saw you."

"Your guess is as good as mine, Nurse Adkins. "Is there any way you could email me your contact information, address of the facility, and a way for me to square up payments?"

"Of course," Nurse Adkins replied. "Let me have your email address."

They spent the next couple of minutes discussing next steps, and Lara hung up the phone with the promise that she would visit the facility when possible.

It didn't take Nurse Adkins long to send the email with the information Lara had requested, as well as brief but succinct directions on how to get there.

It would only take Lara an hour to get there, heading back south toward Boston and slightly west of the city.

Her mother had been so close all along. All twenty-five or so years she had been gone.

And Steve Nadeau had known exactly where she was.

Angry tears welled in her eyes, burning rather sweetly before spilling over down her cheeks. How could he have kept this from her? Was it because she was in a mental insti-tution? What had Mave done to get there?

Lara pondered these questions and more as she showered. Everything seemed so surreal now. Like this was a new world and now she had to deal with it. Lara stared at the clothes in her closet, carefully picking an outfit for the day. Such a thing was always trivial to her, but now she couldn't help but dwell on whether slacks and blouse matched. It normally didn't matter what she wore, as long as it was department regulation and professional.

Lara took time to carefully brush her teeth and rinse with mouthwash. She also tried to tame her hair.

As she stood in front of the coffee machine, waiting for it to brew, Lara considered whether to go to Briargreen now. Having lost the murder case, she wasn't sure if she could handle this new truth bomb that had been lobbed into her life. She considered calling Natalia and Zach, to share in this *Twilight Zone* level of bizarre information.

A quick search from her phone pulled up the Briargreen website. It had a whole three-star rating on Google. It looked quaint from the outside, almost innocuous. It was a brick building, like a late eighteenth century mansion with colonial blue shutters. Wrought iron gates popped out from the sides of the building, disappearing backwards into spacious grounds. There was a whole gallery of pictures showing shrubbery outside, with blossoming flowers and places to stroll and sit. It didn't look like what she thought a mental institution should look like, but the large, brick sign at the entrance to the parking lot said otherwise.

Her mother was alive.

What would she be like? Would she identify Lara immedi-ately as her daughter? No doubt Steven had kept Mave current on Lara's accomplishments. Would she be proud of who her daughter had become?

Would they even get along?

These thoughts and more raced through her brain as she meandered the streets of Eastfall, all the way to headquarters.

Scenes from her life played in her mind like the instant replay of a hockey game. The many weekends she spent with her grandparents made more sense now. Every few weeks, her father would ship her off to spend a few days with her mémère and pépère Nadeau, and he would work his long shifts.

Or so Lara had believed.

When she got older, she rationalized the visits to her grandparents as being a way to spend quality time with them and a way for her father to have alone time. Even as a kid, Lara had always understood the difficult life of a single parent. So many of the kids at school had grown up like her.

Lara recalled arguments between her mémère and father, but they always happened behind closed doors with muffled voices Lara could never make out. Her pépère would try to distract her with games of *Clue*, but Lara wasn't oblivious.

Lara pulled the unmarked car into a parking space and cut the engine. A wind gust kicked up, making the car rock.

No. Lara couldn't do it. Not now.

She would pay what Briargreen required, and once this damn case was solved, only then would she go visit her mother.

Hurrying into the building, Lara tried to make it to her office before being seen by Natalia or Zach.

No luck.

Hearing a door being opened, they barreled out of the conference room, relieved that it was her.

"You're okay..." Natalia said in breathy relief.

Swallowing thickly, Lara tried to gather thoughts to speak. Her mind whirled, too full of this new revelation.

A pair of stunning green and a pair of sultry brown eyes

stared along the expanse of hallway at her, and Lara felt herself cracking. Once, she might have kept this new thing to herself. But now?

Well, shit, she'd had about ten fewer beers last night than she normally might have.

"My mother is alive, and my dad knew where she was the whole time."

One could have heard a pin drop.

"*What?*" Natalia looked absolutely shocked, like a child hearing for the first time that Santa Claus wasn't real. Zach looked perfectly confused.

"Come on," Lara beckoned them into her office and told them what she knew.

"I've actually heard of Briargreen before," Natalia said. "It has a good reputation. That's...holy shit."

"Yeah," Lara sat back in her chair, folding her hands in her lap.

"Can't really relate to this situation, but damn..." Zach said. "What're you doing to do?"

"I don't know," Lara replied softly. "I can't...there's no way I can go right now. I'm just going to give them what they want, and I'll make it there eventually."

"When you do, I can go with you," Natalia offered.

"Thanks. We'll see. It might be something I should do alone, considering the circumstances."

"Of course," Natalia nodded. "But I'm glad...I'm glad you shared this with us, Lara. I know that's a hard thing to do."

Lara had not expected the praise, and she would be dumb to deny that it made her feel slightly less weighed down by the world in that moment. Lara felt so light that for a brief time she considered revealing the weirdness of her house, but thought better of it. They were the only people in her life close to her, and she didn't want to run them off with crazy talk, especially something that could land her in Briargreen right next to her mother.

"Thank you," she replied. "I'm going to get to work on these *other cases* I have. And here..." Lara reached into her bag, pulling out the copies she had of her notes. "These are for Tom."

Zach reached forward for the notes, and held them for a moment, looking down at them like they'd personally offended him.

"You're not really going to stop investigating this, are you? You wouldn't be the person I thought you were if you did."

Lara's eyebrow arched. "Wow...that's a compliment, I'm guessing?"

Zach nodded. He probably didn't hand those out lightly.

"Well...of course I was going to keep looking into things. The mayor did say I could still offer some support."

Zach and Natalia grinned simultaneously, and the damn things were infectious enough to cause Lara to smile as well.

"Now get out of my office. I've got murders to solve, and so do you."

Not to mention, she had a funeral to attend. A mother she hadn't ever known was just going to have to wait.

CHAPTER 29

Armed with a giant thermos of coffee and a resolve that didn't know how to quit, Lara pored over all information on the murders. Natalia and Zach fed her copies of the stuff from the file Jeff McMullens had left behind. By the afternoon, Tom started in on the action too.

"I'm sorry, Lara," he said, voice low as he took a seat in one of her visitor chairs.

"Cap, please," Lara waved him off. "It wasn't your choice. And you stuck up for me. That means a whole helluva lot."

"Yeah, well...you are the one that deserves to take lead on this case. I know I'm capable, but you've got the keenest eye of any investigator I've ever seen. This should be yours." He paused, then slid some papers across her desk. "Here. I believe my minions have been feeding you under the table. Allow me to help."

Lara hadn't felt this sense of purpose in a long time. Like, it finally sunk in that it was okay to have people that believed in her, perhaps even more than okay.

Sometime before lunch, Chief Braddock wandered into her office. She hadn't seen or heard from him since the mayor debacle the previous day. And it scared her that Lara didn't know exactly where they stood.

"Uh...morning, sir," Lara greeted as he made himself comfortable in one of her chairs.

"Lieutenant. You left pretty quickly yesterday." He wore his full uniform complete with shiny eagle pins at his lapels and a gun at his hip.

"Yes, sir. I did," she replied, tentatively.

The chief didn't continue at first. Lara could see thoughts playing across his face, even though the chief was a master at hiding emotions and expressions. "I'm glad you're here."

"Of course I'm here, sir. I've got a couple of robbery cases I need to wrap up."

The chief nodded.

"Good." Those green eyes, twins to Zach's, scrutinized her face and body language. Not in a bad way, just too deeply for Lara's comfort. "You're damn good at what you do, Nadeau. And I'm sorry about what happened. It wasn't my decision to take you off the case, but my hands are tied."

"I understand, sir, you don't need to explain," Lara replied.

"I feel I do."

Lara sighed. "You're the chief, sir, you don't need to explain yourself to anyone."

"That's horseshit. That might be the kind of thing the chief of police does in Boston, but that sure as shit ain't what I do here in Eastfall."

That's when Lara realized there was no other superior she would ever want to work under. Policing wasn't for those in need of coddling, but her relationship with the chief had been one of the most sincere she'd ever had while on the force. His presence in her office told her everything she needed to know. It had taken six months to come to this conclusion, but it was the God's honest truth.

It socked her in the gut, causing her eyes to prickle with

emotion. Like hell she would cry in front of her superior officer.

"It's fine, sir," Lara replied softly, afraid if she spoke louder, her voice would crack. "I promise."

The chief nodded. "Good."

He stood, pausing at the door.

Letting out a long sigh, Lara took a fortifying sip of her coffee.

The last funeral Lara had attended was her father's. And before that, it had been her pépère's. Until her father's death, funerals were just another reason for the Nadeau family to gather.

This one was different. Mostly because she didn't know anyone here, and she'd only met the deceased once. Lara felt she owed it to Jeff McMullens to show up. As it stood, his death was ruled as a vehicular accident. Lara wanted to know for sure whether that was true or not. And she would, soon.

There were a handful of people milling around in the viewing parlor of Weymouth Funeral Home. The large Victorian had been a funeral home for as long as funeral homes had been a concept. The director bounced back and forth, checking to make sure flower arrangements were just right, the refreshments well stocked, and also attended to the comfort of the few family members McMullens had. The director's wife, a woman with a shock of blood-red hair and a kind smile, worked the room, offering condolences and comfort.

Lara grabbed the memorial card that included a short obituary.

It amazed her how someone could live such a fruitful life,

even so young as Jeff McMullens, and have it be summarized in a couple of short paragraphs.

Lara stepped into the line designated for viewing the remains. She was surprised to see it was open casket, as Jeff hadn't exactly looked his best after the wreck. However, she saw when she got within view that the mortician at Weymouth had a real gift.

She would have never known he'd been mangled.

The other angle Lara tried to work was that of suspects. If Jeff had been bumped off by Angylion Pharmaceuticals, as was Lara's theory, chances were some of his colleagues would attend. Angylion colleagues.

Stepping away from Jeff's body, Lara sat down at one of the cushioned chairs lining the walls and scanned the room.

There was Jeff's mother. Lara had overheard a conversation between the mom and the funeral director on her way in, which was how she knew.

According to his obituary, Jeff didn't have siblings and was preceded in death by his father. He wasn't married, and as far as Lara could tell, hadn't had a significant romantic partner.

The rest of the funeral attendees had to be friends and coworkers.

Sure enough, Dr. Emma Michaelson stepped in from the cold, removing her patent leather gloves. Dr. Michaelson was the clinical trial supervisor overseeing the trial Lynn Rickerson had been a potential candidate for. Jeff had been her lab assistant. If Lara recalled, Dr. Michaelson had defended Jeff at the beginning, when he was briefly a person of interest. Lara was glad to see Dr. Michaelson here in support of Jeff.

Not long behind Dr. Michaelson, Dr. Robert Gibbons appeared.

Interesting.

Dr. Gibbons was the Assistant Director of Research and Development at Angylion. He would be considered Jeff's boss's boss's boss and spent the majority of his time in the administration building. Nevertheless, he *was* Jeff's superior and coworker, and probably had made an appearance for propriety's sake.

More people arrived for the viewing, more faces Lara didn't recognize. She kept close watch on Dr. Michaelson and Dr. Gibbons, though, but didn't approach. They stepped up to Jeff's casket, then paid condolences to Jeff's mother, and sat for a time, talking amongst themselves.

"Lieutenant Lara Nadeau?"

Lara's head snapped up, not expecting someone to recognize her. The person who spoke was short in stature, not a hundred pounds soaking wet. He was middle-aged with gunmetal gray hair and milky blue eyes. He wore an ill-fitting suit, and that, coupled with his demeanor, screamed lawyer.

"Yes?"

"I wondered if that was you. I'm Claude King, the executor of Mr. McMullens's estate. Do you mind if I sit?"

God, sometimes she really hated when she was right. Lawyer, indeed.

"No, not at all, Mr. King, please," Lara gestured to the empty chair beside her.

"Thank you," he said as he sat, primly.

"How can I help you, Mr. King?"

"I wanted to discuss a matter with you about Mr. McMullens's will."

"He was kind of young to have a will, wasn't he?" Lara asked.

"Unfortunately, one is never too young for a will," Mr. King replied. Of course he would say something like that. That's how he made his money. "Indeed, Mr. McMullens hadn't established a will until recently."

Alarm bells sounded and red flags waved.

"Was there a particular reason?" Lara asked.

Mr. King shrugged. "I don't believe so."

"Is there a reason why you needed *me*, Mr. King?" Lara asked, wanting the guy to leave her be. One glance over to where the Angylion doctors had been sitting showed empty seats. Lara's gaze whirled around the room but didn't see them. They must have gone.

"Oh, yes, sorry, forgive me. I was going to call you, but someone said you were here. Mr. McMullens bequeathed the contents of a safety deposit box to you."

Lara wouldn't have been more shocked if a gaggle of tap-dancing geese came through the room.

"*Excuse me?*"

"I know. It seemed odd to me too, considering he left the majority of his assets and possessions to his mother to be donated to charity. But there was one thing he was very insistent you receive. He came to me a few days ago to make the necessary changes to his current will. He left the key to the box with me, for safekeeping, to be given to you in the event of his death."

"This didn't alarm you at all?" Lara asked, incredulous.

"No, ma'am. I deal with death and dying on a daily basis. There is nothing that surprises me anymore. And I don't question the wishes of a client. Of course, I did think it odd at the time, and now here we are. But it was a car accident for sure, correct?"

"So says the official ME's report," Lara muttered.

Mr. King said nothing, but instead reached into the interior of his jacket and produced a key from an inside pocket.

"Do you mind if I see your police credentials?"

Lara reached into a pocket of her jacket to pull out her identification. She handed it to the lawyer, who looked over it and some paperwork he'd pulled out.

"Thank you." He handed the ID back to her. "This key will open safety deposit box 36069 at Eastfall National Trust.

Of course, I'll need you to sign some paperwork, but I think we can delay that for another time."

"Much appreciated," Lara replied, reaching out to wrap her fingers around the key. It was an ordinary bank key. She wasn't sure what she'd been expecting.

"Thank you for your time, Lieutenant Nadeau," the lawyer said. He smiled a not unkind smile, stood, and went off to Jeff's mother's side.

During the memorial service and subsequent interment in Eastfall's cemetery, Lara's mind could go nowhere but the key. She needed to get to Eastfall Trust, to get to the contents of the box, and hope someone else hadn't discovered its existence. Images of his bare apartment returned, having been too late to discover what *wardrobe* contained.

Once the services were over, Lara rushed to her car, wanting to get to the bank as quickly as possible.

When she pulled into the lot, she sat in her car for a moment, waiting.

A bank.

She hadn't stepped foot in a bank since the hostage incident. She wasn't sure she could handle it now, but she had to. She needed to prove this to everyone, but most of all to herself. And for Jeff.

Sucking in a deep breath and trying to give herself a little pep talk, Lara peeled herself from the car and headed inside.

Thankfully, there was no one waiting in line, so Lara was able to get right to the front. The bank teller urged her over with a genuine smile.

"How can I help you?" the perky blonde asked.

Five minutes later, after the bank manager had appeared to show her to the vault, Lara slid her key into box 36069 along with the bank manager's. Together, they pulled the box from the wall, and he set it down on the table behind them.

"I'll leave you to check out the contents. When you're ready to put it back, just give a holler."

"Thank you," Lara replied with a slight smile.

Her hands shook as she pulled the chair out to sit in. The box was about the size of a shoebox. Lara wished she knew what it was with her and boxes.

Steeling herself, she reached forward and flipped open the lid.

Inside sat a sealed, standard sized envelope with Lara's first and last name neatly written, and...another book.

Another Goddamn book.

It was old, probably a couple of hundred years old. The binding was loose and coming apart, so with great care, Lara pulled it out. The gilded title on the spine had faded, but what she could make out was nonsense.

Could it be another of Dr. Chappelle's books?

Opting to go for the letter first, Lara slid her fingertip underneath the lip of the envelope, and carefully tore it open.

Nestled inside was a handwritten letter. A quick glance to the end of the letter told her it had been written by Jeff McMullens. And another quick glance to the beginning of the letter told her Jeff had had the presence of mind to include a date, and the date was a few days before his death.

What was it that Alice said?

Curiouser and curiouser.

———

Lieutenant Nadeau,

If you are reading this, then my fears have come true. I am dead.

I know you're wondering what the hell is going on. Why would I leave you the contents of a safety deposit box after meeting you once?

To be honest with you, I'm not even sure.

What I <u>do</u> know is something is wrong with Angylion Pharmaceuticals. I can't identify when my suspicions began, but the administration of Angylion is...off. It's too cookie cutter...too perfect. Of course, the business end of things is legitimate, as far as I can tell, but I'm just a scientist. They provide support and benefits to their employees, follow FDA regulations with clinical trials, and donate to numerous philanthropic organizations.

Despite all this, I can't help but feel there's corruption in Angylion.

As I said, I can't offer definitive proof of what kind of corruption, but the files I left for you on your cruiser should help. It's like a puzzle with a missing piece, and of course, that missing piece is the most crucial. If you look closely at the inventory and supply lists, as well as other financial paperwork, the spending doesn't seem to add up.

As you have already seen, in this safety deposit box is a book. My Latin is horrible, and I never got the chance to have someone look it over, so I don't know what it is.

Whatever it might be, I think it has value to Dr. Gibbons. It came in a shipment to the clinical trial office by accident. I was the one that opened it. The label wasn't addressed to anyone in particular, just Angylion's R & D department. Before I could try and ascertain to whom it was supposed to go, my attention was taken away elsewhere and the book slipped my mind.

The next morning, Dr. Michaelson reported her office had been broken into and ransacked. I knew immediately it had to have been someone looking for the book. I thought if anyone was willing to commit B & E for this thing, then who knows to what other lengths they might go.

It has been a few days since we talked at the cafe. I apologize for the game of phone tag we played. I had hoped you would pick up when I finally called back, but it wasn't meant to be.

I hope you have the strength to look further beneath the veil over Angylion. Something tells me you do. Even though we met once, I feel *as though I know your heart enough to entrust you with this book and all the other documents.*

   I have a science brain, but you have the investigative know-how. I know you will figure it out.

   Whatever this book is, however, you <u>*need*</u> *to keep it safe.*

J. McMullens

After finishing the letter, Lara sat back in the chair, shoulders slumped.

   Lara wasn't sure if she was up to the task of investigating a multinational corporation. Corruption on this scale was like walking into a quagmire. The further you went, the deeper you'd sink until trapped. Cases like this took the FBI *years* to build. One misstep and a judge would throw it out. Not to mention, you'd probably lose your badge.

   Letting out a slow breath through pursed lips, Lara shoved the letter back into the envelope, and along with the book, put it in her bag. She slipped out of the room, and from the bank, feeling the nausea abate the farther she drove away.

   Did she show the book and letter to Nat and Zach?

   Lara didn't want to risk their involvement in something they didn't need to be involved in.

   She wanted to keep them safe.

   The more people attached to this, the worse it could be.

   Priorities, Lara.

   Murderer first, then potentially evil business.

CHAPTER 30

Before heading back to the station, Lara raced back to her house. She rushed in quickly, heading for the staircase. Making a sharp turn, Lara hustled for the attic. It took a couple of tries, but she eventually found the loose floorboard where she'd uncovered the *AB* box. She placed the book and letter gingerly within the dark confines and replaced the floorboard.

When her feet hit the ground floor and before Lara could take a breath, she heard a loud thud.

Tensing, Lara felt goosebumps prickling up the flesh of her arms. The air grew heavy, and she was positive if she turned around right then, someone would be standing there. The sensation of another presence was so tangible.

Whirling around, her honey eyes fell on empty air.

Lara couldn't tell whether she was relieved or disappointed.

At this point, it was hard to even gather up the energy to deny the strangeness of her house. Whatever was there had led her to the book in the attic.

Turning again on her heel, Lara left the house and made for police headquarters.

———————

There were only a few hours left in the workday, but Lara wanted to put them to good use. She dug in, elbow deep in her notes and Jeff's procured files and crime scene reports. At one point, she realized she needed to recreate her thought board, but couldn't do that here. Lara gathered everything and headed home, regrouping in her office where she had her own whiteboard. All afternoon, she worked to map out her victims, the circumstances in which they died, and the locations of the bodies in the city, as well as any connections between them, no matter how flimsy. Lara then added suspects, which weren't many.

Back and forth from her laptop and whiteboard she went, calling up forensics reports and Dr. Rogers's autopsy reports.

There had to be something. Yes, the entire murders were rooted in the mystical, but this was a real flesh and blood person committing these heinous killings. And that flesh and blood person, no matter how careful they were, had to make a mistake somewhere.

Lara took a magnifying glass to the crime scene photos, looked through evidence logs, and read through the forensic reports again and again until her eyes ached from the strain.

It was right there. Whatever she needed to see to make everything click was *right there*. Why couldn't she figure it out?

Knocking at the front door startled her. Glancing out one of the front windows, she saw it was Natalia and Zach. Lara opened the door to be met with them carrying bags of takeout from Bucky's.

Wordlessly, she let them in and led the way to the kitchen.

Neither of them chose to address the giant whiteboard and mess in her office. They settled in the kitchen, purposefully not talking about the case and instead discussing what they would do for the winter holidays.

Once full and completely content, Lara thought about the book Jeff had left her and the book in her office.

Hell, she'd told them about her mom, might as well go for broke.

"I need to tell you something," Lara said. "And you're not going to believe me."

"Try us," Nat challenged.

And Lara did. She told them everything, starting with the small things she'd noticed about the house, to the box she found in the attic, to the woman in colonial clothing at the fall festival, to the dream about the same woman pointing something out in the book, and ended with telling them about the safety deposit box.

To their credit, Zach and Natalia listened without interruption. If they thought her crazy, they were good at hiding it.

"I don't...I don't know what the hell's been going on but... on top of these murders, it's just more weird shit after more weird shit."

Silence reigned over the kitchen. Lara swallowed thickly around the nervous ball lodged in her throat.

"That's...all very strange," Zach hedged. Lara could tell he didn't know what else to say.

"You don't believe me." Lara's stomach sank into her toes.

"No, it's not that," Nat replied. "We believe that you believe. And this explains the few times you seemed distracted. But you've got to admit...the ghosty parts are pretty wild."

"I know it's wild, but...yeah." Lara sighed, shoving another crab wonton in her mouth.

"Did you look at the page in the book yet?" Zach asked.

Lara stopped chewing. "No. I haven't."

In her rush to focus more on the case, she hadn't stopped to think about the book, still open on her desk.

"Well, shouldn't you check it out?"

After a pause, Lara nodded. Yeah, why the hell not?

She left the kitchen to grab the book. She returned and set the tome on the island. Zach and Natalia gathered close, and judging by the looks on their faces, something was wrong.

"What?" Lara asked.

"There's nothing on the page," Zach said.

"What do you mean? There's a shit ton in this book," Lara replied, holding her finger on the page while she fanned through the others. The intricate drawings and flowery language were all still there.

"Lara, I see nothing. The book is empty," Natalia said. Lara's stomach sank.

She fucking hated the look on Natalia's face. Like she was already planning how to convince Lara to get to the nearest inpatient mental health facility.

"Fuck," Lara hissed, before flattening out the book to the page the woman in her dream had indicated.

It appeared to be an incantation. At first, it read as Latin, but right before her eyes, the letters shifted and morphed into recognizable English.

To Reveal A Secret.

What the *hell*?

Shit, it was worth a try.

Lara read the words aloud. Even to her own ears, it didn't sound like English, though she read it in English. When she reached the last sentence, Natalia and Zach scampered back like they'd been electrically shocked.

"Holy shit, what the fuck just happened?" Zach exclaimed.

"Wh-what happened?" Lara asked, voice shaking.

"There...there wasn't shit all in that book, and then all of a sudden..." Zach breathed, still as far away from the island as he could be. It didn't take long for him to shuffle forward cautiously, green eyes taking in the writing on the page.

"You can see it?"

"Yeah, we can see it," Natalia said, evenly.

Now the big questions were—how and why?

Magic?

"I don't know what to do...what to think..."

The three sank to the kitchen floor, backs resting against the kitchen island.

"Ghosts...magic...what the fuck?" Zach breathed.

"How does a person deal with this?" Lara sighed.

None of them spoke as they all tried to process this in their own way. Lara had just performed...magic? How was that possible?

"We've got to find Yoda," Zach suddenly said.

Both women's heads swiveled to shoot him a look.

"What? I don't mean *actual* Yoda, but someone that knows what's up. Someone that can give us some answers. Like Yoda trained Luke."

"*Us?*" Lara asked.

"Yeah, *us,*" Zach replied, looking to Natalia for confirmation. Nat nodded.

It was such a foreign feeling to hear that word. Lara had felt so alone since her father died and didn't think she would ever be rid of that feeling. But here they were, sitting on the floor of her kitchen side by side, two people declaring for *her.* For the second time today, it seemed. They didn't think she was crazy.

"Look, I want to figure this out, but right now we've got more important shit to worry about. There's a crazy person out there using a ritual to gain *ultimate power*, and they're one person away from completing it. If magic is real, then...shit, this ritual could be real."

Natalia and Zach nodded, letting that thought sink in.

"Surely not..." Natalia breathed. It had been a while since Lara had last seen it in Natalia's eyes, but she was...scared. Genuine fear.

CHAPTER 31

A bunch of spineless fools ran The Order.

This wasn't a new conclusion he had reached, however.

They had tried once more to stop his great work. Tried to convince him there was no use in proceeding because the ritual would fail.

Such little faith.

He knew for a fact it would work, had studied the ritual since stumbling upon it in college. Back when he was merely a pledge to The Order.

They were such sycophants. Pandering to their *benefactors* like the ass-kissers they were. The Order hadn't had spine for a hundred years. In the beginning, The Order had such power, such influence. They could topple kingdoms.

Not anymore. They'd grown soft in this new century.

No matter. Only one more for the ritual. One more and he would have the power The Order craved for themselves.

Iustitia.

Justice.

Such an important virtue.

Justice was about balance, and the universe was nothing if not a constant push and pull to keep that balance. It's fitting he would end this ritual with this particular virtue, considering the idea of the ritual was to tip the scales of Justice completely....

His methods weren't orthodox for sure. But at least he was brave enough to get it done.

The Order hemmed and hawed and never pulled the trigger.

Bunch of fucking cowards.

No more. He would be the voice of The Order now. He would lead them into the new age. A new age of change. A new age of power.

Anyone that stood in his way would be removed.

Anyone.

And he would begin with the police lieutenant. The perfect representation of Justice. She was everything that embodied the virtue, though her self-esteem and self-worth were shot to hell. She didn't see it in herself, but he saw it. And he would use that to his advantage.

CHAPTER 32

The next morning, Lara keyed her way into her office. She'd gotten the okay from the chief to work from home on her 'other cases' and there were a few files she needed to grab. She wasn't rooting around long before there was a knock on the doorjamb. Turning, she saw Oliver Bennett standing in the doorway with a cautious smile.

"Hi," he said softly.

"Hi," she replied.

"How're things going?" he asked, taking a cautious step in.

"Okay, I guess."

"Case not going well?"

"It's going," Lara replied vaguely.

"Gotcha," Oliver nodded, realizing quickly Lara still hadn't forgiven him. "We're still good for the Andrews case next week, right? Ready to take the stand?"

Lara nodded, gathering up the things she had come for. Amongst the pile was Oliver's juvenile record. She'd yet to give it another glance over. "All ready. I'll look over the case notes the night before, to refresh."

"Great. I'm counting on your testimony," Oliver smiled wide, blinding, all pearly-white teeth, neatly straightened. The dark stubble on his cheeks and chin only served to emphasize the whiteness. Oliver really was ridiculously handsome. High cheek bones, tall, lithe body....

It was too bad Lara couldn't feel anything in return for him.

"Is there something else you needed, ADA? I've got to get out of here. Got cases to work on, you know."

Oliver's eyebrows furrowed, and his eyes darkened. He didn't like her dismissive tone, but honestly, she couldn't give a shit about whether she offended him or not.

"Really? You're *still* mad?"

"Uh, I mean... I wasn't as mad as before, but if you wanna be like this, I can get mad again," Lara bit back, feeling ire rise.

"Right, fine, sorry for bothering you," he hissed, storming away but not before slamming the door.

Temper, temper. She had more important things to worry about than his ego. Oliver Bennett may be a fantastic prosecutor, but he still had the arrogance of a high-profile defense attorney. Must be something they ingrained in law students at Harvard.

Back home, Lara jumped into it, but not before checking her emails. A new message had come in from the crime lab. Excited, Lara clicked the subject line, opening it. The contents were short and sweet, just as she liked them. It seemed the killer hadn't been as careful with Sierra Fitzgerald as he had been with Lynn Rickerson and Carol Mumford. Within Sierra's uniform, a tech had found a foreign fiber. According to the report, it was high-end fabric, probably belonging to a suit of some kind. They were not able to narrow it further, but they were still looking into it. And, it was something. Lara contemplated the expensive suit thread, adding it to her board under Sierra's picture. Even in death the woman had been a tried-and-true fighter, the kind that would bring down their attacker with them.

At lunch time, while she ate the sad excuse for a sandwich she'd made for herself, she paged through Oliver's juvenile file.

Oliver Bennett had had a rough start to life. Absent father, druggie mother. On the surface, this entire thing read like an inspirational story. A kid that grew up from nothing worked his ass off to make himself into something.

Harvard Law? Couldn't get much more prestigious than that.

Lara came back to the notes about Oliver's mother's death. She'd been in and out of the system for prostitution and intent to buy. She'd been in and out of the hospital almost the same amount of times. It was a wonder she didn't get hepatitis or HIV from needle use. Lara couldn't imagine having a parent like that. Oliver's mom made Steven Nadeau look like a saint.

Her eyes skimmed over the notes from the officer first on scene and then the detective that had picked up the case. Everything from the officer first on scene seemed pretty straightforward. It was the detective's notes that had Lara reading further.

Detective Fratelli hadn't much liked the Bennett family. He wrote about having run-ins with the father before he disappeared, and then having to clean up the mother when she had partaken too much. But when he arrived on scene, he'd thought the location of Oliver's mom's body odd. Not to mention, the needle sticking from her arm. In recent years, Ms. Bennett had taken to shooting up between her toes, though he'd supposed it wouldn't be out of character for her to use her arm again.

Lara polished off her sad sandwich and closed the folder. Detective Fratelli had done his due diligence in including this observation, for sure, and it caused something in Lara's brain to take note. Though Ms. Bennett's death was no doubt a run-of-the-mill overdose, it certainly never hurt to pursue all angles.

———

Hours later, Lara's eyes began to cross. She'd been staring at the whiteboard she'd titled <u>Cardinal Virtues</u> for far too long. Glancing at her phone, she noticed the late afternoon hour and a text message from Natalia inviting her to Bucky's. Lara sent a quick text back, grabbed her coat, and headed into town.

The bar hadn't gotten busy yet, so it was easy to grab a table. Tom had joined Zach and Natalia, and the four of them talked and compared notes over a round of beers.

"We're on the clock here," Lara sighed. "It's only a matter of time before this guy wants to finish his ritual. There's got to be something we're missing."

"A good night's sleep always brings fresh eyes," Tom said sagely. "Speaking of, I'm going to call it a night. I'll see you cats later."

They bade the captain goodbye and ordered another round.

"Don't you think you should slow down?" Natalia asked after Lara had nearly downed half the bottle of Sam Adams in one gulp.

"What do you mean?" Lara asked.

"Well, I don't want you driving back home under the influence."

Lara rolled her eyes. A sort of mania took hold. Just when she thought that two beers would actually be enough for her instead of her usual ten or more, Natalia had to come down on her, policing her intake. Her frame of mind, already aggravated by the beer she had imbibed, only tilted more off kilter.

"Why are you watching what I'm drinking all of a sudden?"

"I'm...I'm not. I just... I thought..." Natalia stammered.

"Thought what? Oh, now that Lara finally talked about her feelings and didn't keep something to herself, that all of a sudden she's fine and perfect?" Lara tried, but couldn't keep the hysteria from her voice.

"You know that's not what I'm trying to do," Natalia said firmly.

"Okaaaaay, ladies, maybe we should—"

"Shut up," Lara and Natalia echoed. Zach shrunk in on himself, giving in with hands raised.

"Look, I appreciate the concern. You haven't gotten all critical of me since you first got here, so I really don't see any reason for you to right now. I'm fine. In fact, I'm going to go home too. Get some sleep. You guys have a great night." Lara slapped some bills on the table for their waitress and stormed from the bar.

"Lara, wait... I'm sorry. You're right, I shouldn't have—"

"No," Lara whirled around in the middle of the parking lot to face Natalia. She hadn't expected the agent to come after her. "Please don't. I should've known that us being around each other for a long time wouldn't end well. It's like a cycle with us. We peak with sex, and then everything goes downhill again. I can't get my shit together, and you harp on me for not having my shit together. That's just how we are. End of story."

"This time feels different," Natalia tried again, a plea in

her tone. "You seem different. I think... I think Eastfall is starting to be a good place for you."

"Maybe. Maybe not. You need to learn to stay away from me, Nat. I really do feel like I'm getting my shit together but...it's a fucking slow process. And with you around, it just complicates things." Lara turned, taking a few more steps to her car, before turning around again. "Just... let's get this case figured out and get you back to Boston. It's best that you're there and I'm here."

Lara got into her unmarked and sped down the road for home.

Once in the driveway and parked, she trudged up the walkway. As soon as her foot hit the first step, Lara froze when the front porch light flicked on by itself. Lara sucked in a breath and let it out slowly. She was too tired for this shit, too physically and mentally exhausted.

Resolved, her feet propelled her forward and into the house.

Inside, it was silent except for the distant hum of the heating system.

"Hello?" Lara called out.

She wasn't sure what she expected in reply, but nothing came.

Before Lara could move toward her office to get back into the thick of it, the light at the top of the stairs flicked on. Her heart leapt into her throat.

The lights were beacons, and Lara couldn't deny anymore that the house was trying to get her somewhere. Placing one foot on a step, she forced the other to move, and then again until she stepped onto the second floor.

Standing at the end of the hallway, Lara waited, and sure enough the lamp in her bedroom clicked on.

Once inside the room, Lara expected to see the woman dressed in colonial garb. But it was empty except for her clothes and other things strewn over the floor and furniture.

The lamp on the other side of her bed illuminated, and Lara rounded the foot of the bed.

At first, she didn't see it. Pants, T-shirts, shorts, shoes.... They were all her things. Some items were clean and some items were dirty. Only Lara knew which was which.

Taking another cautious step forward, her keen, honey eyes scanned the floor more carefully. Then, she got to her knees, peering under the bed and the nightstand.

That's when she saw it.

Underneath the nightstand, as if it had fallen from some-where like a pocket, rolled, and settled there, was a black button.

Leaning in, Lara plucked it from the floor.

Shoving the thing under the light, Lara tried to see if she could ascertain any other identifying factors.

She had no idea how long it had been in her house. It wasn't her button—at least she hadn't noticed any missing from her clothing.

Lara shoved it in her pocket and headed back downstairs. When she didn't get any more signals via the flickering lights, she opted to resume her original plans for the night.

Sleep.

A knock came at the front door. She hadn't been expecting anyone, but then again, it could be Natalia wanting to continue their conversation. Which Lara was so not here for.

She trotted down the stairs and opened the door to find Oliver Bennett. In one arm, he cradled a grease-stained brown paper bag, and in the other, he clutched a twelve-pack of Sam Adams.

"Hey," he said with a soft smile. "It's completely uncouth of me to show up, but I figured I couldn't go wrong with beer and Chinese food. I remember what you ordered that one time—General Tso's Chicken with pork fried rice and an egg roll? I knew you'd be burning the near-midnight oil, so I wanted to help and, you know, bribe you for forgiveness."

Lara blinked owlishly, stunned to find him on her doorstep, let alone on her doorstep with food and beer. She couldn't help but laugh at his last comment.

"Um...sure, sure, come in. We don't want you to get cold," she paused. "Really, we don't want the Chinese food to get cold."

Oliver chuckled as he stepped in the doorway and toed off his shoes.

"Thanks," he said with a smile, standing awkwardly in the entryway for a good ten seconds until Lara got herself together.

"Shit, let me help you," Lara reached forward and grabbed the brown bag, because priorities. She then gestured for him to follow, and they brought their feast to the kitchen. The food smelled so good. She'd forgotten that she hadn't actually eaten dinner.

While Lara cracked two of the Sam Adams open, Oliver pulled the food cartons out of the bag, dividing up the goods. They ate for a few minutes right there, standing at the kitchen island and chatting. She talked about her cases, and he talked about his day in court.

"Have a seat, will ya? I'm going to run to the bathroom, and maybe there's a good movie on TV we can find," Lara said.

"Love this plan," Oliver chuckled, then began putting the Chinese food away in the refrigerator.

Lara headed down the hallway to the half bath, doing her business quickly. After she washed her hands, Lara stepped back into the hallway and stopped when her foot collided with something, kicking it across the floor. There was a soft, barely discernible scraping noise as the object skated along the hardwood and rolled into her office. Peculiar, as she was positive there'd been nothing on the floor a moment ago when she went into the bathroom.

She followed the object's trajectory and soon found where it had stopped at the base of her whiteboard. Squatting down, she picked up the object.

It was a small tube of non-toxic, acrylic paint.

Lara wasn't an artist, at all, so where this had come from, she had no idea.

She took note of the color.

Blue.

The same color drawn across Lynn Rickerson's mouth. The same shade.

The light above her head flickered off and back on.

The book, still open to the page about revealing secrets, began to vibrate gently against her desk. The pages began flipping furiously as though an invisible wind stirred them. It stopped, and Lara took a cautious step forward.

The book hadn't led her into danger yet. Though there was a first time for everything.

The word "Correspondences" was written at the top of the page, in blessed English. Underneath was a brief explanation that a correspondence was a way to categorize plants, herbs, colors, and more into ways that were meaningful. Sympathetic magic, it was called. One could do this based on physical appearance, as well as the properties of the object in question.

Lara moved down the page, until she saw the name of an herb she had heard before. One attached to a crime scene.

Hazel.

Hazel had been found at Lynn Rickerson's crime scene.

Hazel corresponded to...

... Knowledge, according to the book. Seemed appropriate, since she more than likely represented the *prudentia* virtue.

"Hey, I was wondering where you'd gotten off to."

Lara startled at the voice behind her and spun around.

"Thought you might have gotten lost," he chuckled, hands clasped behind his back.

"Uh, nope. Hit the head, and then I thought about something I wanted to look up," she replied, thinking quickly of an innocuous excuse. Her eyes scraped over his person, taking note of what he was wearing. Oliver had come from court, of course. "That's a nice suit, by the way... It's missing a button..."

Her heart hammered in her chest, and she hoped to God Oliver couldn't hear it. It thrummed faster and faster as things began to click in place.

The foreign fiber belonging to an expensive suit that the techs found on Sierra's clothes might be similar to the suit Oliver currently wore.

Which also happened to be missing a button.

Could that fiber have once supported the button she'd found beneath her nightstand? A button she was positive wasn't hers?

Then there was the acrylic paint bottle she'd nearly tripped over, the bottle that *definitely* didn't belong to her.

There were precisely two people that could claim both paint bottle and button. One she knew better than she knew herself. The other she had only met six months ago and had a juvenile record that may or may not be attached to his mother's death.

"Ah... uh, thank you," Oliver hummed, dark brown eyes moving from her to the book.

Something changed as fast as a switch being flipped. The Oliver with the warm smile and kind eyes disappeared, and in his place stood a man with an emotionless countenance. His eyes were dead, no light or life, and his mouth a thin line.

Fear pumped through her veins, mind running in overdrive to think of a way out. Her only exit, though? Right behind him.

Oliver's hands came quickly from around his back. Lara flinched, thinking he'd pulled a gun or a knife on her, but there was nothing in his hands.

That was until he took a couple of strides closer, opened his palm, and blew tan dust into her face.

The effects of it were instant.

Lara lost consciousness. The only thing that kept her from hitting the desk and the floor was Oliver's pair of strong arms.

CHAPTER 33

Lara blinked back to consciousness, head pounding from whatever drug Oliver had administered to render her immobile. Her nose felt dry and sore from inhaling the powder. Her wrists were bound behind her, made useless by her own handcuffs. The ghost of her healed bullet wound screamed from the strain of the angle her arms were bound.

Oliver had made her quite at home in her own kitchen. The dim light over the stove was on, the only source of illumination in the otherwise darkened house. He'd shut off all other lights, including the television.

Shuffling and rattling sounded to her right, and Lara forced her head to turn, though the muscles screamed at the effort.

"Y-You..." she croaked, mouth desert dry.

The man, the ever trustworthy and entirely sweet district attorney, turned from where he rustled in her cutlery drawer and shot a beaming smile her way. The smile frightened her beyond words, as she'd never seen something meant to be happy be so evil.

"Yes, me. Sorry to disappoint you, Lieutenant."

Lara strained and pulled at her restraints, testing them for give. Of course, there wasn't any, and upon inspection of the mobility of her legs, found them duct taped to the good oak of a dining room chair.

Son of a bitch. This dining room set had belonged to her Mémère Nadeau.

"Should've known," Lara moaned, faculties still fuzzy from whatever that tan dust had been. "From now on, I'm going to suspect the lawyer. Can't trust them. No matter what side they're on."

Oliver chuckled, moving from one drawer to the next as though searching for something in particular. "That's a hurtful stereotype, Lieutenant."

"When the shoe fits," she replied, attempting, again, to test the give of her bindings at the ankles.

Nothing.

"This is really nothing personal, I hope you know." Finally, he turned from his searching, rounding the kitchen island to kneel down in front of her. His hands reached forward to grip her thighs, palms gliding up. Once, his touch had made her feel pleasure. Now it made her want to vomit, made her skin crawl. She tried to squirm away, but to no avail. "If there were anyone more worthy, then I would have chosen them. You, however, make my last offering too tempting to pass up."

"Offering?"

"Yes, for a ritual. Well, *the* ritual, really. The one the rest of my brethren are too cowardly to attempt. Oh well. Their loss. They won't be privy to my gains."

The ritual for ultimate power.

Oliver meant to make her the last Virtue.

Iustitia.

Justice.

"How am I worthy of such an honor?" Lara asked, sarcas-

tically. Oliver's mouth twitched into a half smile again as he
stood and walked over to a duffel bag that had to have come
from his car. From the bag he pulled three small Mason jars,
one by one. Each had some sort of hazy, yellow liquid in
them, with a dark mass suspended within.

The missing organ pieces.

"Oh, you are worthy, my dear," Oliver replied, pulling out
a black pouch. Inside was a baggie of some herb she couldn't
name. "In fact, you're the only worthy offering for Justice
within a hundred miles. Your sense of duty is impeccable. All
you care about is the job."

"So, you didn't find out all that shit about me to help me,
as a friend, did you?" Lara asked.

"Nope, not at all. Just doing my research. Needed to know
for sure you were the one."

Of course.

Next out of the bag came another small bottle of paint.
This time gold.

Lara watched him closely as he prepared for the task
ahead. The lump in her throat grew at the realization that she
was going to die. Whatever was in this sick man's head, Lara
couldn't fathom, but if she didn't do something soon, then
this would be her end.

For a brief moment, she contemplated the *what ifs*.

What if she died? Would that be so bad? For over a year,
she'd been floating through life, like a ghost, ruining everything she'd worked hard to accomplish.

What if she died? Would anyone miss her? Everyone she'd
ever loved was gone. Her father was dead, Natalia had broken
up with her and continued to criticize her, Zach was only just
now becoming a friend, her old partner Charlie was back in
Boston living up his retirement...

No matter how much she tried to rationalize her death
being for the best, as she watched him lay out the tools of her

demise, Lara couldn't push down the feeling there was more for her to do.

If she died, who would bring this fucker to justice, putting the other three souls to rest?

If she died, he would once more dig himself below the radar, avoiding detection and arrest.

If she died, who would solve the work started by Jeff McMullens, the mystery of Angylion?

All of these thoughts swirled, giving her the fortitude to continue on, to not let death break her.

But the question was: how would she get herself out of this predicament?

"You gonna at least explain yourself before you kill me?" Lara goaded, knowing the villain was always unable to resist appealing to his own vanity and stroke his ego at his master plan with a resounding monologue. Besides, it fit the profile Natalia had compiled.

"It's a story, for sure," Oliver replied with an almost wistful sigh.

"By all means, start from the beginning. I'm sure we've got time. You never seemed to rush with the others."

"You're right. I knew you were good, Lieutenant. You cannot rush perfection or ritual. Especially not one this important. Everything must be just right."

"And what exactly are we conjuring up today?" Lara asked, while simultaneously racking her brains for any hope of escaping her bonds.

"Ultimate power," was his reply. "It is an ancient ritual never before attempted. First discovered by John Dee, it wasted away in the archives of The Order. No one would dare try it, as its consequences were too dangerous. Cowards. They preach and preach about power and might, but they're afraid to get their hands dirty. It's a ritual based on the four cardinal virtues. The sacrifices must be female, as that is how they are often depicted, and these women must embody the virtue they represent."

"What about Carol Mumford? We found out all about her dirty little secret. Not exactly the epitome of temperance."

"No, she wasn't. Councilwoman Mumford was a special circumstance."

"What about Lynn? Were you the mysterious boyfriend she'd been seeing?" Lara asked, piecing more and more together.

"Yes, I am. Rather pathetic woman. Carol Mumford too. Officer Fitzgerald was the only one that fought back. The other two were weak-willed."

"You really believe this is going to work? I thought you didn't believe in hocus-pocus shit. You wouldn't even let me read you your horoscope," Lara said, trying to free one of her ankles as discreetly as possible.

"I lied, clearly. And it is not shit, Lieutenant," Oliver gritted out, wheeling around to face her with an angry fire in his eyes, the first genuine emotion she'd seen from him all night. "The world is comprised of small minds, minds that cannot even fathom the idea of the supernatural, let alone realize it exists. Only a select few are blessed with the knowledge, with the insight..."

A biting remark was right on the tip of her tongue, but a peculiar sensation at her wrists kept her from responding. A soft tingling encircled them, much like the feeling when a limb falls asleep after ill use. The sensation grew more pronounced, and suddenly, she realized one circlet of the handcuffs had un-cinched itself. Swallowing thickly, heart pounding in her throat, she held onto the loose metal, not wanting it to clang against the chair and give away her good fortune. Adrenaline pumped through her veins, too much to question the how of it all. Survival instincts flared, and Lara knew what she had to do.

"When you say small minds, you mean women, right?"

"Women, sure. And some men," Oliver replied, taking a step or two toward her, a wicked-looking knife in his hand.

"Wow... What woman fucked you up so badly?" Lara goaded, needing Oliver to come just a little bit closer.

Another glint of something maniacal glimmered just below the surface, his lips pursed, clearly perturbed. "My mother."

"Oh, *please*," Lara actually rolled her eyes. "Mommy issues? Really? You couldn't come up with something a little more original than that? So your mother was a drug addict and a whore, big deal. What happened to all that shit about remaking yourself?"

Oliver's nostrils flared, ire growing like a flame stoked with fuel. "My mother was a worthless whore. A druggie and drunk. She beat me, and one day I couldn't take it anymore, so I—"

"Are you done?" Lara interrupted, letting out a long-suffering sigh. "Look, shitty mom or no shitty mom, we all have issues with our parents. Clearly, you're just this side of unhinged that you couldn't get it the fuck together—"

Her words had finally struck the right nerve, and that cool, calculated facade was gone instantly. All that was left was what Oliver was at his very base nature—a bloodthirsty animal. In a flash, Oliver had reared his arm back, the knife aloft, ready to strike. As it came down, Lara's arms shot up, wrists together, catching his arm in its descent. The loose handcuff link dangled in the air, and the only sound in the room was Oliver's surprised intake of breath. Lurching her body forward, Lara caught him off balance, and they tumbled to the floor. The chair was still lashed to Lara's ankles, and in the quick beat where Oliver had dropped the knife, she scrambled for it. A quick slash freed one leg, and then the other.

Oliver was up in a flash, pure rage and fury etched in every tense muscle of his body. If Lara wasn't flying high on adrenaline in that moment, she would have peed her pants in terror. All she felt was the need to run, to survive. Knife in hand, she twirled out of Oliver's way as he lunged for her, and she took off like a shot. Perhaps what she lacked in sheer strength she could make up for in agility. However, Oliver caught her before she could reach the front door. His vise-like grip snatched and tugged at Lara's hair, causing her body to bend back painfully in the effort to keep her hair from ripping from her head.

"You bitch!" he hissed. Lara swung her arm back, trying to catch his arm, his chest, anything to slow him down. Oliver ducked and slid out of the way of her efforts, deftly catching her wrist, grip so tight it made her bones creak. Crying out, Lara reflexively dropped the knife. In the scuffle, one of them kicked it and sent the blade skittering across the darkness of the foyer. Oliver and Lara grappled, his left arm sliding to her front, bringing the inside elbow up and against her windpipe.

"You will not ruin the work I've done," Oliver gritted through clenched teeth, applying more and more pressure. The air stung in her lungs as Lara tried to gasp for breath, but he was successfully cutting off her oxygen supply. The more she struggled in his grip, the tighter it became. In a last-ditch effort, Lara drove her elbow back into his abdomen. It caught but did not seem to affect him much. She tried again, drilling the bone into his solar plexus. The blow worked that time, sending him staggering back a foot.

Lara kicked forward, hand gripping the blessed coolness of the doorknob. Just as she was about to turn the handle, Oliver struck from behind again, arms vise-like around her waist as he jerked her back. Lara yelled, feet leaving the ground as he dragged her back into the kitchen.

"I am going to enjoy killing you," Oliver growled in her

ear, the warm, wetness of his breath making her shudder. "You've been nothing but a fucking nuisance since you came here. Not anymore. I'm not gonna let a meddling cunt like you ruin the work I've done. I deserve this. And nothing is going to stop me."

For a brief second, Lara believed Oliver. There was no besting him physically, and any opportunity she had had with a weapon was gone. She would become the last victim. The last virtue. No one would swoop in to save her, because no one knew. No one suspected.

Oliver lifted her onto the island, clearing everything on top of it with a sweep of his arm. Lara thrashed, tried lashing out with her legs, but he held fast. With a palm flat against her sternum, Oliver reached into his duffel bag, producing a different knife. The blade looked wicked, shining and gleaming in the soft light in the kitchen.

This was it.

This was the end.

Over their heads, the hanging pot rack trembled, the unused pots swaying where they hung. For a moment, Lara thought she was imagining it, some sort of hallucination caused by the preternatural weight of Oliver's hand on her chest, the weight yet again robbing her of normal breath. Black spots popped at the edge of her vision, and little white lights danced before her. It was a moment before Lara realized that the white lights were not from oxygen deprivation. In fact, the white lights weren't lights at all, but odd little puffs of smoke that swirled and twirled around the pot rack.

Beside her, Oliver was murmuring strange words, a language or languages Lara did not recognize. He was beginning the ritual, and any moment now he would strike the final blow, making her Justice.

But the odd happening around the pot rack caused the trembling to become all-out rattling, as though an earthquake rocked the ground beneath them. There was no earthquake, however, just the pot rack gyrating and vibrating as though someone shook it. Oliver, hearing the noise, stopped mid-sentence, head tipping up to see what the source of the noise was. In that moment, a frying pan broke free from the rack and came crashing down on the crown of Oliver's head, knocking him unconscious to the ground. With Oliver in a crumpled heap, the pot rack immediately ceased its movement.

Then there was eerie, dead silence.

Stunned, Lara couldn't move in fear of what could happen to her. The roaring silence filled her ears, blood rushing through her body and up to her head, making her feel faint. Taking a few deep breaths, she forced herself to move, swinging her legs down off of the island. Carefully, she hopped off, tiptoeing away from the unconscious form of Oliver on the floor. Looking from the frying pan to the pot rack and back to Oliver, Lara heaved a sigh, letting out one long, low "*Fuck*."

CHAPTER 34

Blue and red lights illuminated the walls of Lara's front hallway as uniforms and crime scene technicians milled about the first floor. Tom had arrived moments ago, harried and beside himself, his red hair askew, no doubt from running his hands through the strands. Bursting in, her captain swooped forward and enveloped her in the tightest hug she had gotten since her father's last embrace. Sucking in a shaky breath, Lara let her arms encircle his waist, holding on for dear life as tears pricked at the corners of her eyes.

"Jesus Christ, Lara, I was fuckin' terrified," Tom breathed against her hair. "I heard your address over the radio, and I thought—I don't know what I thought, but it wasn't good. How did we not know? Right under our noses..."

"None of us could have known," Lara replied into the solidness of his shoulder. "He was too good at covering his tracks. He was a Goddamn murdering sociopath with the charm of the devil, Tom. I wasn't gonna catch him."

"You don't know that," Tom argued, taking a step back

and raking his hands through his red hair once more. "Look...
You can't fault yourself for not knowing it was him."

"There are three dead women, Tom. And I was gonna be
the fourth. I wasn't anywhere near knowing it was him and *I
was going to be the fourth*."

"FBI, let me through," came another harried, melodic
voice. The uniform keeping track of the comings and goings
at the front door let Natalia pass through the threshold. Lara
let out a sigh of relief, unprepared for the sheer happiness she
felt at seeing the agent. Before she could make to hug her,
Lara noticed Zach right on Natalia's heels, his Havenwood
uniform rumpled and worry in his green eyes. Something
about seeing the two of them side-by-side had Lara's heart
fluttering, and the fact she still had a heart that beat was
enough to make her knees nearly give out beneath her.

"Thank Christ," Zach mumbled as both he and Natalia
came for Lara.

It was a good thing both had a hold of her, because her
knees did give out then and her backside went down onto the
stairs. Lara's arms were wrapped as tightly as they could be
around them both, and she felt a tide of tears bursting forth
through the dam she had somehow kept up.

Natalia could not say anything through her own tears,
burying her face into Lara's neck to hide the fact she was
crying.

"What the fuck happened?" Zach asked, his own voice
cracking slightly.

For a moment, Lara could not begin to explain. She was so
caught up in the fact that these two people really cared
enough about her that they were happy she wasn't dead. For
some reason, that thought blew Lara's mind, that anyone
would care that fucking much. But here she was, in a pile of
FBI agent and patrol sergeant.

When Lara was finally able to find her voice, she

explained what had happened, knowing she would need to give a full statement sometime soon anyway. She lowered her voice when she got to the lights leading her to the button and the paint bottle, and the mysterious movements of the pot rack.

Two uniformed officers came down the hallway from the kitchen, half dragging, half holding up Oliver's body. He was still groggy and half-unconscious from being knocked out, and possibly had a concussion from the weight of the pan. His head lolled on his shoulders, as he tried to lift his head to search for her.

Natalia and Zach stood, blocking his view of her, and watched in silence as the uniformed officers brought him past. Oliver turned his head enough, dark eyes catching Lara's. A shiver raced down her spine at the sheer hatred and anger reflected there.

Because of her, he would not be able to finish his ritual, and therefore, ultimate power remained out of his reach. In a few years, Lara would no doubt be able to laugh at the ridiculousness of it all, but in that moment, Lara had never felt such fear.

As the officer dragged Oliver away, the firm set of his mouth turned to that of a smile of glee. It chilled Lara to the bone. It was the kind of smile that said this would not be the last time she saw him.

Once the bastard had been taken out of Lara's house, Natalia and Zach brought Lara to the kitchen, where Natalia began to fuss over her, saying she needed something hot to drink.

A few minutes later, Lara cupped a mug of hot chocolate in her hands. She didn't really drink the beverage, but its warmth was comforting. A commotion at the front door signaled the arrival of more people. Sure enough, Chief Braddock, Mayor Lothrop, and Charlotte walked into the kitchen.

The chief's emotions were well guarded, but Sam and Charlotte Lothrop looked absolutely horrified.

Probably because their house could have been damaged with a bit of blood and viscera.

"Lieutenant," the chief began. "I'm glad to see you're okay."

Lara had nearly been ritualistically murdered, and that was all the chief had to say?

It honestly reminded her of something her dad would do. He couldn't ever put his feelings into words, so even the simplest of statements was loaded with emotion. Lara forced her lips into a barely there smile in acknowledgment.

She did take a sip of the hot chocolate then. It was still molten hot, but it made her feel something other than numbness.

Charlotte stepped over to Lara, looking as gorgeous and impeccably dressed as always. Real concern showed in her pretty, crystalline eyes. Reaching forward, the blonde placed a soft touch to Lara's shoulder. The touch was more comforting than any words the woman could say.

"We're relieved to see you're unscathed," the mayor said softly. Lara hoped like hell he felt guilty about his decision to keep her off the case. She hoped like hell he felt *something*.

"So he was the one all along?" Charlotte asked.

"Yeah," Lara croaked.

"God, you must've been terrified," Charlotte continued.

Lara didn't respond, merely took another sip of hot chocolate.

"I think we should let Lieutenant Nadeau have the remainder of the evening to rest. We're all done here, techs and such..." Bless Chief Braddock.

"Yes, of course," Charlotte said, pressing a worried palm to her chest. "I'll check on you soon, Lieutenant. Get some rest." Mayor Lothrop ushered her out of the house, and the crime scene technicians disappeared from the kitchen where they had bagged Oliver's things.

A hush quickly fell over the house, only disturbed by the five people that still remained.

"I don't want to see you anywhere near the station the next few days except for when you come to make an official statement. Got that, Lieutenant?" Chief Braddock said, tone not to be fucked with.

"Yes, sir," Lara croaked, swallowing thickly.

"Good," the chief's blue eyes looked from Zach to Natalia. "I trust you won't leave her alone any time soon?"

Natalia and Zach must have given some form of assent, because the chief muttered a pleased "Good" and then was out the door. The flashing blue lights had disappeared, leaving the darkness of the driveway.

"I should get going too," Tom said softly, shuffling from foot to foot. "Don't go and pull any more stunts like this, got it?"

It was meant as a joke, and despite the events of the evening, Lara could not help but chuckle.

"You got it, Cap'n," she mock-saluted.

Tom sighed. Before he made to leave, he stepped forward. Surprising Lara, he placed a soft kiss to the hairline at her forehead. It was a very fatherly gesture, something Lara had seen him do to Lola. It made tears spring to her eyes again, but like hell, she beat them back.

"'Night," she said softly, as he turned to leave. If he had heard her, Tom made no sign, and disappeared out the door.

"Come on, let's get you in bed, huh?" Natalia said softly.

Stuck still in hazy shock, Lara nodded, allowing herself to be moved, lifted, turned, and led upstairs to her bedroom. It crossed her mind she didn't want Zach to see the messiness of her room, but she brushed the thought away. Like it fucking mattered how untidy the room was.

The hot chocolate had disappeared, as had the blanket that had been wrapped around her shoulders. Lara was shoved, and her backside hit the mattress. Shoes disappeared as did the jeans she had been wearing. Calloused hands swung her legs into the bed, and more delicate fingers brought the blankets to her chin.

"Try and get some sleep, huh?" Natalia whispered, coming into focus right in Lara's line of vision. The FBI agent bent over the side of the bed, her beautiful face a damn welcome sight.

Lara was fucking happy to be alive.

Happy she *felt* alive.

The numbness of grief, depression, and despair had cut off Lara's ability to feel anything.

Amazing what a brush with death could do for one's perspective.

The lamp light was clicked off, and her vision plummeted into darkness.

"Wait," she slurred, the adrenaline high wearing off, sending her body into shut-down mode. "Please don't go..."

Lara wasn't sure who she talked to. Maybe just Natalia. Maybe the both of them. But before she could clarify, her heavy eyelids shut and blessed exhaustion took her into oblivion.

The blaring brightness of the early-afternoon sun woke Lara from dreamless sleep the next day. A quick bleary glance over at the alarm clock on the nightstand said it was nearly one o'clock in the afternoon. The events of the night before slammed back into her memory, and Lara shot up.

She was alone in her bed, though the other side looked rumpled, as though someone had lain there. Glancing around,

Lara noticed the clothing and other objects that had been on the floor were picked up. It sure looked a hell of a lot neater than before.

Thuds and clangs from downstairs filtered up to her. Lara extricated herself from the bedsheets. In her sleep, she had turned and tossed, somehow wrapping herself in the sheets like a mummy. Her legs felt wobbly when she stood, and her body ached from the treatment it had been given the previous evening.

But she was alive.

There were no pants within reach on the floor for Lara to slip into, so she had to search in a drawer. Once she found a clean pair of sweatpants, Lara stepped into them and then padded downstairs barefoot.

Natalia was in the kitchen, the source of the thuds and clanging noises. The agent was trying to cook with about three pots going on the gas stove, and a lot more happening on the kitchen island.

Where Lara had nearly been killed.

But she was alive.

The smells wafting and filling the room were delectable, and Lara knew instantly Natalia was cooking an old de Benedetto family pasta sauce recipe. Lara's mouth watered, and her stomach grumbled. Natalia had yet to notice Lara's appearance, and she used this opportunity to duck into an alcove near the living room.

The television screen had been turned on to Jerry Springer, and there was Zach, sitting on the couch in a fresh pair of jeans and a T-shirt, hair slick from a shower.

Lara's heart squeezed, watching him smile and chuckle in amusement at the ridiculousness on the screen.

Goddamn, she was alive.

"Hey, I didn't hear you come down," Natalia appeared

behind her, causing Lara to jump a little in surprise. Whirling, she tried to put on a smile.

"Hi."

"Hey," Zach greeted, materializing next to her.

Damn, the both of them moved quickly.

"How'd you sleep?" Natalia asked.

Lara shrugged, "Okay."

"Good," Natalia replied. "'Okay' is good."

Her honey gaze moved from Natalia to Zach, unsure of what she had done to deserve to have two such people in her life. She had done nothing but drink and fuck up the past year and more, with no moves to try and right herself. She had nearly bashed a man's face in, and nearly botched the first major murder investigation the city of Eastfall had ever seen in its history.

But these two had been there. In some way or another, they were still here.

"Yeah, I think it will be okay," Lara replied softly.

CHAPTER 35

Eastfall's Saint Michael the Archangel Catholic Church seemed grim against the backdrop of the cloudy, freezing November evening. The building looked more like the setting of some sort of gothic horror story than a church. Sucking in a steadying breath, Lara shoved her hands in the pockets of her peacoat and trudged forward. Once more, she had forgotten her gloves, and in just the time it had taken for her to get to the front steps, she could not feel her fingers.

Figured.

Inside, the building was silent except for the faraway echo of voices. Following the signs to one of the meeting rooms, it did not take Lara long to locate the right one. About twenty or so people milled about the room. There was a table set off to the side with meager refreshments, and in the middle of the room, chairs were arranged in a circle.

Lara had always hated circling up. High school, college, it didn't matter. It felt too intimate. And made it easy for people to stare.

The urge to bolt came over her, but just as she was about

to turn around and make like a tree, a figure blocked her path.

It was the parish priest.

Gulping, Lara was positive that he had clocked her intent in one quick glance.

She hadn't been to church in years, not since she'd been confirmed. Organized religion had never felt right to Lara, but she had gone through all of the sacraments like a good little Catholic girl, in order to appease her father. He had grown up with Catholic guilt drilled into him since day one by the nuns at school and his own parents.

"Welcome," the priest said with a small, welcoming smile. "We're about to start if you'd like to take a seat? Maybe grab some coffee first?"

Lara wondered if she was the only new face here. Did she stick out like a sore thumb?

"Y-Yes, thank you," Lara stuttered, before turning on her heel and heading to the refreshment table. It wasn't that she particularly wanted the coffee, it was just something to do so as to not be the center of the priest's attention. The coffee smelled burnt, probably slightly less disgusting than the swill they used to brew at her precinct in Boston.

But it was something warm and oddly comforting.

The priest headed for the circle of chairs, pausing to greet people on his way.

The guy was just over the hill, with a shock of steel-gray hair and a full, thick beard the same color. He was youthful in a way, but age-old wisdom lurked in the dark depths of his eyes. He wore the traditional casual dress of a priest—a long-sleeved button up shirt tucked into black dress slacks with the ever-present white color. The only hint of color Lara could see was the flash of brightly patterned argyle socks.

There was something about the guy. He exuded calm.

Lara could feel it permeating the room, soothing her frazzled nerves just enough to get her to the circle and in a seat.

"Alright, we'll start this week's meeting with a prayer," the priest began, commanding silence and the attention of the ring of people. It did not take him long to drum up a brief prayer, culminating in asking for God's blessing, as all priests did.

"Amen" rippled around the circle at the close of the benediction, and Lara found herself murmuring the word as well.

"As most of you know, my name is Father Miguel Lopez, and I am the parish priest here at Saint Michael. As always, I want to preface the fact that this is not a formal Alcoholics Anonymous meeting. It is merely a support group for those seeking to quit and wanting community. It isn't even about bringing God in. It's simply an effort to better ourselves and find our right paths again." Father Lopez paused, dark eyes immediately landing on Lara.

"We have a new face amongst us tonight. If you wouldn't mind introducing yourself, that would be great."

Lara cleared her throat and fidgeted in her chair until she forced herself to sit straighter. These damn cheap foldable chairs were always the same, no matter what church you went to.

"My name's Lara," she said.

"It's nice to meet you, Lara. The rules are simple—this is a no judgement zone, and you can share as much or as little as you want. If you're just here to listen, that's fine, but never hesitate to speak up. I have found the more one puts into something like this, the more one gets out of it."

Lara nodded, but did not volunteer anything else.

It was a step in the right direction—showing up.

Only time would tell whether she shared or not, but as the meeting progressed, and she heard the stories of the others sitting in the circle, Lara could not help but think that perhaps she could get through this. She had forced herself here, *for her*, to make Lara Nadeau better.

And, well, if part of it was to feel as though she could make her father proud? Who could blame her?

————————

Fingers dug into aged wood and pried up the loose floorboard. The book from Jeff's safety deposit box remained untouched, along with the letter he'd written her. Carefully, Lara lifted the book out, and brought it downstairs. Using her cell phone, she snapped a couple of pictures, including a few pages on the inside. After, Lara thumbed back through them, and once she was satisfied, she called up the email app on her phone and sent the photos off.

By touch alone, Lara felt the book had the same sort of energy the grimoire did, the book she had found in her attic. This suspicion had led her to get back in contact with Dr. Archibald Chappelle at Boston College, who was all too happy to look over some photographs. Whatever book it was, Lara's intuition told her it was one of the thirteen, the *Books of Forbidden Knowledge*.

Until Lara knew more about them, she needed to keep them out of sight and safe. Grabbing both the book from Jeff McMullens's safety deposit box and the grimoire, Lara climbed the stairs once more, and then again into the attic. It was filled with junk, and Lara would use that to her advantage.

The grimoire went back into the space beneath the floorboard. With some help from friends, Lara decided it would be best to keep the book away until she learned how to use it properly. In fact, in this very moment, Zach was no doubt scouring the Internet looking for Lara's 'Yoda,' despite the fact that both she and Nat were convinced a real witch wouldn't advertise herself online.

The book from Jeff's safety deposit box went deep into the stacks of junk. Lara found an ancient hat box that had one moth-eaten hat that she quickly discarded. In place of the hat, she put the book, then hid the box amongst the plethora of antiques. Again, best to keep it hidden until she knew more about this one. Not to mention, it would be better to keep the books separate, if they are as sought after as Dr. Chappelle seemed to think.

Once this task had been accomplished, Lara headed back downstairs and sat at her desk. She called up her email, especially one from Mayor Lothrop who had sent over some scans about the house. As she waited for what Dr. Chappelle would return with, she read about the house and its occupants over the years.

Swallowing thickly, Lara eventually found who she believed to be *AB*.

Anne Buchanan.

Anne Morgan, née Buchanan, had been the wife of the original owner of the land, Michael Morgan. According to the papers provided by Mayor Lothrop, Anne had long been suspected of being a witch, but was foremost the town healer. The marriage between Mr. and Mrs. Morgan had been the stuff of fairy tales, and according to legend, Mrs. Morgan died not long after Mr. Morgan. Together, they had several children who grew up to have children of their own.

Was Anne Buchanan Morgan her spectral heroine?

As if hearing Lara's thoughts or peering over her shoulder, a couple of thuds came from the attic. What once might have scared the shit out of her now had Lara smiling.

"It's nice to meet you, Anne," Lara spoke aloud. Another couple of thuds returned Lara's sentiment.

Her email dinged, showing a reply from Dr. Chappelle.

Lara's eyes skimmed over the contents but focused on the words that seemed to confirm her suspicions. Dr. Chappelle indeed believed this to be another of the mysterious thirteen books of the *Books of Forbidden Knowledge*. Also, according to his cursory look at the pictures, he believed the book to be the volume he'd spoken about in their meeting, the one found in an attic twenty years ago. Not unlike her grimoire. That book was the *Mysteria Corporis*, or *Mysteries of the Body*. It supposedly contained medical knowledge ahead of its time, including a cure for cancer. The problem, again, with these books was that a lot of them were written in languages no one could translate.

Tricky.

Sighing, Lara closed the email and sat back in her desk chair.

Everything came back to these books, including the looming menace that was Angylion Pharmaceuticals.

It would take careful investigative work, and a lot of help, to figure out the end game here.

But Lara was confident.

Reaching for the plate next to her, Lara munched on a chocolate chip cookie. They had been baked for her by one of Lynn Rickerson's coworkers, Jennifer Cassidy, in thanks for rooting out her murderer.

The cookies may be the physical embodiment of thanks, but Lara took heart from the mere fact that Lynn, Sierra Fitzgerald, and Carol Mumford had been avenged.

If she hadn't been able to avenge these women?

Well, what good would she have been as Justice?

CHAPTER 36

The office was dark, save for the singular lamp illuminating one corner of the spacious room. The CEO had opted to draw the shades over the wall of windows, blocking the view of the quaint historic downtown of Eastfall. Two figures occupied the room, the CEO and his assistant head of Research and Development, Dr. Gibbons. Both spoke in hushed tones. The CEO, behind his large oaken desk, was beyond frustrated. So much that he had opted to take it out on the poor underling sitting in the armchair in front of him.

"Bennett was a liability we should have handled a hell of a lot sooner. The boy nearly jeopardized all we've accomplished. Not to mention McMullens meddling and sharing secrets. But I had him taken care of. How in the hell could he have gotten his hands on all that material?"

"I wish I knew, sir. We're still looking into it. Bennett is behind bars now, with no chance of parole, thanks to our court connections. He'll rot like Manson."

"He was such a promising acolyte," the CEO sighed, truly regretful at the loss of his proudest recruit. However, proud no more.

"Our benefactors have requested he be kept alive... For now. They believe he may yet serve a purpose."

"Is that truly wise?" Dr. Gibbons asked. "He is a compromising loose end."

The CEO shook his head. "No, I don't think we have anything to worry about. His loyalty to The Order, however misplaced, is unshakeable. I will give him credit for that."

"Unshakeable loyalty or not, in the right circumstances, he could open his mouth and blab."

The CEO bristled. "Are you questioning my decision? Our bene-factors' decision?" Gods, he hated having to talk to the benefactors. They were easy to anger and very impatient. It took a lot of energy, both mental and physical.

Dr. Gibbons shrunk back, nearly curling in on himself at the very thought of what could happen to him for his insubordination.

"N-No, sir. I just... I worry, as always, for the safety of The Order and all we have built."

"It is my constant worry," the CEO sighed again, massaging his forehead with firm fingertips.

"What of the lieutenant? Lieutenant Nadeau?"

"I'm blown away at the audacity of Bennett choosing her for Justice. The woman is a complete incompetent. It would have done better to go for the FBI agent."

"He also made the mistake of selecting Mumford for Temperance," Dr. Gibbons couldn't help but chuckle.

"And that was the pitfall," the CEO shook his head, sinking back into his chair. "He went for irony... And that's the problem with these old manuscripts. You just never know how they should be interpreted. Besides, the only power he would have gotten was a rush of adren-aline. He may believe he is worthy of The Order, but he doesn't possess one drop of blood that would allow him to succeed at such an endeavor. Besides, he didn't have a complete ritual. But that didn't seem to matter to him, however, when I informed him of such."

"Bennett was...misguided, sir," Dr. Gibbons said, attempting to reassure. *"That ritual has never been successfully attempted, and there is reason why. He did not listen when you, and I, told him there was a missing piece. A piece probably lost forever."*

"No matter. The police have handled it for us. They will chalk it all up to his being mentally unfit. No one will know the connection. Should not know the connection."

"We hope," Dr. Gibbons replied, jaw clenching for a moment in nervousness, realizing he should not have said such a thing out loud to his master.

"Regardless, it matters not. All pieces will fall into place very soon, and with her on our side, we will be unstoppable."

"Her," Dr. Gibbons shuddered.

"With her timeless power, and our connections and influence, there will be nothing to stop us from realizing the mission of The Order. Imagine it... We will be the members, in the long history of The Order, to succeed. Anything we could ever want will be ours for the taking."

Long nights of scheming not unlike this one, in darkened offices and behind closed doors, was what had gotten them to this moment. Their vision was within reach, and with just a few more moves, they could declare a checkmate. Both the CEO and Dr. Gibbons knew it, as they had made it their life's mission to reach this moment. Oliver Bennett had been a speed bump, but his actions would not completely slow down or stop what they were about to do.

From Old World to New World, The Order had traveled far and sacrificed much. They had built a multinational conglomerate, Angylion, from the ground up, but its corporate headquarters could be nowhere else but Eastfall. Eastfall was a special place, more special than people realized. In fact, the fewer who knew, the better.

Now, just a matter of making sure the lieutenant steered clear of them...

CHAPTER 37

P art of getting through life was sharing your victories and your sorrows with those close to you. Lara had begun to learn this from Father Lopez. The road to recovery is a path one didn't have to walk alone. *Life* was not a path one had to walk alone.

Despite this valuable lesson she had learned, this wasn't the kind of situation Lara wanted to share with Natalia or Zach.

The outside of Briargreen Mental Institution looked just as their gallery of pictures depicted on their website. The inside, though, was like any hospital, only more secure. The sterile smell cloyed at Lara's nose as she stepped up to the visitor window. The entryway was pretty barren, with only a few chairs in the waiting room. There were two doors besides the entrance. Both only opened by keycard access.

An attendant sat behind the partitioned glass, looking bored and practically asleep. It was still early morning, and the man clearly had not had enough cups of coffee.

"Can I help you?" he asked, in a tone that relayed the fact he was not thrilled to be there.

"Um...is Nurse Janice Adkins available? My name is Lara Nadeau."

The man shuffled some papers around, until he found something that must have caught his eye.

"She sent down a message that we would be expecting you. I'll give her a call, and she can escort you."

"Thanks," Lara said.

The man pushed a sign-in sheet through the small opening at the bottom of the pane of glass. Lara took a second to fill out the sheet, and then the visitor sticker. Peeling it from the sheet, she pressed it against the left breast of her peacoat.

While she waited, she took a nearby informational pamphlet about the facility and began to read.

Briargreen Institution had existed in some way or another since the 1770s. It was the first of its kind in this region of Massachusetts. The hospital specialized in the severe mental illnesses. Lara couldn't help but recall scenes from *One Flew Over the Cuckoo's Nest*, complete with Nurse Ratched and a young Jack Nicholson.

One of the doors opened and out stepped an older woman, probably in her fifties, with graying hair and kind eyes. She was plump, like the stereotypical grandmother image. Her scrubs were plain but stylish.

"Ms. Nadeau?" she asked.

Lara nodded. "Nurse Adkins."

Both women clasped hands.

"Welcome to Briargreen. You ready to meet her?"

No words were exchanged as Janice let Lara through the secured doors and through a maze of hallways. The noises were frightening, but then again, Lara was not used to such an atmosphere. In this part of the building, there was an undertone of something else beneath the sterile smell, and it made her feel queasy. As they walked, Lara caught sight of the grounds out back through open window frames, and along the interior hallway were plenty of alcoves built in to act as sitting areas for visiting family.

Actual visitation hours wouldn't start for another few hours, but because of the circumstances, they had allowed Lara to come earlier.

The deeper into the institution they traveled, the more she could hear her heart hammering in her chest, blood rushing. Lara had never felt more nervous in her entire life, not on her first date with Natalia, not the first time she had to testify in court for arrests she'd made, and not prom night either.

The moment of truth came when Nurse Adkins stopped in front of a closed door. The nurse paused, turning back to Lara.

"I never did ask," Lara cut in before Janice could say anything. "Why is she here?"

Janice got this indescribable look on her face, somewhere between hurt and something else. "She admitted herself about twenty-five years ago."

"What?"

"I had just begun work here as a nurse. Mave...well, this has never felt like a place for her, but she insisted many times over the years that this was for the better. Something about protecting others."

"And the doctors have supported this?"

"For sure... Her paranoia developed into delusions. Over the years we tried discharging her, with her permission of course, but she always relapsed. This is a long-term facility, so we always have the room for her."

"As long as the money keeps coming, right?" Lara replied bitterly, not directed at Nurse Adkins in particular.

"I am sorry."

"It's fine. Payments will be made." It only seemed right to

use the inheritance she had received from her father to help support her mother. It was what he would have wanted, Lara was certain.

Nurse Adkins's lips pursed, as though she wanted to make a remark, but kept silent instead.

"You can have as much time with her as you want. Know that she is very lucid and will know who you are. If you need me, the nurses' desk is down that hallway and to the right."

Lara nodded, her heightened nerves choking off her ability to respond. Nurse Adkins seemed to understand and took her leave. Lara watched her disappear down the hallway, before turning to face the stark white of the door.

She wasn't sure how long she stood there, getting up the gumption to go in.

Jaw clenched, Lara pushed through the door, and into the dimness of the room.

It was decorated starkly, which did not surprise Lara. There was one tranquil looking painting of some flowers on the wall, a separate bathroom, a desk, a nightstand, a twin bed, a ratty old armchair that looked like the twin to her father's, and a couple of lamps. It was dark in the room except for the illumination of one lamp near the desk. A woman sat there with her back to Lara. The woman's hair was the same color as Lara's own except peppered with gray strands. She was slight, thin, as though she didn't eat enough.

Lara stood, rooted to the spot, hands clenched at her sides.

Did she go forward? Did she say something? Did she wait?

Nothing about what she had seen of the woman so far was familiar to her, and that made her more confused and conflicted.

"I'm glad you came," the woman at the desk said, her voice a whisper, like the tinkling of bells. Slowly, she turned to face Lara. The face that looked back at Lara's was not unlike her own. Perhaps Mave's features were a little more delicate, but the hair was the same, the chin, the honey eyes...

"Things have been set in motion, my dear daughter. Things that can't be undone. There is much for you to learn, and little time to teach you."

"What the hell is going on?" Lara finally found her voice, words crackling on her emotions.

"The end of us all, Lara."

ACKNOWLEDGMENTS

This novel was a long journey. The story started vastly different from where it ended, but I hope the main themes still pervade throughout. I wanted a flawed but kick ass lady to bring the thunder to a misogynistic creep. One way or another, it happened.

I would first like to thank the person that pushed to make this all possible. Kathryn, you've been cheering me on from the sidelines the entire four years it took to get to this point. It's your fault for getting me into this whole mess in the first place, inspiring me to take writing further than just a fun hobby. You paved the way for this novel to be possible with your own success, talked me off the ledge too many times to count, and helped me work through hashing out plot points. I can't thank you enough. Without you, this book wouldn't exist.

A giant thank you to my mom for birthing me, and always being my biggest cheerleader. I know how much you love James Patterson, and while Lara probably isn't as cool as Alex Cross, I still hope you enjoyed this.

Thank you to my family. Every single one of you, in some

way, has supported me and encouraged my writing. There are so many bits of my family's French-Canadian traditions sprinkled throughout this novel that I hope you guys caught all the references.

My deepest appreciation goes to my editor, Lauren Hughes. You truly helped to push this novel further than I thought it would ever go. Your support and compliments through the process helped spur me forward.

Huge shoutout to Caroline Teagle Johnson for designing the most stunning cover I think I could have ever wanted for this book. I can't wait to work with you for Book 2. Got any pictures of swords handy?

Thank you to S.E. Davidson, my mapmaker, for taking my horrible sketch of Eastfall and making it into something gorgeous and actually legible.

Thank you to the Happily Editing Anns for proofreading this thing. My most favorite comment will forever be "The Sam Adams in my fridge don't have twist-off caps."

Lastly, I would like to Juno, my loyal fur baby. She stayed, resting in her bed, the entire time I wanted to pull my hair out over edits. Thank you for always being a calm little pocket in my crazy storm.

ABOUT THE AUTHOR

J.R. Lesperance is an emerging author of paranormal thrillers and romance featuring strong female characters.

To keep up with J.R.'s latest news and releases, check out her website at www.jrlesperance.com and various social media sites below.